SYNOPSIS

Repeated references to the colors—red, white, and blue—in message traffic from Asia, the Middle East and Northern Ireland tweek the interest of an intelligence analyst in an organization created after 9/11 to keep the President of the United States 'up to speed' on suspicious activities world wide. Detailed analyses and investigations by special agents discover that the Secretary of State, who lusts to be the first female in the Oval Office, has been handed an unprecedented opportunity to eliminate the four men blocking her path to the White House through a series of almost simultaneous assassinations, thousands of miles apart. Abetted by her father, they arrange for Irish and Islamic terrorists, the North Korean Navy and a Chicago mobster to carry out the assassinations. An elite team of three men, a retired submarine Admiral, a former Seal, and a former All-American football player turned computer whiz, who along with the President are the only ones who know the full extent of these seemingly unrelated plots, is tasked with coordinating among their peers in Europe, the Middle East and Asia, the steps to counter and defeat the threat, without having their efforts become a media feeding frenzy. Complicating their efforts is the short time fuse of less than six weeks to successfully complete their assignment!!

DEADLY AFFAIRS OF STATE

ED NOVAK, JR.

© Copyright 2006 Ed Novak, Jr.
All rights reserved. No part of this publication may be reproduced, stored in a retrieval system, or transmitted, in any form or by any means, electronic, mechanical, photocopying, recording, or otherwise, without the written prior permission of the author.

Note for Librarians: A cataloguing record for this book is available from Library and Archives Canada at www.collectionscanada.ca/amicus/index-e.html
ISBN 1-4251-0970-3

Printed in Victoria, BC, Canada. Printed on paper with minimum 30% recycled fibre. Trafford's print shop runs on "green energy" from solar, wind and other environmentally-friendly power sources.

TRAFFORD
PUBLISHING™

Offices in Canada, USA, Ireland and UK

Book sales for North America and international:
Trafford Publishing, 6E–2333 Government St.,
Victoria, BC V8T 4P4 CANADA
phone 250 383 6864 (toll-free 1 888 232 4444)
fax 250 383 6804; email to orders@trafford.com
Book sales in Europe:
Trafford Publishing (UK) Limited, 9 Park End Street, 2nd Floor
Oxford, UK OX1 1HH UNITED KINGDOM
phone +44 (0)1865 722 113 (local rate 0845 230 9601)
facsimile +44 (0)1865 722 868; info.uk@trafford.com
Order online at:
trafford.com/06-2729

10 9 8 7 6 5 4 3

This novel is dedicated to E. Parker Smith and Max Templeman, long time Kiwanis friends, who will live forever in my fond memories.

TABLE OF CONTENTS

Dedication iii
Table of Contents v
Forward. vii
Acknowledgements ix
Cast of Principal Characters xi
Prologue 1
Chapter 1—The Game Starts. 12
Chapter 2—Glenn Reminisces 16
Chapter 3—Glenn meets the Admiral 23
Chapter 4—The Conspiracy Unfolds. 28
Chapter 5—Enter the "Hacker" 32
Chapter 6—The Colors are Identified. 35
Chapter 7—To Pearl Harbor and Japan. 42
Chapter 8—To the United Kingdom 50
Chapter 9—To Israel 61
Chapter 10—Assessing the Conspiracy. 71
Chapter 11—Madam Secretary. 80
Chapter 12—Putting it all Together 89
Chapter 13—Briefing the President 94
Chapter 14—Putting the Counter-plan in Place. 99
Chapter 15—Laying the Trap 103
Chapter 16—Updating the President 108
Chapter 17—The Pot Boils Over 114
Chapter 18—Send for the Navy and the Marines. 119
Chapter 19—Marching Orders 126
Chapter 20—Kevin meets Senator Willis 132
Chapter 21—M16 Targets the IRA 139
Chapter 22—The Admiral goes West Again 145
Chapter 23—Mossad Zeroes in on the 'Chameleon'. 154
Chapter 24—The Admiral goes to Sea 164
Chapter 25—The Action Starts 171
Chapter 26—Saving the Senator. 175
Chapter 27—Mossad Eliminates the 'Chameleon' 182
Chapter 28—The IRA takes a Hit. 187

Chapter 29—Submarine Action in the Western Pacific... 192
Chapter 30—Madam Secretary's Dream is Shattered 204
Chapter 31—Unwinding 208
Chapter 32—Planning the Final Solution.............. 210
Chapter 33—Giving Thanks 217
Chapter 34—The Final Solution 219
Chapter 35—Headlines and Honors.................. 226
Epilogue 229
Glossary 233

FORWARD

Within the worlds literature and journalism, it is plagiarism when an author appropriates the majority of another author's work and publishes it as his own creative effort. On the other hand, if an author borrows bits and pieces from a host of other authors, it is called research, but, it is also said that "imitation is the highest form of praise".

Prior to putting pencil to paper, this author was an avid reader of the works of Colin Dexter, Agatha Christie, Ian Fleming, Tom Clancy, Richard Marcinko, Clive Cussler, Jack Higgins, Dale Brown and several other writers of mystery and intrigue. It was inevitable that vague similarities to what was read would find their way into this story as guidelines and a skeletal matrix that eventually became this original (I hope) work.

The author, who writes in the future (when this work was started) has a flexible license to create scenarios that might be impossible, unrealistic or ridiculous in the present setting and time frame. Opinions, persons and strategies are adapted to the events at hand and are not always in agreement with the 'never happen' or 'never done that' philosophy. Historical events and those persons who lived in and through past times and events are referred to in this work to put the story line into perspective, and to add a semblance of credibility to the tale.

The main character is not a James Bond nor a Sean Dillon, not a Dirk Pitt nor a Jake Grafton, and certainly not an Indiana Jones. He is intelligent, world wise and street savvy, brave without being foolhardy, patriotic to the core and politically incorrect, more than willing to take acceptable risks in doing his job and physically capable of handling the situations into which he is thrust.

His superior is a firm believer in the old adages—'that the best defense is an unstoppable offense' and 'do your enemy before he does you'. The mission of his organization is to provide appropriate governmental officials with the information necessary for them to be pro-active rather than reactive to impending crises.

This novel is a work of pure fiction, dealing with a scenario that the author feels has not been previously put into print. The author seriously hopes and prays that it will never become a reality.

ACKNOWLEDGEMENTS

The author wishes to thank his good friends and fellow Kiwanians, Warren Kane and Edd Nolen, both long time denizens of Capitol Hill for their input on the ways and intricacies of the Federal government. Special thanks are due to award winning author Donna Andrews and the members of the BNRestonCritiquers group, who reviewed selected chapters of this novel and made many valuable suggestions to improve the reader friendliness of the text. Thanks and deep appreciation are especially given to my wife, Natalie Novak, who patiently suffered through reading the original script and its many revisions, ensuring that the action moved smartly and did not have the effect of a strong sleeping pill. Finally my son, Edward A. Novak, III, deserves kudos for being my severest critic, offering important suggestions to prepare the final manuscript for presentation to the publisher.

CAST OF PRINCIPLE CHARACTERS

INSTITUTE FOR INTELLIGENCE ANALYSIS
Vice Admiral USN (Ret) Vincent T. Billig (Director)
Glenn Stark (Senior Field Agent)
Kevin 'The Hacker' Jablonski (Super Computer Whiz)
Miss Natalie Eagleton (Admiral's Secretary)

U.S. GOVERNMENT OFFICIALS
Randolph Alexander (President of the United States)
Michael Flaherty (Vice-President of the United States)
Representative Sidney Rosen (Speaker of the House of Representatives)
Senator Byran Willis (President Pro-Tem of the Senate)
Maureen Kavanaugh (Secretary of State)

UNITED STATES NAVY
Admiral Mark Kane / Riley (Chief of Naval Operations)
Vice Admiral Thomas Kiesel (Commander, Seventh Fleet)
Rear Admiral Harry Drapcho (Commander, Naval Forces Japan)
Rear Admiral James Tonelson (Commander Naval Forces Marianas)
Captain Richard Simpson (Commander, Submarine Squadron Seven)
Captain Bart Savage (Commanding Officer *USS Sea Lion*)
Captain Gary Hall (Commander, Air Group, *USS Vinson*)
Commander Charles DeGarmo (Commanding Officer, *USS San Francisco*)
Commander Frank McDade (Commanding Officer *USS Scranton*)

UNITED STATES MARINE CORPS
General Kendall Golden (Commandant of the Marine Corps)

UNITED STATES AIR FORCE
Colonel Leonard Gillespie (Commanding Officer, Anderson AFB Guam)

BRITISH COUNTER-INTELLIGENCE (MI6)
Sir Malcolm Oliver Middleton (Director)
SgtMajor Ian MacGregor (Officer-in-Charge, Belfast Office)

ISRAELI INTELLIGENCE (MOSSAD)
Brigadier Jacob Templeman (Director)
Rebecca Zelman (Senior Assistant)

IRISH REPUBLICAN ARMY (IRA)
Patrick "Paddy" O'Rourke (Expeditor)
Sean Gilhooley (Terrorist)
Jack "Jocko" McCarthy (American Sympathizer, Father of Secretary of State)

MUSLIM JIHADIST
"Chameleon" (assassin)

NORTH KOREAN NAVY
Captain Kim Dac Hyun (Commanding Officer, *Red Vengeance*)

PROLOGUE

BELFAST, NORTHERN IRELAND
October 13, 2006

The Shamrock Pub was located in a part of Belfast that had no tourist attractions and very little visitor traffic. Owner Paddy O'Brien did not advertise in any of the travel publications and the pub was not on the list of pubs recommended for tourists to seek out. Paddy's desire for anonymity was evident by the absence of a sign or lettering on the windows. The only identifying mark was a shamrock shaped window in the front door.

Paddy's was a neighborhood pub, with a clientele consisting mainly of locals, their families, and occasional out-of-town guests. The outside windows were rarely washed, except by Mother Nature, which kept the patrons hidden from the curious passer-by. The atmosphere within the pub closely resembled that of the saloon in the TV series "Cheers". All the regulars were known to Paddy, to each other, and the pub staff by their first names.

Those occasional, and unwary, tourists who wandered into Paddy's were greeted with a sudden decrease in the usual hubbub, piercing stares sizing them up, followed by a general ignoring of their presence. While these misguided pilgrims were not prevented from entering the pub, they were not made welcome and their early departures were actively encouraged. Those, who bellied up to the bar, were served their swift pints quickly and silently by a bartender who collected payment upon delivery of the potables. There was no such thing as running a tab. As the tourists sipped their beverages, the regulars on both sides gradually moved away from them and the barman shifted to a remote end of the bar from where he ignored any and all attempts to get his attention for refills. The brave souls who opted for table seating were served by a sullen bar maid who seemed to disappear once she was paid for the first and only round of drinks. Any attempt to strike up a conversation with the locals at adjoining tables was not too politely rebuffed. The average stay for a tourist was less than fifteen minutes.

One of the notable exceptions to the usual cold reception given foreigners was Jack McCarthy, known to the regulars as "Jocko". His salt and pepper flat top hair cut and weather beaten tanned face immediately set him apart from the locals. None the less, he was always greeted with civility, but rarely with warmth because he was never able to shed his American mannerisms. He was usually greeted upon his arrival by Paddy himself, who escorted him to his personal booth, dubbed his social office in the rear of the pub. This booth was strategically placed where its occupants were out sight from the rest of the bar's patrons.

This day was no different. On entering the pub, McCarthy caused no more of a stir than a few nods of recognition. No attention was paid to the large brief case he was carrying. Paddy stopped drawing a pint of Guiness as soon as he saw Jocko and immediately passed the partially filled stein to another barman. He came forward to greet his favorite Yank with a broad grin that revealed several missing teeth, reminders of his violent youth. They greeted each other with customary bone crushing hand shakes, that were unspoken tests of strength and endurance. As usual, neither man could claim a victory, so they broke their grips and gingerly flexed their hands and fingers.

On their way to the social office, Paddy whispered, "Jocko, I've got a few lads I'd like you to meet. Don't be put off by their demeanor, they appear aloof because they don't warm up to strangers immediately, but they're professionals and just the men I think you are looking for." Jocko noted that there were three young men, ages between thirty and forty, seated in the booth obviously waiting for them.

"Jocko," Paddy exclaimed, "I give you the Gilhooley brothers, Sean, Seamus and Liam. It is good men that they are." The three young, physically fit men did not rise nor extend their hands to Jocko. Their unsmiling, expressionless faces did not change as they acknowledged Paddy's guest with simple nods. When Paddy and Jocko took their seats in the comfortable upholstered booth, a bar man arrived with five pints of Guiness stout. Paddy opened the meeting with his patented toast, "To the English, may their lives be short, and their deaths painful." The five men raised their glasses and chug-a-lugged the dark brew, as was the customary response to the toast. They had no sooner placed their empty glasses on the table when they were replaced with a second round.

Paddy, then explained, "Jocko, since our last meeting, when you gave me the skeleton of your grand plan, I've given your proposal a great deal of serious thought. I met with the principals of the local IRA and they were intrigued with the idea of rubbing it into the faces of the Brits through the Yanks. We dusted off all of our contingency plans to welcome the Queen, should she ever dare to set foot in our fair city, and reviewed everything from a missile strike, to a letter bomb, to an Al Capone style Valentine's Day party. The final consensus was that to be sure of hitting the mark, within a small impact area and narrow time frame, it would have to be a bomb. It would have to be of sufficient power to do the job without wide spread effects and of the type that could be set off by someone with a clear view of the target. Enter the Gilhooleys, they are the best of the best for this sort of job." Throughout Paddy's introduction, the Gilhooleys said nothing nor did they take their steely eyes off McCarthy. Jocko felt as if he were undergoing a three-dimensional MRI scan.

Paddy drained his glass and rose to his feet. "Enough of the pleasantries, it's time for you, me and Sean to get down to business. Let's go into my inner sanctum. Seamus and Liam will amuse themselves out here." As Jocko was entering Paddy's office, he glanced over his shoulder and saw that the younger Gilhooley brothers were already joined by two auburn haired colleens.

Paddy's private business office was exactly that. The furniture was expensive, but not gaudy. The chairs comfortable but not plush, and the walls were adorned with various guns, swords, knives, and large mounted animal trophies that Paddy had shot himself. The only picture was a depiction of the Easter Monday battle between Irish patriots and the British. Conspicuous by their absence were any pictures, plaques, or any other items of a personal nature. When Jocko had once commented on the décor, Paddy had replied, with a cold expression on his face, "Jocko, I want the people that I entertain in here to be well aware of just how serious a man I am, and no one will ever discover who my friends, associates and benefactors are just by looking around." Jocko was suitably impressed.

As the three men settled in, Paddy poured them each a sizable shot of Irish whiskey but without a toast this time. During the brief time it took to leave the booth and be seated with their drinks, Jocko sized up the sullen young man he had just met. He was obviously the eldest of the brothers and their leader. His demeanor and dress were non-descript. He could mingle in a crowd without attracting a second glance. His stony face and steely eyes never changed. "Yes," Jocko thought to himself, "I wouldn't want to make an enemy of this man!"

Sean Gilhooley was likewise taking the measure of the American, but his conclusion was less complimentary: "A soft Yank, too used to all the good things of life, too used to having his own way and not much use in a hand-to-hand situation."

Paddy's keen eyes recognized all these maneuvers and he moved quickly to defuse the electricity he felt in the air. "Jocko, I'm sure that you have questions, but first, let me tell you a story. Once upon a time, there was a happy family in Derry.

Mother and father were proud parents of three sons and two daughters. It happened that on one fine Sunday, the family was out for a stroll, when they suddenly found themselves caught in a cross fire between the Brits and the IRA. The family dove for cover behind a brick wall. While their parents and sisters hugged the ground, the boys, fearless and adventurous as teenagers will be, scrambled away to another protected spot to get a better view of the action.

What they saw next made their blood boil. As a British soldier stood up to throw a grenade, he was hit and the grenade wobbled off in the wrong direction and exploded in the midst of the family behind the wall. In one horrible second, the boys had lost their parents and beloved sisters. In that instant was born a terrible hatred of anything and everything English. In time, those lads became ardent members of the IRA and eventually, the fiercest and most successful fighters against everything English. If you haven't guessed it already, that family was the Gilhooleys and Sean here is now the head of the family and the leader of one of the most accomplished bomb squads in the IRA."

Throughout the recitation of the Gilhooley family history, Sean sat in stony silence, sipping his whiskey without any display of emotion. Jocko also sat in silence, smoking his pipe. When Paddy had finished, Jocko acknowledged his understanding with a simple nod of his head. Paddy now took a big sip of his whiskey and keeping his eyes on Jocko said, "I've had my say, now you can ask your questions."

Jocko took his eyes off Sean, turned to Paddy and asked, "Paddy, I'm not happy about what appears to me to be a lack of security. How can we be sure that nobody is on to us? Wasn't it a big gamble for us to meet out in the open in the pub? How can we be sure that we weren't seen by the wrong person? This whole session seems too casual and too laid back for my peace of mind!"

With a smirk on his face, Paddy replied, "Jocko, Jocko, you've been watching too many cloak and dagger telly shows and movies. To everyone in the pub, you are the rich American from Boston, who has deep pockets for the cause. The lads here are infrequent visitors from the west counties. Hardly anyone knows them by sight, but if I sit with them, they have to be okay. Got it?" Without waiting for Jocko to answer, Paddy continued, "This is not the CIA, KGB or MI6. We have no fancy iris scanner, finger print screeners, laser cameras, hidden metal detectors, or a squad of heavies with bulging shoulder holsters scattered about the premises. We don't need them! As a matter of fact, all that electronic crap only draws attention. They would be as out of place here as the Queen herself. We keep things simple, but we make sure that unwanted strangers don't want to come back. If a stranger does return, we do a background check and if anything suspicious turns up, we pass it on to the IRA for action. Locals, who are infrequent visitors get vetted if they keep showing up. Only those who pass the vetting process are accepted as legitimate patrons. Those who don't pass just seem to be accident prone, and we rarely see them again. Have you noticed the red and green lanterns at the ends of the bar? Well, they are not nautical decorations. If a copper or one of the Queen's Scottish lackeys enter, the green light goes out and the red light comes on and stays on until the hostiles leave. The regulars know what the red light means and they mind their Ps and Qs until the buggers leave. We don't spit in their faces or in their beer, but pay full price for their drinks. Nothing is on the house for them. We let them stay as long as they want and we don't pressure them to go. After all," Paddy added with an evil grin on his face, "We're just a typical fun-loving Irish pub. Of course we have an occasional brouhaha, but what pub worthy of being called an Irish pub doesn't. They are usually short and without weapons. My boys can recognize the signs that precede the fisticuffs and hustle the combatants out the door before it becomes a matter for the constabulary. This is a <u>clean</u> house!"

Paddy took another sip of whiskey and continued, "Nothing but serious business is conducted in here, but mind you, this is not a war room nor is it a strategy planning room. It is a room for negotiations where proposals are offered and considered, and recommendations formulated and passed on to the higher-ups. Consider me a facilitator, if you will. You, Jocko, want to buy something. Sean can deliver what you want to buy. I moderate the proceedings during which, by the way, no haggling is permitted. You set a price that you will pay for what you want. Sean will either accept or reject your offer. If need be, one counter offer is made. If no agreement is reached, we shake hands and that's as far as it goes. If a deal is struck, all further negotiations are conducted elsewhere as arranged by the principals. Of course, the simple facts of the meeting, successful or not, are passed on to the local IRA. They keep a close watch on whatever transpires in their bailiwick. Today's proceeding, however, might very well be an exception to that rule. The fewer people who know what we will discuss, the less the risk that the beans will be spilt, as you Yanks say. Now, you ask, does it work? Yes it does. We have never been raided, no one has ever been arrested after leaving here and nothing has drawn the attention of the coppers." At this point, Paddy leaned back in his chair and raised his hands like the parish priest proclaiming, "Let us pray."

Jocko leaned forward to empty the ashes from the bowl of his pipe and voiced the concern that he hoped would not destroy the meeting, "Paddy, 'tis a fine operation you run here and a fine testimonial that you give the Gilhooleys. But I need more specifics on their experience, capabilities and expertise in matters as serious that I will propose."

Sean shot forward from his chair, reaching for the front of Jocko's shirt shouting, "You son of bitch Yank, how dare—" That was a far as he got. Paddy, anticipating his reaction, had immediately jumped up from his chair and thrust one of his large meat hook hands against Sean's chest pushing him back into his chair.

"Cool down Sean, me buckaroo," he said in a tone of voice that clearly indicated that he was in charge. "Jocko, here, is ready to pay a handsome sum for the job he wants done and he's entitled to be sure that he's going to get what he's willing to pay for. Answer the man!"

While this test of wills was being played out, Jocko calmly

refilled his pipe, lit it and settled back into his chair, without ever once taking his eyes off Sean or blinking an eyelid. Paddy took all this in and thought to himself, "Jocko me lad, you've been around the block a few times, haven't ye? I'll bet that in your younger days you had a set of king sized balls."

Sean also noted Jocko's unexpected failure to panic, something he was not used to and accepted, begrudgingly, that here was a man very much like himself. "All right, Yank," he spat out, "at the time we lost our family I was eighteen, Seamus sixteen, and Liam fourteen. I let it be known that we wanted to hook up with the IRA. In due time, we were contacted and introduced to the lower echelon ranks of the Derry IRA. Liam was too young for any serious assignments, so he became a runner. Seamus broke in as junior bodyguard for the offspring of the higher-ups, and I was trained to be a real bodyguard and later an enforcer. One of my mentors was an explosives expert. The tales of his exploits intrigued me so much that I requested to be assigned to the 'big bad boys' as the explosives experts called themselves. My mentor, who still had all ten fingers, told me that to become one of the BBB, I first needed to learn all about explosives, how they were constructed, what they were made of, how they worked, and how to handle them as safely as possible, before I ever laid hands on a device myself. On his recommendation, I joined the British Army and volunteered for the Royal Engineers. Thanks to my mentor, I had learned enough basic knowledge and familiarity with explosives to be accepted. I completed all the required training and eventually my brothers followed in my footsteps."

"We pulled a few strings to be assigned to the same Explosive Ordnance Detachment. Desert Storm was our final exam and we passed with booming success. In the next few years, we went all over the world to get experience working with our French, Italian, German, Israeli, Japanese counterparts, and even your own U.S. Army. By 1996 we were considered an elite unit and assigned to Northern Ireland. To be assigned to conduct operations against our own people was too much for us, so we retired as it were, and were warmly welcomed back onto active duty with IRA. To keep our image low key, we were posted to the Western counties. By my count, we've got thirteen major and about twenty-two minor bombings to our credit. As you no doubt noted, the three of us still have our ten original fingers."

"When Paddy put out the word that he was looking for volunteers for a special job, we were recommended to him for a few good reasons: One: we're good at what we do, Two: we've never turned down an assignment, Three: we've never failed to deliver, and Four: we're lucky. Does that satisfy you, Yank?" The last question was as much of a challenge as a glove slap across the face.

Jocko had never taken his eyes off Sean, matching the younger man's stare. He now leaned forward to empty his pipe without giving any indication that he was impressed with Sean's curriculum vitae. He turned his gaze to Paddy, whose expression was asking, "Well, Jocko?" Jocko nodded 'yes' and the wheels began to turn.

Jocko placed his brief case on the table and opened it. "English pound notes as agreed," Jocko said, adding, "the equivalent of nine thousand American dollars down payment." Sean's eyes started to twinkle and he leaned forward, ostensibly to count the money. Paddy stopped him by shaking his head and wiggling his left index finger, "Now, now, Sean me lad, no need for that. I trust Jocko, and if I trust him, you trust him!" The twinkle in Sean's eyes faded away as quickly as it had appeared.

"As you say, Paddy," he growled, "but I need to know the target, the action date and the level of security the opposition will be able to mount against us."

Jocko shot a quick glance at Paddy, who nodded yes. Jocko leaned forward, almost nose to nose with Sean, and in deliberate tones stated, "The Vice-President of the United States."

"Well now," Sean whistled, "A worthy target, and a formidable challenge, just our cup of tea. But tell me Jocko, why would a fine upstanding Yank like yourself want to do in such a high government official of your own country?"

"Easy," Jocko replied, settling back into his chair, "Carlton Flaherty is the driving force within the U.S. government against self/home rule for Northern Ireland."

Sean let out a high pitched whistle, "Well now, not only a monumental challenge, we have ourselves a true enemy. This is <u>war</u>!" His face literally beamed as he savored the anticipation of the coup. He asked, "Will we have to go to America to do the job and when do you want it done?"

Jocko answered, "I can't give you all the details at this time, but the action will take place right here in Belfast sometime in late November. I'll keep you updated through Paddy, on the nuts and bolts of the operation, you can trust me on that."

Paddy rose to his feet and exclaimed, "It looks like we are all agreed. Let's seal the bargain with a toast." He poured three sizable potions of his best Irish whiskey, neat. Sean and Jocko now also rose and lifted their glasses to Paddy, as he pronounced the toast, "Erin Go Braugh—confusion to the enemies of Ireland." The three conspirators drained their glasses in a single swallow and prepared to leave the room.

As the three men re-entered the pub's main bar, Jocko nodded to the Irishmen and strode purposefully toward the exit to the street. Sean turned to Paddy's social office and an expression of exasperation crossed his face when he saw that his brothers were nowhere to be seen. Paddy also noted their absence and went immediately to a house phone behind the bar, punched in a single number, barked a few short orders and hung up. Within a few minutes, Seamus and Liam came bounding down a flight of nearby stairs. This particular staircase was blocked off by a thick rope, from which hung a sign, stating in capital letters, "FOR MEMBERS ONLY, NO EXCEPTIONS!!!!!" The last non-member, who dared try to ascend those stairs, left the pub in an ambulance to have his broken leg casted at a local hospital. The younger Gilhooleys ignored Sean's glare and the three of them accompanied Paddy back into the private office, from which they left the pub as they had entered it, through Paddy's private entrance. Paddy immediately locked the door after them, reset the security code and returned to his duties as the genial host of the establishment.

What occurred next would have caused Jocko to have serious doubts about his confidence in Paddy's security and severely shaken Paddy's egotistic faith in his security procedures. At a far corner of the bar, a morose patron, giving all the outward appearances of having drunk too many pints, fumbled in his pocket for his cell phone, punched in three numbers, waited for a few seconds, replaced it in his pocket and drained the last of his Guiness. He waved awkwardly to Paddy, who acknowledged the wave by shaking his head. The patron then wove an unsteady path through the pub and on exiting, lurched to his vehicle. Once inside the Land Rover, he laid his forehead against the steering wheel, giving the appearance of a sot trying to clear the cobwebs before attempting to start the engine. What he was really doing was dictating into a mini-voice recorder a complete and detailed report of everything that he had witnessed in the pub, stressing the unexpected appearance of the Gilhooleys and the fact that Jocko had left his brief case behind. He noted, with satisfaction, that Jocko's tail had followed him from the parking lot. He added recommendations for tightening the surveillance on Jocko, that a 24 hour surveillance of the Gilhooleys be started and that a watch on Paddy's private entrance be added. The report would be on the desk of the head of the local British counter-terrorism unit by the time he arrived in his office the next day. Something big was afoot and the authorities needed to find out exactly what it was, and to be quick about it!

CHAPTER 1

FAIRFAX, VIRGINIA
October 22

The totally unpredictable schedule of my occupation made any opportunity for a serious romance something I only dreamed about. My unkempt 'street person' appearance on my return home from an assignment and my habit of hibernating for a few days, to readjust to living in a friendly environment, scared off all the young ladies living in the same condo complex that I did. I was referred to as 'the grizzly bear who lives in the cave on the third floor'.

I had been home from my last assignment in Kabul for about a month, long enough to become humanoid again. My scraggly black beard was now neatly trimmed and my greasy shoulder length hair was shampooed and cut to a more acceptable length. Frequent trips to the gymnasium and hours relaxing in the Jacuzzi completed readjusting my 'bent' psyche. After updating my pistol qualifications at the FBI pistol range at the Quantico Marine Base, I was ready to seek out pleasurable activities while awaiting my next assignment.

I was enjoying a visit to the Smithsonian's Udvar-Hazy Center at Dulles airport and was gawking up at the Concorde when I tripped and crashed into a very pretty young lady. Neither of us was knocked off our feet nor were we injured. A profusion of apologies were mutually exchanged and I learned that Cindy Lou Davies was a stewardess — oops, flight attendant for a charter airline that specialized in foreign charters. Dusting off my rusty social graces, I did the gentlemanly thing to compensate for my awkwardness and invited her to lunch at Macaroni's in Reston. It turned out that she was between flights and that we had mutual interests in the multitude of recreational activities offered in the nation's capital. On successive days, we were able to take in a play at Ford's theatre, attend a special Navy band concert at the DAR Constitution Hall, and enjoy a dinner cruise on the Potomac, before reality claimed both of us. Needless to say, my parents were overjoyed when they learned of Cindy.

The rat race started again on a Sunday in mid-October, a typical Indian summer day when the weather was ideal for a picnic in the park. I had returned home from a Wizard's basketball game. If the truth be known, the only reason I went to the game was that I had won the ticket in a raffle at a Kiwanis club luncheon at which I was a guest earlier in the week. Baseball was my passion and I would have preferred to have been at RFK stadium watching the Nationals play, but their season was over and I couldn't gracefully decline the ticket I had won. For me, nothing, that could take place on the court, could ever compare with the electric tension of a perfectly pitched game, or the exhilaration evoked by a grand slam home run. Be that as it may be, all thoughts of the game had faded by the time I had reached the Dunn-Loring Metro station, one stop short of the end of the Orange line in Vienna. The late afternoon was still hot and humid, so I was glad that it was only a short walk across Gallows Road to my condominium, in a new recently opened development that catered to an upwardly mobile and trendy crowd of budding future CEOs and a bevy of single female government employees.

On entering the refreshing coolness of my condo, the flashing light on my answering machine reminded me to take my cell phone out if its charger. Unlike James Bond, who never went anywhere without some sort of an exotic communications device that always went off at the most inopportune times, I always left my phone at home whenever I was going to be in circumstances that would preclude any sort of a rapid response to an urgent summons. On activating my answering machine, I was greeted by the sultry voice of the Admiral's secretary. Hers was the voice that could calm the most irate Senator or lobbyist who was demanding to talk to her boss immediately, if not sooner.

The message was short and simple, "Glenn, you have an appointment with the Admiral at 0800 on the day after tomorrow, TTFN (ta-ta for now)." It was so typical of the Admiral—not, "He would like to see you," or "Confirm if you can be here for an early morning meeting," or "Can you call for an appointment tomorrow?"—just a curt command to which I was supposed to reply, "Aye-aye Sir." I celebrated my reprieve from a Monday commute to Ashburn by calling Cindy Lou to set up a picnic in Rock Creek Park for the free day. It goes without saying that we had an enjoyable time.

On the morning of the 24th, over my usual breakfast of a sticky bun and two large mugs of high octane coffee, I mulled over the best way to drive from Dunn-Loring to Ashburn. The uncomplicated route was to go up Gallows Road to Route 7 (Leesburg Pike) and head west. The more complicated, but possibly faster, route was to get off Route 7 at the Dulles Toll Road, take it west to Route 28 and then head north to get back on 7 again. I finally realized that it didn't make that much difference either way, because, like Coach Lombardi, when the Admiral scheduled a meeting for 0800 AM, he really meant 0745, and the poor soul who slowly meandered in at 0750 was in for a Class "A" chewing out for being late. That meant, in order to insure that I was in his office by 0745, I had better be on the road by 0630 (almost the middle of the night for me). It was only about a twenty-five mile trip, but you never knew what the early morning rush hour traffic would be, especially on a weekday morning. So I opted for the uncomplicated route.

My usual routine for my trips to the 'office' was to fill a large thermos with high octane brew and tune into the morning show on WGMS, the classical music station for the nation's capital. As I put my red Miata convertible in gear, I sadly missed going to the old office at Dupont Circle in the District because that trip was a short ride on the Metro and a chance for a few more minutes of shut-eye. The weather was clear and warm, and surprisingly, the traffic was light. I lucked out, for Dennis Owens was making one of his frequent fill-in appearances on the morning show and he was in rare form. His wry sense of humor, his patter and his treasure-trove of trivia questions made the trip that much more enjoyable. As I passed the turn off for Wolftrap, my thoughts went back to the very first time that I had responded to a similar curt notification of an early morning appointment with the Admiral.

CHAPTER 2

January 2003

My father was a State Department ambassador, so I grew up in several foreign countries where I learned to speak several languages, including a variety of Arabic dialects. My fluency in the major tongues of the world helped me greatly in graduating, with honors, from the Georgetown University School of Languages and Linguistics. I supplemented my scholarship by enlisting in the Naval Reserve and upon graduation I applied for OCS. My academic record and favorable enlisted evaluations landed me in Newport Rhode Island, where I became a late twentieth century version of a 'ninety-day wonder'.

Upon commissioning as an Ensign in the Naval Reserve, I reported aboard the *USS Rodney M. Davis*, a recently commissioned *Oliver Perry Hazzard* class gas turbine guided missile frigate, to start a three year tour in the Operations Department. In spite of all of its 'state of the art' navigational, propulsion and stabilization systems, King Neptune frequently demonstrated to us mere mortals that he, and he alone, ruled the oceans. Halfway into my tour, I decided that I had had enough of rocking, rolling and pitching, so I applied for and was accepted for

SEAL training. I survived 'hell week' and successfully completed BUD/S training, but not with the credentials to be recruited by the likes of Dick Marcinko to join a merry band of 'shooters and looters'. This did not damage my ego, because I had never subscribed to the macho image of—"live fast, die young, and have a handsome corpse."

In subsequent years, I did my share of hairy and scary operations, like participating in the reconnaissance of, and clearing of obstacles to the Marine's invasion of Kuwait (which never happened) during the wee hours of the morning before the start of the real Desert Storm invasion of Iraq. Following the end of the desert war, I became an underwater world traveler, exploring the territorial waters of North Korea, mainland China, Vietnam and all of the 'hot' spots in the Red Sea, the Persian Gulf, Gulf of Oman and the Gulf of Aden. I almost became a permanent resident of that Indian Ocean paradise known as Diego Garcia. A few of my jobs were really dangerous and life threatening, to me as well as the enemy. I was awarded a Purple Heart and a Bronze Star, but I could never wear them because someone might ask me how I earned them and if I answered, I would have had to kill the questioner.

I eventually reached that point in a Reservist's career when I either went Regular Navy, reverted to Ready or Inactive Reserve status or resigned my commission. I opted out. My decision to leave the Navy was made easy by my perceptions that the military was more interested in training 'huggy-kissy' humanitarians rather than warriors, that selections for promotion and command were based heavily on the espousal of equal opportunity, that sensitivity training was more important than honing combat skills and that more and more of our operations were being initiated by politicians and micro-managed by desk sailors who had never ventured into harm's way. The Captain conducting my separation interview commented, "I see that you're eligible for promotion to Commander, and from your record, you're a 'shoo-in'. Why do you want to get out?"

I then vented twelve years of frustrations and gave him the 'whole nine yards'. When I had completed my litany of reasons for getting out, his only other question was, "Are you through?," and when I said, "Yes," there was a sad expression on his face as he signed my papers, shook my hand and wished me 'fair winds and following seas'.

I had almost two months leave on the books and was still entitled to pay and allowances, so I decided to travel and see some of the places and do some the things that I had been dreaming of doing for years. Towards the end of my separation leave, I found myself in the nation's capital and was resting in my room in the Willard hotel when the phone rang. A voice, deep inside me, told me to ignore it but my curiosity about who would be calling me in a city where I knew nobody overrode the feeling. The pleasant female voice first confirmed that I was me and assured me that it was me she was calling. She identified herself as the private secretary to the Director of the Institute for Intelligence Analysis and told me that the Director wanted to interview me in his office at 0800 the next day. Presuming that I would show up, she then gave me directions on how to get to the Institute, which was located in the Dupont Circle section of Northwest Washington. The same deep voice inside me was telling me to say, "No way!," and to "Hang up before you get yourself into something way over your head." But I was intrigued by the invitation because I knew who the Director was, (every body in the Navy knew who he was) what his reputation was and my curiosity was flying sky high.

The only question I asked was, "Do I wear my uniform?," since I was still considered on active duty. The answer was an emphatic, "Don't you dare! Uniforms are forbidden around here." After I had hung up, second thoughts started to run rampant through my mind. "How does he know enough about me to want to see me in person?," "How did he know I was here?," "What does he want of me?" and "Why was he so sure that I would agree to meet with him?" Needless to say, I did not have a restful night's sleep.

During the short taxi ride to the Institute, I mused on the man I was about to meet. Vice Admiral Vincent T. Billig, USN (Ret) was a legend among naval submarine and intelligence circles. He played on one of the few Naval Academy football teams to beat Notre Dame and the caption under his picture in the Naval Academy yearbook for the class of 1963 summed up his illustrious academy years with the "most likely to become Chief of Naval Operations" accolade. His choice of duty upon graduation was to enter the submarine service. After graduating from submarine school, he earned his dolphins aboard the *USS Blueback*, a diesel powered boat, before progressing to the nuclear powered fleet.. The future Admiral completed command tours in Fast Attack boats and Polaris and Trident 'boomer' boats, sailing in every one of the world's oceans. It was during this period in his life that his social status changed from very eligible bachelor to confirmed bachelor, but he never lacked for female companionship. Several of the ladies he dated tried in vain to pierce his anti-matrimony armor, for his only true loves were the sea and the Navy.

On one of his fast attack patrols, he had successfully tailed a Russian 'boomer' on its Atlantic deployment, from the time it left her Barents Sea home port to the day she returned home, without ever being detected. That feat won a Meritorious Service Medal for him and a Meritorious Unit Citation for the boat and her crew. It was also a key factor in his being 'deep selected' for promotion to the rank of Captain. I had the good fortune to travel on one of his commands as an embarked guest and to experience first hand his competence as a commanding officer, his genuine concern for the well-being of his crew, and his readiness to 'bend the rules' to make the incursion into enemy territory safer for me and my team mates. When he was forced to come ashore in an administrative billet, he changed his submarine designator to that of the intelligence service. I always felt that he had chosen to be involved with intelligence, with headquarters outside the Pentagon, rather than ride a desk in the Pentagon, because he was too out-spoken concerning the apparent lack of valid on-site intelligence reports (similar to those he been tasked to gather), and took up the cause to reverse that trend. He continued to be described as a mixture of Hyman Rickover, "Bull" Halsey, and Ernest J. King, but unlike King and Rickover, he did not enjoy the full favor of the White House. The owners of the egos, he had bruised in doing his job, successfully blocked his promotion to full Admiral, so he 'hauled down his flag' and retired after forty years of continuous Naval service. The picture on the front page of the Navy Times issue reporting his retirement ceremony, presided over by the Chief of Naval Operations and the Chairman of the Joint Chiefs, showed him wearing what looked like the chart of the Navy medals and ribbons on his chest. The only three personal medals that were missing were the Purple Heart, the Prisoner of War Medal and the Congressional Medal of Honor.

The events of 9/11/01 proved that he was ahead of his time, when he was advocating more intense collection of on-site intelligence by humans, and the meticulous evaluation of the gathered facts by a panel of experts who would report directly to the President of the United States. In the aftermath of 9/11, the President was disgusted with the failures of the various 'alphabet soup' intelligence agencies to correctly interpret the now obvious warning signs that preceded 9/11, and to alert him of the catastrophe that was imminent. He conceived the idea of an independent committee whose function would be to analyze the data collected by the various intelligence agencies and to report to him directly what was going on, where it was going on, and who was behind the goings on. He also wanted this select committee to evaluate what impact these goings on would have on the United States. The President's key supporters in Congress attached a series of riders to several of the resolutions honoring the heroes of 9/11 and the legislation designed to prevent recurrences of 9/11, giving the President the authority to form such a committee. To ensure continuity in the leadership of the committee, one of those riders set forth a ten year term of office for the chairman of the committee.

Armed with the enabling authorizations, the President called upon his old friend and shipmate, Vice Admiral Vincent T. Billig, USN (RET) to accept the first chairmanship of the new committee. The two of them then fleshed out the skeleton of the committee that became the nucleus of the Institute for

Intelligence Analysis. Admiral Billig charged into his new job with the same eagerness and resolve that had been his trademark as skipper of a fast attack boat. Under his leadership, the committee soon became a premier body of professionals, whose one and only duty was to keep the Oval Office and the Joint Chiefs of Staff 'up to speed' on current events, subversive plots, and terrorist threats that were of immediate importance, right here and now. The committee's success led to it being renamed the Institute for Intelligence Analysis and the Admiral became its first Director.

My musings ended as the taxi arrived at the Institute. I presented my ID card to the security guard and passed through the metal detector without setting off any bells or whistles. The receptionist in the deserted, and funeral parlor like lobby, told me that I was expected and directed me to take lift number 3 (read English accent) to the third deck (third floor). I later found out that she was a 'black belt' and the second line of defense against any unfriendly intrusions into the building, should anyone get by the security guard. Her primary job was to smile sweetly at tourists who were allowed in the lobby and to tell them that there was really nothing for them to see other than the pictures on the walls depicting naval battles from the Revolutionary war to the present, and that guided tours of the building were not available. She was so adept at not sending tourists away disappointed, that no one had ever written a letter of complaint. This morning she smiled at me and went back to what ever she did to occupy her time.

When I got off the elevator on the third deck, I found myself in another lobby, about half the size of the ground floor lobby. It was presided over by the private secretary who had called me the previous evening. She was older than the young English lass in the reception lobby, but she was definitely all woman, in her expensively tailored suit and very stylish hairdo. It was not quite 0800, so I was invited to take a seat on a very soft and comfortable leather couch. At precisely eight o'clock I heard a clock behind the doors to the inner office strike eight bells. As the last bell sounded, Miss Eagleton (as the name plate on her desk proclaimed) nodded towards the door of the Admiral's sanctum and said, "You can go in now."

On entering the Director's office, I was struck by the simplicity of the décor, to be exact, the lack of the usual trappings of most Washington offices. Conspicuous by their absence were plaques of honor, celebrity autographed photos and framed citations. A large portrait of Winston Churchill scowled down on the Director from behind his desk. The Prime Minister was flanked on one side by "Bull" Halsey and on the other side by Vince Lombardi. I learned later that whenever the Admiral was asked if he had a patron saint, his quick response was, "Sure I do, there he is—St. Vincent of Lombardi." Directly across the room were the only other wall decorations, a portrait of the President, between portraits of General Patton and Admiral Nimitz.

The Admiral was seated behind his desk that held a red phone, a white phone, a black phone, an intercom, a super sophisticated computer and one of the latest video phones. I learned later that the red phone was a direct line to the Oval office, the white a direct line to the Pentagon office of the Chairman of the Joint Chiefs, while the black phone connected him to the rest of the world. There was neither an in nor an out box and no stacks of paper in view. Apparently, items of business were taken care of immediately or delegated to the appropriate section for action. He was speaking into the black phone and motioned me to have a seat at the small conference table, strategically placed within arm's reach of his desk. The phone conversation ended and the 60+ year old man, who looked 40, with a physical profile that shouted that he could (and probably did whenever he had the urge to do so) complete the annual physical fitness test with flying colors, stood up and moved over to the table and greeted me: "Good Morning Commander Stark, good of you to come here today." (as if I had a choice). His handshake was so firm that it seemed like my hand had been gripped by a vise. With the pleasantries completed, he took his seat at the head of the table, activated a hidden call button and made small talk until Miss Eagleton brought in a coffee service and left the room without speaking a word.

CHAPTER 3

After we each had a swallow of delicious coffee, the Admiral took a large, plain manila folder from a well concealed drawer in the table. He then came right to the point and in a tone of voice that left no doubt that he was in charge stated: "O.K.—ground rules--#1-I talk first and you listen, #2- I'll answer most of your questions before you ask them, and #3- when I'm done—it's your turn." Talk about taking a broadside before you even know you're in a battle. At that point I didn't even know that I would have questions, but who was I to argue with the man.

With his face completely devoid of expression and his steely gray eyes zeroed in on my face, he began: "First, how did I hear of you and how did I learn all about you? About two months ago, a four stripper friend of mine in San Diego called me after he had completed a separation interview with a man he described as a 'hot runner', who had all the qualifications to work for me. Second— 'why me you ask'? Since being tipped off about you, I got your service jacket and after digesting it I contacted several of your former commanding officers, who confirmed that what they had written about you in their fitness reports was the 'straight skinny'. They all agreed that you should be recruited for the Institute. In the past two months, I've kept tabs on you, giving you time to cool off, and when you showed up here in the District, I felt that the time was right for us to meet face to face."

He then opened the manila folder and extracted the original of my Officer's service record, a clear demonstration of the amount of 'pull' he possessed. It was rumored that so many people owed him so many payback favors that he wouldn't live long enough to call in all the markers. Without great ceremony he leaned forward, opened the jacket and took out a written sheet of paper on which he had obviously made lots of notes.

He then started to read from his notes, like a prosecuting attorney reading a list of charges. "Stark, no middle name, Glenn, age 33, single-never married, height 5'11," weight 187, brown hair, brown eyes, no distinguishing facial features, no tattoos, no distinguishing marks or scars, physically fit–graduated from Georgetown University with a major in languages and a minor in partying, served a tour as Communications Officer and Assistant Operations Officer at sea, volunteered for SEAL training and survived. Decorations—Navy Achievement Medal, Navy Commendation Medal, Meritorious Service Medal, Meritorious Unit Citation, Presidential Unit Citation, Bronze Star and Purple Heart—among others." At that point, he looked up from his notes and added: "I haven't the slightest idea of what you did to earn those honors, nor do I care to know. The fact that you did earn them, and are still living says enough about your character and moral fiber."

He then returned to his notes and continued reading aloud: "In the zone for Commander, but declined to augment into the Regular Navy and chose to resign his commission." He took a deep breathe and snorted his displeasure at the last two comments. He then went on, "significant personal comments—enthusiasm that never wanes in the face of adversity—leads from in front, not behind—fierce determination to complete an assigned mission, regardless of the danger involved—truly cares for and looks out for his men, not politically correct—and tolerates poorly fools, incompetents and yes-men." He replaced the sheet in the folder, slammed it shut, and thundered, "End of service!"

He then folded his hands on top of the jacket and with an

expression on his face, like the cat who had just swallowed a canary, proceeded in a much milder tone, "Which brings me to question 3, what do we do here? We read other peoples mail, that's what we do here. The old 'cloak and dagger' style of intelligence gathering doesn't cut it any more in this day of electronic wizardry. In this office we don't subscribe to the old Victorian code of ethics that said, 'a gentleman does not read another gentleman's mail', there are no gentlemen any more. Political and military ethics of today are, 'do your enemy (or potential enemy) before he does you'. To 'do them before they do us', it is mandatory for us, I mean the USA, to know what is going on anywhere and everywhere in the world, and lately, even in space. We accomplish this by listening in on every type of communications known to man, sorting them out, decoding them when necessary, and keeping everything in 'real time'. My people here do this so well that it is not uncommon for me to read a message before the addressee. This is how we keep a jump or two ahead of the 'bad guys'. Our peers in all the other agencies that deal with intelligence send us what they can't figure out and we take it from there. When even we can't be sure of what we're dealing with, we send out field agents to wherever the source of the quandary is to get 'down and dirty', face to face, and one on one with the 'bad guys'. Now to question #4—what do I want of and from you? Well, for one; you have mega-balls, two; you have a thick skin, three; you aren't afraid to speak you mind, four; you don't have a 'politically correct' bone in your body, and last; you're a survivor and you're lucky. I want you to work for me!"

Having dropped the bombshell, he went on to explain, "All the electronics and gadgets that are connected to all the antennae that you see on the roof of the building, are just that—gadgets that did not have the intellectual capacity of robot #5 from the movie "Short Circuit". Once the gadgets collect the raw data, it is the job of our analysts, working over hot computers in air condition cubicles, to digest the raw input, chew on it from several viewpoints, thereby arriving at an informed and highly accurate analyses of the pieces of information. If they came up short, they sent for the likes of you!" How was that for a thumbnail job description.

After a few more deep breaths, he went on, "Those analyses become the bases of briefings to all sorts of officials, at all levels of the bureaucracy who are supposed to give the muckity-mucks, who have a need to know, what they need to know, along with rational recommendations on what actions the muckity-mucks should take in response to the situation discovered." He pounded his fist on the table, and continued, "All the sophisticated electronic gadgets in this building, or in the world, can't read fear or hatred in a man's eyes, detect a tremor in his voice, see a bead of sweat forming on his brow nor notice the start of a nervous tic. Only another living human being, in a face to face confrontation, can see these details that can spell the difference between the truth and a pack of deliberate lies, intended to confuse and/or cause us to make big mistakes. In short, we must have, now have, and will continue to have HUMINT, human intelligence, to complement our whiz kids. That's where you come in, we need real live people, willing to risk their lives by going into dangerous situations, in order to confirm whether or not the intelligence we gather is for real, or a pack of lies to deceive us." In other words, he used his agents as his legs, and he wanted me to become one of his legs.

He went on to describe 'his' Institute as a modern day mix of the Bletchley Park and Pearl Harbor's Station Hypo snoops, civilians and military people, who decoded Germany's and Japan's coded message traffic, and helped to win WWII. He stressed that it was important in today's world to read <u>everybody's</u> mail, in whatever form, domestic and foreign, to stay 'up to speed' on what was being hatched anywhere in the world. I sort of got the idea that it was now my turn when he asked, "Do you have any other questions?"

Being a practical chap, with no source of income once my terminal leave was up I asked, "How much?" He leaned back in his chair and broke into a smile that went from ear to ear. It literally screamed, "I knew it, I knew that was going to be your question." Without batting an eyelash, he quoted a pay grade, several steps above my LCDR stripes, accompanied by perks and bennies that I had never knew existed.

I asked my last question, "How much time do I have to think it over?"

Very benignly he answered, "Take all the time you need— five minutes should be enough."

The prospects of continuing to use my linguistic talents and the skills I had acquired as a SEAL, as well as becoming used to the life style my new found level of financial security could give me, were too much to refuse. I joined his team and became an under-cover agent— a spy!

In the following years, I assumed a character totally different from the spit and polish SEAL officer. I let my hair grow longer, grew a full beard, got myself a deep <u>total</u> body tan, and got accustomed to wearing grubby clothes. It was not unusual for me to be sent to spots like Teheran, Baghdad, Aden, Damascus, Amman, and Islamabad, where I was constantly in the company of 'dirt bags' who wouldn't hesitate a second to kill me, if my cover was ever blown.

CHAPTER 4

ASHBURN, VIRGINIA
October 24

The traffic west on route 7 was not bad, so I made good time and was in no danger of being late for the meeting. I had just passed the intersection of route 7 with route 28, and moved into the right lane for the turnoff into University Center, probably named for the Loudoun campus of George Washington University located there. The university was the first structure built there, but then new construction boomed to include the new headquarters of several companies formerly located in the District. In 2004, it became evident that we had outgrown the Dupont Circle address and a move to bigger quarters was necessary. The Admiral had prevailed upon the Government Accounting Office and the Office of Management for the Budget to begrudgingly cough up the funds for our new suburban home. The Ashburn location was selected because of its proximity to Dulles airport, its accessibility to several major highways, and because, at that time the price was right.

Someone in the Bureau of Idiotic Nomenclature had found out that there were so many Ph.D.s on staff that the payroll looked like the faculty of the nearby university. So they tried to rename the Institute the ACADEMY for Intelligence Analysis, and change the Admiral's title from Director to Dean. The Admiral vigorously and successfully fought against the proposed name changes. It took all of the negotiating skills the Admiral possessed in abundance, plus the weight of his reputation and his calling in of several 'markers' that he held to overcome the name changes. It was the title 'Dean' that caused much of his resistance to the re-designation attempt. It was well known that he was turned off by the supercilious demeanor of many high ranking academicians, and therefore few bureaucrats dared to cross swords with him on the subject. So, the Institute remained the Institute and the Admiral kept the title of Director.

The new building was a four story steel and glass structure, constructed in a style that was disrespectfully termed 'modern ugly'. But it served its purpose. Entrance into the sprawling parking lot was through a locked gate that was opened by pressing your left thumb against a sensor. If you had the correct thumb print, the gate opened. If your thumb print was not on file, an alarm sounded and a security vehicle carrying at least two well armed security guards suddenly appeared to question the legitimacy of your visit. Once through the gate, I drove into the garage under the building where department heads, senior staff, and VIPs had assigned stalls. Access to this garage was past a gate house, presided over by another security guard. The magic 'Open Sesame' ticket to pass the guard was a special plastic ID card that the guard ran through a sensor in his kiosk. These special cards were replaced at irregular intervals. One time visitors were met at the kiosk by a staff member who had the final say on whom the guard admitted. I had no trouble getting into the garage and headed for the section of the Senior Staff parking area, where people like me who only went there on demand, parked in unmarked slots. Access to the upper levels was by elevators, one of which went only to the fourth deck and required yet another card to enter the cage and start its ascent. Talk about security, yssssh. The fourth deck, dubbed the "bridge," was only about one-half the size of the other levels. It was divided into several sections: a reception area, the offices of the Director, and his second-in-commandSgtMajor the Vice-Director, commonly called just 'Vice', and a combined auditorium and lounge that was used for staff meetings and receptions for really important VIPs. Beyond the enclosed area, on the roof of the third level, was an array of dishes, radars, and other paraphernalia typical of a 'spook shack'. Being a prudent man, I presented myself to Miss Eagleton at 0730 who greeted me with a relieved smile that whispered, "Thank God you're on time." I was pleasantly surprised to see that the English receptionist from the old building lobby had obviously been promoted to be the private secretary to the Vice. She was seated at a desk that was almost as big as Miss Eagleton's and greeted me with a cheery, "G'day mate". I bet she had recently seen a Crocodile Dundee flick. With 13 minutes to kill before H-hour, I helped myself to a cup of deliciously aromatic Columbian coffee and wondered what was waiting for me.

Frequent visitors to the Admiral's office were familiar with the scene that they saw on entering his office. If there was no beverage on the desk nor a chair in front of the desk, it meant that your stay was going to be short, either to give concise report or to receive an equally terse assignment and depart. If there was a straight-backed chair in front of the desk and a steaming mug of coffee on the desk, you were probably there for a discussion, but don't get too comfortable or take too long to drink your one mug of coffee. Most of those meetings were over in less than twenty minutes. If on the other hand, there was a pot of steaming coffee, several cups, and an assortment of donuts and Danish pastries on the conference table, you were there for a long session that was going to be very serious and probably convoluted. Today, the conference table held a large coffee urn, 3 large mugs, and a tray filled with donuts, Danish pastries, bagels and an assortment of cream cheese. There were also cushioned chairs instead of the usual wooden uncomfortable chairs placed around the table. It was going to be a very long morning!

The Director was at his desk and talking on the white phone. He nodded his greeting to me and pointed to the table. I took a seat and started going through the large folder that was in front of my place.

CHAPTER 5

I had barely settled into my usual chair, to the Admiral's left, when the telephone call ended and the Admiral arose, stretched like a cat getting ready to pounce on a mouse, and casually, too casually for him, ambled to the table. He poured himself a full mug of coffee and plopped resoundingly into his chair at the head of the table. I had barely opened the file, when he surprised me by sayingSgtMajor "Take your time with your coffee and be sure to sample a sticky bun."

He added, "That file is the result of a month of painstaking work by the "Hacker" who will be joining us soon, I hope. He'll give you a full briefing, and update me on anything of importance that has taken place since he hand delivered the folder to my office late yesterday afternoon."

I had no doubt that the Admiral had stayed up late last night, reading and digesting each and every word contained in the report. The folder had obviously never left the Institute, as it was tagged, "Top Top Secret". A small yellow sticker stated, "For Authorized Eyes Only" and "Don't Touch Me If You Want To Live". So the Admiral had a sense of humor after all. The mention of the "Hacker" whetted my curiosity and I automatically raised the level of my attention, "up a few notches" as

Emeril Lagasse would say.

I had never met the "Hacker," but his reputation was well known within the 'spook' community. He was respected as the apotheosis in the field of cryptology and computer science. There never was a code, no matter how complicated, like the German 'enigma' that he could not crack, and no computer system had up to now been devised that he could not hack into, regardless of its sophistication or security guards. To put it simply, he was the best of the best, with no peer. It was this reputation that motivated the Admiral to engage his services, treat him royally, shower him with 'perks' and 'bennies', and pay him an emperor's salary for his expertise. The Admiral thought he was worth every penny to keep him working for us exclusively.

I'd never met the man, but I had conjured up the image of a small, thin man, with a receding hair line and wearing thick glasses. I felt sure that his hand shake would be wishy-washy and that he would speak in whispers. I suspected that I would have to get a hearing aid if we were to spend much time together. As this image faded, the intercom buzzed and Miss Eagleton announced, "He's on his way."

The Admiral muttered, "It's about time." As we turned our attention to the door, it suddenly burst open and the breathless figure of a young man rushed into the room, apologetic for being late. I later learned that he was almost never on time and that he was the only person who got away with being tardy. Just like Paul Horning was Coach Lombardi's favorite, the "Hacker" was Admiral Billig's 'Golden Boy'. That he was so blessed was further made evident when the Admiral delayed starting the meeting until the "Hacker's" respiratory rate had returned to normal. He was also allowed a few sips of coffee and had a few bites of a Danish. My immediate gut reaction to his appearance was, "So much for my ability to conjure up pictures of someone I had never met." The man, who had joined us, had just a trace of a limp, was at least 6 foot 4 and weighed a solid 240 pounds. He wore no glasses and had a full head of black hair. He looked more like an All-Pro football player than a 'spook'. As I later found out, my rapid reassessment was not that too far off.

Kevin Jablonski had played college football for Notre Dame. During his first three years, he started every game, alternating easily between tight end and wide receiver. At the end of his Junior season, he was an unanimous choice for first string All American and winner of the Heisman trophy. The pundits had already projected that he would be the first player to win the Heisman two years in a row, since Archie Griffin of Ohio State had done it in 1975-76. He was felt to be a cinch to repeat as an All American and to be a first round NFL draft choice.

All these hopes, dreams, and aspirations had come to a screeching halt just before his Senior year when he inadvertently barged into a convenience store hold-up. His size, his booming voice and his ability to out-scowl even the likes of 'Mean Joe Green' had caused the gunman to panic and to immediately shoot him. A large caliber, high velocity bullet slammed into his left thigh and ripped into the middle of his femur. The shot was at close range and the caliber of the bullet caused a devastating injury. The femur was broken into two widely separated segments, the ends of which were shattered, and massive soft tissue damage was done. "Sic Transit Gloria". It took almost 2 years of orthopedic and neurological surgery, physiotherapy and the full nine yards of rehabilitation skills to enable him to walk again using neither cane or crutch, albeit leaving a small limp. During the arduous and complicated convalescence, he had done everything he could to stay physically fit, a task he had doggedly and painfully pursued and finally mastered. He also changed his major from physical education to cryptology and computer science to keep himself mentally fit during the long months recovery. He took his studies as serious as his football career, and I was now looking at the finished product.

The Admiral had winced when Kevin had shaken hands with him and as we were introduced he shook my hand with a vise like grip that he must have perfected to keep the football from being stripped from his hands. Needless to say, I did more than wince, and after checking to see that I still had five functioning fingers, we finally got down to work.

CHAPTER 6

Just as he was about to start the meeting, the Admiral suddenly stood up. All the coffee that he had drunk since early morning had finally caught up with him, requiring a trip to the 'necessary'. As he headed in that direction, he said "Glenn, Kevin and I both know what's in the folder, while I'm busy, go through it,——and, Kevin—comb your hair." I used the lull in the action to pour myself another mug of coffee and to liberally garnish a poppy-seed bagel with pineapple cream cheese. Kevin did as he told, and went to a sink in a far corner and combed his hair.

On finally opening the file, I noted that it contained four sets of colored paper– red, white, blue and yellow. The red sheets had the most entries, printed on both sides, that were transcripts of messages, all originating within the offices of the North Korean Trade Commission. This Commission was a relative new-comer to the Washington scene, whose stated purpose was to get for North Korea the same "Favored Nation Trading Status" as was enjoyed by the Red Chinese. The messages were all sent to the same addressee—The North Korean foreign office in Pyongyang. There was no incoming traffic, indicating a curious one way correspondence. They all had the phrase '*Red Storm*' scattered throughout the body of each message.

The white sheets held transcripts of messages that had originated in the Syrian Embassy, all of which were addressed to the Syrian foreign office in Damascus. There were frequent references to '*White Lightening*', and as with the North Korean message traffic, there were no return messages

The blue sheets contained typewritten copies of transatlantic telephone conversations between a "Jack" in Boston and a "Paddy" in Belfast. An alert 'snoop' at the New England desk of the firm had picked them up purely by accident, but was sufficiently 'tweaked' by their conspiratorial tone and frequent referrals to '*Blue Streak*' to open a file. Some times we do fall into the stuff and come up with a jewel. These conversations were also of the one-way variety. "Jack" had done all the talking, and "Paddy" had listened, contributing only grunts that sounded like 'yeahs' and 'nahs'.

The yellow sheet had very little written on it, none of which made sense to me. I then re-read each section more slowly and thoroughly.

The first intercept on the red sheets was dated 2 September 2006 at 2358. My first thought was, "Who was the idiot doing business at midnight on a Saturday," until I realized that it was about noon the next day in Korea. It was a short message, "*Red Storm* on track, proceed with plans according to schedule." Since that first transmission, there were five others, all with the buzz phrase '*Red Storm*' somewhere in the body of the message.

The intercepts on the white sheet started on Sunday, 3 September 2006 at 0500. Again, I thought (to myself of course), "Have the Arabs gone off the deep end too," until I recalled the time differences between the USA and the Middle East, and the fact that Moslems did not observe 'Sunday Routine'. The key phrase was, "*White Lightning* almost certain to strike in the third week in November. More details to follow as they arise." There were only three follow up messages, indicating that definite details up in the air.

The content of the blue sheets suggested that "Jack," whoever he was, was running the show and that "Paddy" was some kind of an agent for a band of freelance IRA reprobates. The first tape that was picked up by chance was also direct, "*Blue Streak* definitely heading your way. I'm coming over there next week to confirm the financial arrangements." The conversation took place on October 2nd, 2006 at 1100. "Jack," at least, seemed to like doing business during the day. There were only two other recordings that made it into the file, both dealing with travel reservations.

Before I could start on the yellow sheet the Admiral had returned and took up right where he left off, with only a very short pause to refill his coffee mug. "OK, Kevin, you have the floor, tell us what your 'little gray cells' make of all this." He then settled back into his chair, lit a cigar, closed his eyes, and started to blow smoke rings. He knew what was coming. On the other hand, I was all ears.

Kevin began, 'Let's start with the North Korean stuff first. Remember, what I'm going to say is part presumption, part obvious conclusions, and part educated guesswork. But, that's what I get paid for. It doesn't take a rocket scientist to figure out that the North Koreans are cooking something up that will probably take place late in November, somewhere in the Western Pacific. We're not sure at this time whether '*Red Storm*' is a code name for an operation or a person, but an educated guess is that '*Red Storm*' is a person, and that some sort of a naval operation is involved. I guess that because, as far as I can determine, there is nothing of importance scheduled to take place on the Korean peninsula in that time frame, not above or below the 38th parallel.

The other two locales, Northern Ireland and the Near and/or Middle East, always have something boiling. Since neither the Northern Irish nor the land locked Arab nations have any sizeable naval forces, we conclude that whatever is going to happen there, is going to take place on land, but we haven't completely ruled out an aerial event. One can never be sure in dealing with these mind sets whether a suicide bombing or a hi-jacking is being planned. For the present, my educated guess is a ground action. Like the problem in the Pacific, all that we are pretty sure of, is that something of big importance will take place in Northern Ireland and the Middle East. I can't narrow it down any further at this time, but they are probably going to go down close together. I'm positive that '*White Lightning*' is a person, but I can't be sure about '*Blue Streak*'. We'll keep our ears in the air, and update the package every day."

Throughout the briefing, my 'little gray cells' were moving at warp speed. What a jumbled up puzzle we had to solve. The Director then asked, "Glenn, any questions?, and by the way, don't worry about the yellow sheet, it is just all the date/time groups of the other colored sheets listed in chronological order. You'll notice that there are some entries that don't match the red, white, or blue ones, entries that don't make sense at present, but anything that falls into the time frame we are investigating deserves mention. Kevin will keep us up to speed as he checks out the times and dates."

I nodded my head, "Yes," and spoke up. "How many people know what's on these papers? How many copies of this folder are there? Are each of the sections of the folder worked on by specific teams, or is it a collective effort? Finally, are there any indications that there is some sort of a grand conspiracy underway?"

The Admiral opened his eyes and sat forward in his seat, but before he could take the stub of the cigar from between his lips, Kevin jumped in again. "As far as I know, only the three of us are privy to the whole ball of wax and this is the one and only folder. The New England, Far East, and Middle East sections are all working independently. I specifically don't want them comparing notes, but who can say. I can't eliminate all the scuttlebutt but these people are all professionals who realize that their jobs are to give me their reports with as many cross references that are even remotely related, and I take it from there. The only collective effort is here (as he tapped his skull). I'm the only person who sees all the inputs, unless the boss asks for independent input, which he hasn't done so far. Every scrap of paper that comes into my dungeon is shredded right there by me when I'm finished with it and I personally take the shred box to the burn room and watch the contents go up in smoke. Can I give you a 100% guarantee that someone has not made a copy of any original before giving to me, no I can't, but remember, every piece of paper that we work with has a special indicator that shows up if it is run through a photocopier, and nothing has showed up so far—satisfied? And lastly, there is no indication that the 'bad guys' are talking to each other. Each group appears to have its own agenda, that they are working on alone."

The Admiral finally got to have his say, "Kevin has it right, the staff members who intercepted the communications and those who decoded them have accomplished some epic work in penetrating the highest security codes of North Korea and Syria in a short period of time. The translators are second, third, and fourth generations of Americans of Asian and Middle East descent, who burned a lot a midnight oil to keep everything current and accurate. A lot of time and effort went into dissecting "Jack" and "Paddy's" conversations to ensure that there was no voice or word code involved, or double meaning in 'Paddy's Irish vernacular. Through all the Admiral's accolades, I could see the 'Hacker's' fine hand, coordinating the workings of the separate sections and probably doing a sizeable portion of the work himself.

By now, the cigar stub had been crushed out and the Admiral took the conn. "The elements of a newspaper reporter's work revolves around finding the answers to these questions—-Who, What, Where, When, Why, and How. So what do we have here?

Who — I agree with Kevin that the whos are people, I'll tell you why I think so later—

What — Something of extreme international importance is afoot, but exactly what we aren't sure, but I have an idea that I'm keeping to myself for the present—

Where — In three different places that we're sure of—

When — Probably in a window between the 15th and 30th of November this year—

Why — I don't know exactly yet, but the hair on the back of my neck tells me that that they are

	all tied up together, and spell big trouble for us—
How —	Probably terrorist type attacks. Kevin has given us skeleton to build on, so let's start brain-storming a few possible scenarios."

"Now let me give you some hot information that isn't in the folder. This is for your ears only. It has not been officially announced yet but the President, himself, not the Secretary of State, will represent us at the Far East Trade Summit in Tokyo in November, and he will pay a courtesy call on the Governor of Guam on the way out. Over the objections of the Secret Service, the Vice-President will represent us at the wedding of the Irish Republic's Prime Minister's daughter, also in late November and then head to Belfast for a very short visit with family members who still live there. And very soon, an invitation from the Israeli Medical Society will be extended to Representative Rosen, the Speaker of the House to be the principal speaker at their annual meeting in late November in Jerusalem. So we now have some flesh to put on the bones—

Who —	Most probably the three highest ranking officials of our government—
What —	Not sure, harassment-demonstrations-physical assaults, who can say—
How —	Up for grabs"

"We have our work cut out for us. It's time for the HUMIT to go to work. I've been itching for a long time to get out from behind that desk over there and here's my chance. I'm heading West to Pearl Harbor and then on to Yokosuka to speak directly with the Navy brass and spooks out there…. Glenn, you have a reservation on a flight from Dulles to London tomorrow."

He reached into the table's drawer and pulled out a thick airline ticket packet, and slid it across the table to me. He continued, "MI6 in London, and Mossad in Jerusalem will be expecting you, but they don't know why you're coming. They may have an inkling, but they are playing it cool. Kevin—you're to take personal charge of the New England section. Move it to Boston if working on location might facilitate discovering who "Jack" is.

But keep your fingers in all the other pies at the same time. And finally, to answer your questions, (remember-he's an expert in answering questions before they're asked) we are keeping this 'in house' at present. Too many government agencies working on the same case exponentially increase the risk of a leak. Until we have the full picture, the three of us are the only players."

He signaled the end of the meeting by picking up the folder and placing into his safe. As he turned back from the safe, he looked at us with a twinkle in his eyes, "What are you two waiting for?—GO!" It was a good thing that he wound up the meeting at that point, because the coffee urn was empty, all the pastries had been eaten, and my bladder was sending me urgent messages.

CHAPTER 7

HAWAII
October 25

In keeping with his desire to keep the present operation under wraps, the Admiral opted to travel as inconspicuously as he could, so he flew commercial from Dulles to Honolulu via Los Angeles on a non-government issued ticket using up some of the scads of frequent flyer miles he had accumulated. He even flew as Mr. Billig in civilian attire. Even though flying first class, the two back to back five hour flights put a strain on his usually unflappable nature, as evidenced by the scowl on his face upon de-planing in Honolulu, which made him stand apart from all the other happy tourists. He was met in the arrival lounge by an aloha shirt garbed Navy driver, who took him, in an unmarked government sedan, to the Senior Officer's Quarters at the Makalapa complex, just above Pearl Harbor. It was only 10:30 PM Hawaiian time, but his body time was 3:30 AM Eastern time so the Admiral immediately hit the sack. Before turning in, he called Admiral Peter Robinson, Commander Pacific Fleet, to let him know that he had arrived and to give him a thumb nail synopsis of the questions that he desperately needed answered.

October 26

At exactly 0800, he was ushered into Admiral Robinson's office, followed by the Admiral's steward carrying a pot of Kona coffee and a tray of fresh tropical fruits. The two admirals were old buddies, so they greeted each other like long lost friends, with little formal Navy protocol. While they were still on their first cups of coffee, Admiral Robinson's Intelligence officer arrived and began a 'heads up' presentation to Admiral Billig. Sounding like a college professor delivering a lecture, he laid out what they knew about "Operation Red" as they called it—

Yes — fleet intelligence was aware of frenzied goings on in North Korea,

Yes — it did appear that a naval operation was being planned,

Yes — the tentative operation date was late in November,

No — they didn't know that the Secretary of State was not going to represent the United States at the Trade Summit,

No — since there was no North Korean presence in the islands, they were not working with 'right now' information, but they were getting daily updates from Japan that were almost 'right now',

Yes — they were paying strict attention to all Communist bloc shipping in the Central Pacific Ocean,

No — the 'buzz' words *Red Storm* did not show up in any ship messages, either incoming or outgoing. The traffic was concerned with weather conditions, but what used to be sporadic reports were now being sent every 48 hours to North Korean Naval Headquarters.

There was a short question and answer period with Admiral Billig doing the asking. The answers he received confirmed a few of the ideas that he was sure of in his own mind, and reinforced the need for him to continue on to Japan. After the Intelligence Officer had taken his leave, letting out a sigh of relief as he passed through the door, the two flag officers concocted a special communications network that plugged Admiral Robinson's 'spook' shack directly into the Admiral Billigs's office in Virginia. The purpose of this was to focus specifically on anything that could be related to the forth coming North Korean naval operation. With the meeting concluded, there was just enough time for Admiral Billig to board a nonstop flight to Narita International Airport in Japan. The same driver, who had picked the Admiral up the previous evening, was waiting for him right outside the ComPacFlt office, again in civvies with an unmarked vehicle. On the short trip back to the Honolulu airport, the Admiral had a twinge of remorse that his time on Oahu was too short for a meal at John Domini's, his most favorite restaurant on the island.

Prior to leaving the East Coast, Admiral Billig had arranged a meeting with two other old friends, Vice Admiral Thomas Kiesel, Seventh Fleet Commander, and Rear Admiral Harry Drapcho, Commander Naval Forces Japan. This meeting was set up as a social call, using hand written letters sent by regular air mail, to play down the serious matters to be discussed, and to avoid speculation about the unscheduled visit by Admiral Billig. Reading between the lines, the language of the letter said, "I've got a hot potato on my hands and I need to meet with both of you to pick up some 'on-the-spot' news. I suggest that we meet ashore, and away from headquarters to avoid any chance of starting any 'scuttle-butt'."

JAPAN
October 28

To further avoid calling attention to himself, the Admiral went through the usual Japanese customs and immigration procedures like any other American business tycoon. Once into the massive arrival lobby of Narita airport, he quickly identified the civilian Japanese driver, who was waiting for him near the counter where U.S. Navy personnel gathered while waiting for the 'blue' bus to the Yokosuka Naval Base. He was lead to an unmarked executive Toyota sedan and was whisked to the naval base, some 25 miles south of Tokyo. As soon as they were on the Shuto Expressway, the driver contacted his dispatcher to confirm that his passenger had arrived and was enroute. When the Admiral saw the Tokyo tower in the distance, he wondered if he would be able to get back to Tokyo in time to see a performance of the Takarazuka all girls dance troupe, but decided that the enjoyable show was a luxury he would have to forego this trip.

He then unlocked his briefcase, re-read the updated 'red' file, and started to put in order the questions he needed answered. Towards the end of the commute ride, he sadly realized that jet lag was more tiring than he had expected and reluctantly accepted the fact that he getting a little old to be a field agent. He silently thanked Miss Eagleton for scheduling his first meeting for after the evening meal hour to give him a chance to reset his physiological clock. He was well aware that both of the admirals he was going to meet with had agendas of their own to attend to during regular working hours. So after freshening up in the posh VIP suite in the BOQ, he took himself to one of his favorite restaurants, Yasohachi's yakitori shop, which was within walking distance from the base's main gate, in the Ginza section of the city of Yokosuka.

At precisely 1930, he arrived at Admiral Drapcho's home, as did Admiral Kiesel.. CNFJ had complied with the Director's request for a low-profile meeting by arranging it as a small informal reception for the Seventh Fleet Commander and all three flag officers were in civvies. The main purpose of this preliminary session was to explain in detail why my Admiral was there, what he needed to learn, and to impress on his colleagues the necessity for utmost secrecy. His flag colleagues were very familiar with the way that Admiral Billig operated, so there only a few issues that had to be ironed out by affable compromises. It was decided that further meetings would take place in Admiral Drapcho's headquarters because the main intelligence shop was ashore. Admiral Kiesel would be kept 'up to speed' at every step of the way.

October 29

At exactly 0730, it making no difference that it was a Sunday, Admiral Billig was in CNFJ's conference room, sipping his second cup of coffee and chatting with Admiral Drapcho's aide, when the 7th fleet and naval base Intelligence officers joined him. Because he didn't know these captains personally, there was a brief moment of Naval protocol to be observed. As soon as CNFJ was finished with his own morning briefing, he also sat in. Admiral Billig, who was the senior officer present, immediately launched into his famous (or infamous depending on where you sat) head-to-head approach to any situation. As was his custom, he was reticent to reveal anything other than what he wanted to reveal.

His opening volley succinctly reviewed the data in the updated 'red' file. He then fired a question to the both captains, "Either of you pick up anything new in the past 24 hours?" He got the same answer from both of them, a terse "No sir". Their responses were obviously not what the Admiral had expected and he showed his displeasure with a guttural, "Hmmmpf." The two captains looked at each other, and started to squirm, something captains rarely did. Almost through clenched teeth, Admiral Billig growled, "Okay, what do you have that I don't?"

The CNFJ intelligence officer began his brief, his self confidence returning the further he got into his presentation—

- "Yes — my people in the 'spook cave' have been picking up weather transmissions from the Red Chinese to North Korean Naval HQ, which are then relayed to a base in the northern reaches of the Yellow Sea to a particular vessel that we don't have a handle on as yet. But we have learned that her C.O. is Captain Kim Dac Hyon, a very senior captain and a 'hard line' party member. He is outspokenly anti-American because his family suffered badly during the Korean War.
- Yes — Everything we've picked up indicates a late November deadline of sorts." The Com7 intelligence officer agreed with his CNFJ counterpart

and added— "We've started surveillance of the base in question using submarines attached to our ComSubRon 7 based here in Yokosuka.

No — We haven't put that information on the air, because it is not complete, and we didn't want to stir up the waters until the surveillance was completed."

Admiral Billig snorted another "Hrumph, a little irregular isn't it, to keep that kind of stuff under your hat?" The Com7 intelligence officer continued—

"Just following my boss's orders, sir.

Since SubRon7 was doing most of the 'leg' work, I've taken the liberty of bringing COMSUBRON 7, Captain Richard Simpson with me. He's in the waiting room, can we have him in?"

CNFJ took a quick look at Admiral Billig, who nodded a 'yes' and then said, "Come in Captain." The newcomer must have standing with his hand on the door knob, because he was in the room as fast as if he had walked through the wall. Captain Simpson was a very capable, knowledgeable, and respected major unit commander in 7th Fleet's family. Like most submariners, he had no excess pounds on his lean frame and the tightness of his short-sleeved khaki shirt on his upper arms clearly showed that he was in top physical condition. The necessary introductions were made and Captain Simpson immediately picked up the briefing where the intelligence officers had left off.

The content of the information he imparted to the Director quickly erased any jet lag symptoms that were lingering and peaked his 'little gray cells' into a high frequency mode.

"Yes — SubRon 7 is aware of and up to speed on the increased message traffic.

Yes — we are aware of the new base at the upper end of the Yellow Sea, satellite photo reconnaissance confirming the location of the new base.

Yes — As soon as I had learned of the new base, one of my boats had laid a SOSUS[i] underwater shipping

---

i   SOSUS= *Sound Underwater Surveillance System*

detection field across the southern end of the Yellow Sea. The South Korean navy is monitoring the field from Chejudo, an island at the mouth of the sea.

No — As yet, no shipping of any consequence had passed the net.

Yes — There is activity at the new base consistent with a submarine support facility. Aerial surveillance has detected the presence of a submarine that had not been adequately camouflaged.

Yes — As follow-up, I've been routinely deploying Los Angeles class fast attack boats into the Yellow Sea to keep tabs on the new arrival. So far, we know that the boat is a Russian built, nuclear powered Akula class boat. By comparing her sonar signature with those in our library, she used to be part of the Red Chinese navy and before that she was in the Russian North Sea fleet. She was recently in overhaul for the installation of a sub-surface to air missile launch system.

Are we concerned about it? You bet we are. She has been conducting sea trials shooting off training missiles. As yet they haven't fired at actual targets. It looks like the Chinese are training the Koreans, and they are hard at work."

The CNFJ captain then concluded the briefing by stating, "South Korean Naval Intelligence has learned that the boat's name is Korean for *Red Vengeance* which may have special significance."

As the briefing had progressed, everyone had taken special notice of the deepening dour expression forming on Admiral Billig's face, which was now a scowl, He gave the appearance of a thoroughbred race horse, straining at the starting gate of the Kentucky Derby. Admiral Drapcho then contributed what was probably the newest bit of information to Admiral Billig's growing file, "My counterpart in Guam, Rear Admiral Tonelson,

Commander Naval Forces Marianas, has reported an increased presence off Anderson Air Force Base of the same type of fishing trawlers that the Russian navy deployed there during the Vietnam conflict. In reality, they were early warning weather and intelligence platforms. Nowadays, they are flying the North Korean flag."

As soon as the briefing was over, Admiral Billig took his leave, leaving his colleagues wondering what had upset him and where was he going from there. On the return trip to Narita airport, he decided to skip a stopover in Hawaii and got himself a first class seat on a non-stop flight to New York. He had to get back to his office <u>right now</u>! Once settled into his seat and at cruising elevation, he started to review what he had gleaned on his whirlwind trip. Several of the reporter's questions seemed to be answered—

WHO— the President, but how the hell did the Reds know he was coming? There had to be a leak high up at the Cabinet level, but who?

WHAT— an assassination attempt, most probably a missile attack on Air Force One.

WHERE- somewhere over the Pacific Ocean between Guam and Japan, probably at a place where the ocean was so deep that debris would never be recovered to pin-point the cause of the disappearance of the Presidential jet.

WHEN— in late November, just prior to the Asian Summit Trade Conference.

WHY— most probably to prevent the most out-spoken opponent of granting North Korean favored nation status from attending the summit.

The thirteen hour return trip was just as tiring as the trip out, due to part of the flight being a 'red eye', and the speed at which the Admiral's brain was racing. He wondered "What have Glenn and Kevin discovered, and how soon could the next vital meeting with his staff occur?" Things were definitely starting to fall into place.

CHAPTER 8

LONDON
October 25

On these spur of the moment transoceanic flights, if not going under cover, I always appreciated Admiral Billig's insistence that the travel be in first class to insure that his agents were as fully rested as possible at the end of the flight. For this particular flight, he had suggested (read ordered) that I use my blue passport rather than my Official Government one to keep a low profile. My flight from JFK to Heathrow, on board a fully modernized 777, was more than comfortable. Even though the first class cabin was full, the service and attention of the cabin crew made the seven hour flight seem like it had just taken off when it landed. It was past 10:00 PM by the time I got into London, but I had enough time for a late night repast at T.G.I. Friday's in Piccadilly. The night was so mild that I decided to walk back to the totally non-upscale St. Giles hotel, which at one time was a YMCA, and indeed, part of the facility was still a youth hostel. But it was ideal for my purposes, shrouding me in anonymity midst a throng of tourists. Then it was time to hit the hay and reset my body clock.

October 26

After a hotel breakfast that was not fancy, but filling and easy on my gastric lining, I took the tube to the Thames near Parliament. MI6 headquarters were conveniently located near both Parliament and #10 Downing Street, and like the Institute, displayed no outward indication of what took place inside the walls. The lift to the top floor was noiseless and fast. As I stepped from the cage, I found myself in a brightly lighted large foyer. The only articles of furniture in the room were cushioned chairs lining three of the walls and a large mahogany desk in the center of the room, which was presided over by a very English executive secretary. I introduced myself and she greeted me with a smile and a, "Good morning, Sir, the Brigadier is expecting you." There was no trace of an English accent. As she was greeting me, she touched her intercom and said simply, 'Sir Malcolm, your American guest is here," and instructed me to "go right on through."

The living equivalent of James Bond's "M" was Brigadier Sir Malcolm Oliver Martin, whose name was followed by a string of letters almost as long as the alphabet. To the diplomats who visited his office he was "Sir Malcolm". To his staff and peers he was "The Brigadier". Behind his back (very far behind his back) he was frequently referred to as "Sir Mom," and in the field, far removed from England, he was simply "Mom".

Tall, with just the hint of a maturing waist line, Sir Malcolm sported a shock of snow white hair and a snow white beard, both of which were fastidiously groomed. His facial features were best described as 'plantagenous', and his hazel eyes sparkled brightly even when he was in the midst of delivering a dressing down. His suit, shirt and tie were Seville Road tailored and color coordinated, and the crease of his slacks was sharp enough to cut your finger. Indeed, he could have easily been mistaken for a university headmaster instead of the highly efficient spymaster that he was.

When I entered his office, the décor of which was just like my Admiral's, designed for work rather than socializing, he was seated behind a huge mahogany desk. On the wall behind him was a portrait of Winston Churchill glowering over his shoulder. The only other decorations in the room were the Union Jack, and the battle flag of the Royal Marines. He quickly rose from behind his desk and we met in the middle of the room. His handshake was just as strong as the Admiral's and left my fingers numb for a few seconds.

"I see you got here fine, and as far as I can determine, totally incognito. Other than a brief note from Immigration describing you as a 'first cabin businessman on holiday', no other notice was made of your arrival. As a matter of fact, you blended so well into the tourist scene that I don't even know where you spent the night." (The cloaking people in our travel section had worked another miracle.) Pleasantries were exchanged and refreshments, British style teas, scones and jellies quietly appeared and after sampling the goodies, we got to work. Sir Malcolm motioned to a work table that was positioned in front of a large picture window with an unobstructed view of Big Ben.

Once we were seated in well cushioned arm chairs, he leaned forward and sighed, "Right you are, and what do you have for me, and what are you going to ask from me?" Quid pro quo right from the start.

I went over, in detail, the increasing volume of voice traffic between a chap called "Jack" in Boston, and a bloke called 'Paddy' in Belfast. I also explained that a presumed code phrase, *'Blue Streak'*, was somewhere in every communication and that there were frequent references to the latter part of November, coinciding with the forthcoming marriage of the Irish Prime Minister's daughter. Sir Malcolm listened to me in silence and I could almost hear his computer-like brain sorting out the details and pigeon-holing them.

His only comment was, "It's good to see that your intelligence gathering and assessments have improved since the nineties. Yes, our man in Belfast has been keeping his eye on Paddy, a disreputable front and provocateur for the IRA. We read them as planning a welcoming party for the Prince of Wales, when he attends the wedding of the Irish Prime Minister's daughter.

Quite an undertaking when you consider that the IRA has never, to date, pulled off such a monstrous stunt SgtMajor but if the al-Qaeda could attack New York and Washington, this might be a first. Also our sources in the Mid-East are getting worried that the Palestinians are planning something big for the same time frame. Could be that the IRA is hiring a Muslim suicide-bomber to do their dirty work. Those bastards don't give a damn about dying, which makes them very difficult to defend against. Also, too, they work cheap, but the IRA coffers appear to have fattened dramatically in the past few weeks."

After a sip of tepid tea and downing one-half of a jellied scone, he continued, "We're trying to plan for every contingency. We have convinced HRH to wear body armor and he has a top fashion designer working with our armor chaps to come up with a uniform that won't make him look dumpy. He will be wearing a uniform cap that is actually a Keflar reinforced helmet, very fashionable of course." Sir Malcom suddenly stood up and walked to the huge picture window and drank in the fantastic London skyline while sighing prodigiously. When he returned to his seat he continued, "We presume, of course, that one of your former Presidents will be your government's official representative. I do hope that it will be the elder George Bush."

Now it was my turn. I wiped some crumbs from my chin and began, "Sir Malcolm, very few people know this, but our Vice-President will represent the U.S. and he will make a brief half day trip to Belfast after the wedding to dine with family and friends before returning home the same day. He will not spend the night in Ireland. The reason that his attendance has not been publicized is that the Secret Service takes a very dim view of the President and the Vice-President being out of the country at the same time. The Irish government has been discretely informed of this and they have been very cooperative by not listing him in any of the public relations releases. They say only that there will be a high government official representing the U.S. At the very last minute it will be announced that Vice-President Flaherty will represent us. As you are well aware, President Alexander is firm in his decision to attend the Asian

Trade Conference in Tokyo at about the same time."

"The Secret Service would go ballistic if they knew the truth and then any semblance of security would go out the window. The plan is to announce that the Vice-President will be making an aerial inspection of the eastern U.S. and Canadian air defense facilities. The usual cadre of Secret Service personnel will accompany him but we'll supplement the usual throng of journalists that follow him everywhere with several 'journalists' from some of the lesser media. They will actually be a Special Forces Anti-terrorist team. No one will be given the true flight plan until Air Force Two is over Canadian air space. He will have Air Force fighters escorting him over land and Navy jets will escort him across the Atlantic. A carrier task force, on a training mission in the North Atlantic, will provide operational and tactical support as needed. The escorting units will not open their sealed orders until Air Force Two is in the air. Like your Prince's, Vice-President Flaherty's trip will be as short as possible. The reason that we are taking these extra-ordinary precautions is because, as you well realize, he is a real thorn in the side of the IRA because of his very vocal opposition to the withdrawal of a British presence in Northern Ireland."

Sir Malcolm immediately sat bolt upright and muttered, "I say." In a voice that suddenly dropped twenty degrees in warmth, he started his side of the 'quid pro quo', during which his brain was processing mega-bytes of thoughts and information. "Well, now we have a really sticky wicket on our hands. Not only do we have to worry about HRH, but your VP as well. There's a lot more here than meets the eye. My new gut feeling is that the target of the Irish stew-pot is your Vice-President rather than our Royal, but we can't take any chances. We will prepare to protect both of them. We are well aware of his opposition to us packing up our kit and leaving Northern Ireland, like we did Hong-Kong, but what purpose would his assassination serve? Your President has already made it known that he supports Mr. Flaherty on this subject. Surely, there has to be a hidden agenda somewhere to risk such a bold venture!" I told Sir Malcolm that the boys and girls in the back rooms of our Institute were hard at work to answer that question, but I also opined that the IRA doesn't always act rationally when presented with a golden opportunity to bring world wide attention to their cause.

Another pot of tea, stronger and darker than the first arrived, and I enjoyed the view of the same London skyline that Sir Malcolm had enjoyed a few minutes earlier. Sir Malcolm was furiously pecking away at his computer and carrying on several conversations using his office intercom and telephones. After about fifteen minutes, the room became silent and he rejoined me at the work table. His voice was now excited, "Right, you need to get closer to the action. I've just arranged a flight for you from Gatwick to Belfast in this afternoon. Since you Yanks aren't too welcome over there at the present, you'll be traveling on a British passport, just to avoid any possible unpleasantness. My secretary will have it for you before you leave here. Seeing that John Bull is still the power in Northern Island, I don't think that any one other than the girl at the British Airways check-in desk will ask to see your passport. But, as you Yanks say, 'better safe than sorry'. You'll have time in the taxi from wherever your kit is to Gatwick to go over your cover. It's one that we've used in the past without raising any red flags."

"Once you land in Belfast, you'll be met by a very tall Scotsman with a very large moustache, wearing a brightly colored kilt and carrying a well used bag pipe. It's all part of the game. I won't tell you how he will recognize you, but he will, and he'll run the show for you over there. In real life, he is a Royal Marine, not a bandsman in the Scottish color guard. SergeantMajor Ian MacGregor is the Officer-in-Charge of the best anti-terrorist unit we have left in Northern Ireland." He suddenly jumped up and proclaimed, "Well then, we both have lots of ground to cover, so let's be at it. SgtMajor will make all the arrangements for your visit and your departure to wherever it is you're going when you leave the UK. SgtMajor will also keep me posted on the goings on in his cricket field and, I'm sure, will fill you in on what he has discovered in his zone of responsibility. You'll find that he reacts quite rapidly and forcefully to events as they take place. Good to have met you, young man, take care, and by the way, if you know where you're going from here, let my secretary know. When she gets the word from SgtMajor when you are departing Belfast, she will make all the proper arrangements." His parting handshake was even stronger than his greeting one, telling me that he had the bit in his teeth, and was moving into high gear.

I did not see much of the English countryside on the trip to Gatwick because I was busy acquainting myself with my new identity. I was a musician and a dealer specializing in bagpipes, such a deal. As Sir Malcom predicted, the young lady at the British Airways check in desk at Gatwick, whose name tag read 'Megan O'Shea', took only a brief look at 'my' passport, and waved me on to the departure lounge without saying a word. Brits traveling to Northern Ireland didn't seem to rate the usual Irish hospitality. The short flight across the Irish Sea was uneventful. My greeting at the Belfast airport was not very low key. Coming out of the jet way and entering the airport proper, I was met by a giant of a man, with the widest handle-bar mustache I had ever seen, wearing the brightest red plaid kilt that was ever made and carrying a battered bagpipe.

His greeting was nothing like you would expect from a Sergeant-Major in the Royal Marines, "Laddie," he thundered, "welcome to the old sod, we've been expecting you." Still not sure of what I was getting into, I quietly muttered something like, "Good to be here," and he led the way out of the airport. I always travel light, carry-on bag only, so we proceeded directly to the parking lot. I was amazed at how little attention was paid to us, especially him. I guessed that was how he greeted all his visitors.

In the parking lot, he directed me to mutely painted Land Rover, stowed my bag in the boot and his instrument in the back seat, and we 'hit the road'. Once we were on the highway, his personality changed dramatically, and he came a Sergeant Major of the Marines. In a very slow and smooth voice he said, "Glad to meet you, I have to hand it to you, you took the charade back there without blinking an eye, you're a pro, I can tell. That little bit of play acting back there was for the benefit of the

IRA watchers, who meet all flights from the U.K. Across the years, I've become well known for meeting fellow musicians in that manner, so it doesn't give the 'micks' reason to start digging into things they should stay out of. I got a lengthy concise message (how's that for an oxymoron) from Sir Mom. It was so accurate that I feel that we've been friends for years. By the by, you're staying at my digs, such as they are, where we can do our thing away from the office, which the IRA watches like a hawk. Every suspicious stranger they pick up on gets a complete vetting. You'll be staying with me as befits a long lost friend rather than an official visitor."

I congratulated him on his acting ability, following which we finished the trip to his digs in silence, while I enjoyed the Irish country side and scenery. Once inside the small, modest house that he called 'digs', he ushered me into his parlor, put a pint of cold Guiness stout in my fist and excused himself to "get out of my costume and into something more comfortable." More comfortable turned out to be a simple turtle neck sweater and slacks, both black, a striking contrast to the colorful figure I met at the airport, so I figured that we were in a working mode, and indeed we were.

"Sir Mom filled me in on why you're here, what he knows of circumstances from where he sits, and how he expects us to work together. So, here's what we have so far going on over here in Belfast. We have been listening in on the same phone conversations that you have, and have narrowed the point of contact to a local pub in the part of town that tourists rarely see. It's called "Shamrock Pub" and Paddy, Patrick O'Rourke, is the owner and principal bar man and a dyed-in-the-wool IRA member high up in the pecking order. His pub has become the meeting place for a rather belligerent section of the IRA, so belligerent in fact that the Sein Finn wants nothing to do with them and leaves them alone, hoping that the sleeping dog will continue to sleep. The regulars to the pub would like us to believe that they are nothing more than good old fun-loving, beer drinking sons of Ireland, but we suspect that they are responsible for some of worst terrorist attacks committed in the past few years. They don't wake up and bite often, but when they do bite, it is nasty. These particular blokes seem to be the lads who take on the nastiest jobs, have the reputation of tackling anything, and love every minute of the chase." The pints of Guiness were drained, so he got fresh bottles from the kitchen.

"Because they don't crawl out of the woodwork very often, we haven't been able to prove anything, and the best we've been able to do is keep them under close surveillance and once in a while, throw a spanner into their plans and save a few lives. We also keep a sharp eye on visitors to that part of the city, especially the foreigners who call at the pub, and one of the more frequent callers, whom we keep a very close watch on is one Jack McCarthy of Boston."

At that, my brain screamed, "We just hit the jackpot."

SgtMajor went on, "We know that he is the father of your illustrious Secretary of State and a big time fund raiser for the IRA back home. The frequency of his visits has gone up in the past six months and the only place he visits is the pub and then returns to the USA. I can give you a list of his visits for the time frame in question, if that interests you."

I indicated to the SgtMajor that I was indeed interested, and made a mental note to myself to have the 'Hacker' get on his case, as only he could do.

SgtMajor continued, "We've seen a couple of characters lately, who are not known in this county, but our field agents in the West tell us that the Gilhooley brothers have the reputation of being top notch bomb experts. We think that they might have been imported as a welcoming committee for the Prince of Wales on his trip here next month. Now, Sir Mom said that *'Blue Streak'* might have a different meaning to you, is he correct?"

I finished off my second Guiness and told my host that I was becoming more sure that *'Blue Streak'* was our Vice-President, and that the 'Veep' would be making a 'whistle stop' to Belfast after the wedding in Dublin.

"Now the fat's in the fire," he exclaimed as he jumped up and retrieved a thick folder labeled "Bombings" and started to rapidly turn pages. "Ah, here we are. Look at this lad," as he handed me the picture of a young man, who to all intents and purposes looked like a doctoral candidate in Philosophy, which he was. "Benign looking, isn't he," mused the SgtMajor as a wicked grin spread across his face. "Sean Gilhooley's philosophy is that of mayhem, destruction and anything else that you can think of—definitely not the kind of student you would sit with in a coffee bar to discuss Plato."

As my eyes ran down the list of crimes that he and his brothers had been linked to, but without sufficient evidence to get a conviction, it was clear that this joker was capable of anything, including cold blooded murder.

The rest of the evening was spent going over as much common knowledge that we could dredge from our combined corporate memories. I also learned to my gastric delight that the SgtMajor, even though a confirmed bachelor, was also a gourmet cook. He prepared a sumptuous repast that went well with more Guiness stout. By the end of the meal, we came to the conclusion that we had gone as far as we could with what we knew to be fact, not conjecture. There was much scrounging for each of our departments to do in the next few days. I asked SgtMajor to get word back to Sir Malcolm that I was ready to proceed on my way Israel, the next stop on my schedule.

He answered flatly, "No sweat, you lie low here tonight, and I'll have you on your way in the morning."

ENGLAND
October 27

Being a man of his word, the black clad SgtMajor returned to his digs in mid-morning, transformed himself into the Jolly Red Giant, and returned me to the airport. He had already arranged for my return trip to Gatwick, instructing me to proceed directly to Heathrow, and head for the British Airways First Class Lounge. I would be met there by one of Sir Malcolm's staff with further details. SgtMajor's parting shot was, "Don't worry laddie, I'll be keeping a 24 hours a day watch on those bastards myself starting today. I have a feeling that we will be seeing each other again in the very near future." I half expected him to clap his heels together and give me a snappy salute, but that would not be in keeping with our charade.

The flight across the Irish Sea was without incident and I had no problems getting through Gatwick. The shuttle bus ride to Heathrow passed through some very beautiful English countryside, but it's beauty was lost on me, as I was busy getting my 'ducks in a row' for my next meeting. As promised, one of Sir Malcolm's deputies was waiting for me at the reception desk in the British Airways lounge. In short order he relieved me of "my" British passport, gave me back my own, and briefed me on the details of the flight to Jerusalem, where I would be met at Ben Gurion airport by a chauffer, who would be displaying a sign 'BOHICA TOURS'. I thanked him for the hospitality of MI6, and gave him my request that they get a message off to Admiral Billig to get the 'Hacker' busy digging up all the dirt that he could on Jack McCarthy, with special attention to his trips to Belfast in the past six months. Sir Malcolm's aide said that the message would be on its way after Sir Malcolm reviewed the latest update regarding his inquiries, and incorporated them into the message. I spent the next hour enjoying the creature comforts of the lounge, British telly, and bar snacks. It also gave me time to realign my thoughts regarding the problem at hand. Several of my questions had been answered, and I had to get them in order:

— Who, was undoubtedly the Vice-President,
— What, was his demise, probably during a massive terrorist bombing
— Where, obviously in Belfast,
— When, during his short visit to family in Belfast, and
— Why, the best reason for the planned attack seemed to be retaliation for his opposition to the plan to have the Brits pull out of Northern Ireland.

It was not a pretty picture, but I feared that things were going to get worse very soon.

CHAPTER 9

JERUSALEM
October 28

The trip from Heathrow to Ben Gurion airport, which was closer to Tel Aviv than Jerusalem, was smooth, with not even so much as a bounce to trigger the turning on of the Fasten Seat Belt sign, once it was turned off, until its reappearance indicated that we were in the final approach to the airport. The weather over the Mediterranean was overcast, so I used the time to 'log a few ZZZ' (take a nap). The landing was smooth as silk, but the heat of the Near East was a striking difference from the misty and foggy British Isles. Once inside the terminal, the air conditioning was a welcome relief. The presence of uniformed military personnel, armed with an assortment of loaded automatic weapons, was very different from the minimal security of U.S. airports and even Belfast airport. There was a no non-sense attitude all around me that confirmed that I had arrived in an area of the world where unrest and the threat of terrorist attacks were a way of life, and where jokes about airport security were not tolerated at all.

To my relief, there was minimal delay going through immigration and customs, even using my private citizen passport. Upon entering the arrivals lobby, it took me only a few minutes to pick out the BOHICA TOURS representative, who was a petite woman in a crisp chauffeur's uniform, sporting one of the widest smiles I had ever seen. Her welcome, in flawless English, was just as warm, if not as raucous, as that of the Jolly Red Giant. We left the air conditioned comfort of the terminal and quickly traversed the short distance to the limousine parking area. Even though it had taken only about five minutes to get to the limo, I was sweating profusely, while my welcoming committee of one was as cool as she was in the terminal. The trip to the airport security building was relatively quick, as it was strategically located in the airport industrial area. This was not the main Mossad headquarters, which were housed in downtown Jerusalem, but one of several branch stations located near to potential terrorist targets. Its primary mission was that of rapid response to emergencies in and around the airfield.

The tall, muscular and fit personnel, of both sexes, all had that determined look of self-confidence and competence that told me that this was not a place where practical jokes were tolerated. My driver, whom I later learned was assigned specifically to pick up VIPs, was obviously well known by sight to all the personnel manning the security check points. In almost no time at all, I was ushered into the working office of Brigadier Jacob Templeman, the head of Mossad, whose authority was equal to that of my boss and Sir Malcolm.

The office was more of a command post rather than a reception or ceremonial office. Banks of TV monitors and computers lined three walls and were all presided over by alert and attentive young men and women. The fourth wall was covered with maps and floor plans of all the buildings in the area. It was obvious that the personnel were accustomed to the Brigadier conducting business in the room, because they paid little attention to him and seemed to ignore me. I suspected that they only looked 'laid back', but were fully capable of turning into a SWAT team, if a 'situation' arose in the room.

Brigadier Jacob Templeman was a man in his fifties and still fit as a fiddle, with not an ounce of fat on his frame. His handshake was another in the series of knuckle-busters I seemed to be getting these days. From the Admiral, I had learned that his family had fled from Hungary in the middle of the last century to escape Russian reprisals for the ill-fated revolt. His father had relocated his family to the middle of Philadelphia, where the Brigadier and his siblings were raised as Americans. The Brigadier was the product of the American public school system from grade school through high school and graduated Magna Cum Laude from Temple University. He then did postgraduate work in Israeli colleges, majoring in the history and traditions of the Hebrew nation. It was during this period in his life that he decided to emigrate to Israel, as he put it, to get closer to his roots. He had served with distinction in several of the short wars between Israel and her Arab neighbors and had rapidly risen to his present position of authority. Because of his American background, he spoke English with a Philadelphia twang and was fond of using idiomatic language (aka slanguage) in conversation with American guests in his office. He was also fluent in Hebrew, which he spoke without an American accent.

"Take a load off your feet, plop yourself in the big overstuffed chair over there and give your butt a chance to lose its numbness after all the air miles you have been logging recently," the Brigadier suggested with a twinkle in his eyes. He chose a large leather executive chair that I suspected was for his use exclusively and when he leaned back, the recliner mechanism took over and with his hands crossed on his flat abdomen, he bade me to 'lay it on me'.

As compared to the thickness of my 'blue' folder that had increased in size in the past thirty-six hours, my 'white' folder could have easily fit into a schoolboy's three ring binder. I had reviewed its contents on the flight from London and was able to talk without having to open the folder or use notes. I told him that we had been intercepting and decoding a series of top security messages from the Syrian Embassy in D.C. to their foreign office in Damascus. They kept referring to a '*White*

Lightning', with references to several dates that seemed to have narrowed down to a fifteen day window late in November. We suspect that something big and important is going to happen in Jerusalem. I did mention Sir Malcolm's theory that the IRA was possibly negotiating with the PLO, or a similar organization, for a 'suicide hit man' to assassinate the Prince of Wales. During my short spiel, the Brigadier had filled a large bowled pipe with aromatic tobacco and lit it with what looked like a miniature flame thrower. I later found out that it was a model of the latest Israeli field flame thrower. A cloud of fragrant and sweet tobacco smoke soon swirled around his head.

The Brigadier didn't say a word while I had the floor and gave no body language sign that he was aware of the messages or what importance, if any, he was attributing to them it. I couldn't have been more wrong. When he was satisfied that I was finished, he sat up, put his elbows on the table and proceeded to give me a short history of recent terrorist acts that seemed to have occurred around the times that the messages had been received in Damascus. He thought that while these acts appeared to be random and sporadic, they were probably a prelude to a larger attack. It was my turn to sit quietly to hear what he had to say.

He took in a deep breathe and began, "Okay Kemo Sabe, as you have probably deduced, we live in an armed camp. Terrorism and counter-terrorism are ways of life for us. Unfortunately, we usually find ourselves reacting to the attacks, because many of them appear to be 'off-the-cuff' adventures of splinter fundamentalist fanatics. The sad thing is that so many of their young people, mostly men, are ready and willing to sacrifice their lives as martyrs to placate Allah, hoping to obtain a place of honor in the afterlife they believe in. I guess it was the same with the Japanese kamikaze pilots who wreaked havoc on the Navy off Okinawa towards the end of WWII. By the way, there is no such thing as an insignificant piece of intelligence that crosses my desk (so he had read my mind). You'd be surprised, no I take that back, you'd be pleased to see that our department is very like the Institute you work for, with one significant exception. Alas, we do not have a "Hacker" like yours on our staff. We must get ourselves from point "A" to point "B" by going through point "C". We eventually arrive at point "B," but usually twelve to fourteen hours after your "Hacker" has gotten there and moved on to his next puzzle. Now, to the '*White Lightening*' 'traffic:

— Yes, we know all about them, but as far as we can tell, there have been no exchanges with the IRA, so whatever is coming down will be in my backyard. These fanatics do not look upon a 'one on one' suicide attack as a sure ticket to Allah's bosom. Their usual philosophy is, that unless the intended victim is someone of international importance, the more people they take with them, the greater will be their reward. By the way, I don't think that reward will be in what you and I call Heaven.

— Yes, while these attacks are random, and seemingly unrelated, the most feasible reason for them is to draw attention away from the real target.

— Yes, we agree that something big is probably going to come down late in November, probably when Pope Benedict is scheduled to make a good will visit to us. The details are still fuzzy. We hope that the Vatican will give us at least a forty-eight notice, so we can activate the security plan we've hatched to protect him. We all know that the 'good guys' always wear white and the Pope always wears white, so we are presuming that '*White Lightning*' refers to His Holiness. We fully intend to send him back to Rome in as good a condition as when he arrives.

— Yes, we have a team of investigators here, and in every known center of terrorism in this part of the world tracking down who the players might be."

"Oh, by the way, we are acutely aware that the level and magnitude of all these unpleasant incidents seem to escalate every time your Secretary of State holds a press conference, where she appears to be giving her endorsement to the idea of a separate Islamic State within Israel." I started to protest, but before I could open my mouth he went on, "Now simmer down before you jump on my back, we know that she doesn't speak for your President but every time that she opens her mouth lately, we brace for a fresh outbreak of terrorist activities. We sure wish your President would muzzle her as soon as possible."

"You've probably guessed by now that I've usually got something up my sleeve, if I had a sleeve, but I deal with more than one hot potato at a time. Let's meet the agent I've assigned to take what we call 'Action White Knight' as her primary case until it is resolved." He leaned forward and flicked a switch on his desk top intercom and after his aide had answered the call, gave an order, "Send Becky in," as if he was expecting her to be waiting for his summons, which she probably was.

The young woman, who entered the room, could only be described as a 'stunner', five feet eight inches tall, about one hundred twenty-five pounds with a svelte figure that would have been comfortably at home in a James Bond movie. She seemed to float on air as she approached us. Before the Brigadier could introduce us formally, she said, "Hi, I'm Rebecca Zelman. I'm pleased to meet you, Glenn, it'll be a pleasure to work with you. I learned all about you from the Brigadier." Her handshake was firm, but not the bone-crushing variety, her smile was warm and very friendly, and her voice was sultry and sexy.

By this time the Brigadier had risen, waiting for a lull in the action to get a word in edgewise. With a touch of sarcasm in his voice he said, "Well, now that you two are old buddies, let's get on with more serious concerns. Becky will be a little of everything for you, interpreter, point of contact with me, guide for you through the armed camp that is twenty-first century Jerusalem, and when the you know what hits the fan, she will be there to either turn the fan off or sweep up the fallout. I've arranged for you to have exclusive use of the office next door and unlimited access to our computers for whatever is needed to assist you. I'm leaving you in good hands, and Derek, turn down the rpms of your sex drive. Becky has that motor revving effect on all, and I mean all, the men the first time they meet her."

With that, he sat down again and turned his attention to his computer screen, telling us that we had been dismissed. Becky led the way through a connecting door into a sparsely furnished office, much smaller than the Brigadier's. She ignored the leather chair behind the desk, choosing instead a leather sofa and indicated to me that I was expected to join her on the sofa.

While all this was transpiring, my brain was in overdrive, "Oh boy, what have I gotten into. She knows all about me but I didn't know she existed until ten minutes ago,— and we're expected to be a team. I'm going to have a few groups for the Admiral about not being clued in to who I had just met."

It didn't get any better as she proceeded to bring me 'up to speed' on what her people had accomplished so far. Her voice lost the sultry tone and became all business, "Since we got your department's inquiries about the '*White Lightning*' message traffic, we've moved the investigation to the front burner —

— We've been aware of the 'white' message traffic almost from the first day the first one was picked up by our watchers (read=electronic snoops)
— What concerned us was the increased local traffic between Damascus and known unfriendly fanatical groups, which one listener described as an "electronic feeding frenzy"
— Of even more concern to us was that several of the addressees were people we've never heard of before. Either some deep 'moles' have been reactivated or there are new players.
— There was even a mini-summit among the leaders of several of the more militant fanatics a fortnight ago in Teheran. It didn't last long, it must have been weeding out session because since then there have been only two groups getting mail, but they are two of the most radical fundamentalist fanatics. Last week, one of the groups either pulled out or was dropped and now there is the only one getting copies of the messages from your capital. Since then the volume of traffic between them, Damascus, and Tehran has tripled, which is a big red flag signaling that something very big is in the wind."

"As the Brigadier indicated, we have narrowed down the list of potential targets down to the Pope. The only other large scale event scheduled here in the same time frame is the annual meeting of the Israeli Medical Society. It doesn't make sense that attacking a bunch of doctors who treat their people as well as ours would get them favorable publicity, but who knows how their minds work."

While she gave her vocal chords a rest and my reeling brain a chance to slow down to warp speed, it suddenly dawned on me that she was briefing me, rather than the other way around. "What would you say," I asked, "if I told you that the Speaker of our House of Representatives, who just happens to be Jewish, will be coming here to give the final speech at that medical meeting. It hasn't been formally announced, but it is a 'go'. Could he rather than the whole medical society or the Pope be your 'White Knight'? Or better yet, could they both be targets!

Becky's eyebrows arched and a frown appeared on her forehead. She stared up at the ceiling for about two minutes, collecting her thoughts, and when she came back to earth, she had already formulated a plan of action.

The tone of her voice became excited as she warmed to the chase, "You bet it makes a difference. We can now definitely eliminate everybody else as targets and also forget about a suicide mission. The suicidal attacks are usually random attacks by fanatics seeking glory or publicity. Taking out the Pope, or one American, even an important American, would not stir up the kind of backlash that killing a dozen or so prominent Jewish doctors would. It also means that an indiscriminant bomb attack is out because it would be almost impossible for a bomber to get close enough to either man to assure success. Our security would prevent that. It also means that we have to start looking for a specialist in focused assassinations. Now that we've come this far, my job will be to ferret out which of their assassins will get the job. It's going to have to be someone who is not well known to us, who can move about with impunity, and is expert in several methods of instant murder on a small scale. I have a starting point. Now, I'll start working on our supply of informers to see who fits the bill. Give me a couple days, and I'll get back to you."

As I later reflected on this 'power' meeting, it occurred to me that Becky's razor sharp mind ran at super warp speed and she possessed that unique ability to absorb a huge number of seemingly unrelated tidbits, get them into the appropriate pigeon holes and pull a plan of action out of the mess. The meeting came to an abrupt end, as Becky suddenly stood up, got a shit-eating grin on her face, shook my hand and whisked me towards the door, with a parting assurance that "I'll be in touch, through special channels of course."

The Brigadier had already left the building on other business and seeing that all my mission objectives had been met, my driver, who had patiently cooled her heels until Becky had closed the door behind me, got up, smiled her usual sweet smile and stated, "I'll escort you back to the first class check-in counter at the airport. You have first class reservations on the next flight to Munich and a connecting non-stop flight to New York."

Everybody seemed to know what I was going to do before I knew what I was going to do,– what a revolting development. I could only marvel at the speed of the events that had taken place and what was already planned. I was thoroughly impressed by the wide ranging foresight that the Brigadier and Becky possessed. I figured that degree of proficiency came with the territory when you were perpetually in the 'hot seat'.

The flights across the Mediterranean and the Atlantic were long and boring and with waiting time in terminals, it took me two days to get home. The movies were typically FFM (fun for the feeble minded). The meals, even though they were served on china, on cloth covered tables with silver rather than plastic implements, would not have inspired a gourmet to call them anything but drab. I used the time to catalogue what I had learned —

— WHO – our Speaker of the House, the Pope just didn't fit in with the scenario that was evolving
— WHERE and WHEN – at the meeting's final banquet, the only time he would not be constantly moving about, and the only time that he would be alone—at the microphone

— HOW– unknown at this particular time
— WHY– probably because he was Jewish and American and to embarrass the Israeli government and teach us lesson

With that piece of housekeeping completed, I dozed off into a dreamless slumber. The best part of the return trip was the shuttle from JFK to Reagan National. It was less than ninety minutes in duration and I was coming home, and eager to meet with the Admiral and the 'Hacker' to see what they had come up with. By the time I reached my condo, it was well into the wee hours of the next day so I hit the hay, and logged a 'sleep around', a 12+ hours snooze.

FAIRFAX
October 30

When I rejoined the land of the living, it was well into the afternoon. Since my refrigerator was almost empty, I went to the food court at Tyson's Corners for a combination breakfast, lunch, and dinner. I coined a new word for my meal—a 'brunchner'. On returning to my condo, I ignored the flashing light on my answering machine until I had opened a bottle of Samuel Adams ale and settled into my comfortable overstuffed chair. I was now ready to catch up with the present..

Among the messages were offers of no-fee credit cards, discount Caribbean vacations, affordable life and long term care insurance (that one made me chuckle), total lawn care, and even a few that had just silence before the connection was broken. The last message on the tape was the one I was looking for—Miss Eagleton's sweet voice informing me that there would be a meeting in the Admiral's office at 0800 on Monday morning, no other details. It was taken for granted that I would be there. The day off to work off my jet lag was greatly appreciated. Obviously, the Admiral wanted to be well rested from his whirlwind Trans-Pacific trip before we sat down to plan the next steps. Cindy Lou, unfortunately, was not in town, so I was able to spend a rare day at complete leisure, catching up on paperwork.

CHAPTER 10

ASHBURN
October 30

Arriving at 0730 in Miss Eagleton's office, I went through the motions of tossing my imaginary hat to an imaginary hat and coat rack. She humored me with a smile and mouthed a silent, "Good morning, he's waiting for you," and gestured with her thumb towards the entrance to the 'bridge' as she frequently called the Admiral's office. Once through the portal, I could see that the setting for a long session was in place. The same three chairs were in their usual places at the work table along with a tray of bagels, croissants, and assorted Danish pastries. A large twenty-five cup urn of coffee, filled to the brim, was bubbling away.

My cheery, "Good morning," was greeted by a grumpy, "If you say so." He was still suffering from jet lag, so it was going to be one of <u>those</u> mornings.

Before I had finished pouring my first cup of the mind jolting fluid that the Admiral called 'coffee', Kevin entered the room with arms loaded with several different colored folders. Behind him, I heard Miss Eagleton set the security lock on the door and a quick glance at the phone banks showed that all the plugs had been pulled from the wall, even the 'hot' line to the President. I sighed inaudibly at the prospect that it <u>really</u> was going to be one of <u>those</u> mornings. In keeping with his way of doing business, the Admiral, who was already seated at the head of the table, raised his head, and said, "Let's do it," calling the meeting to order at 0750. So what else was new.

The first order of business was an exchange of information that Admiral Billig and I had gathered in the last week. We both spoke pretty much from memory, with only occasional references to notes. Kevin sat silently through our reports just soaking up all the tidbits of data and mentally shuffling them into the report he was going to give once ours were concluded.

Kevin took the floor and laid out the results of the background check he had done on Jack McCarthy, as I requested after my session in Belfast. As usual, the skill of the man in defeating the most intricate and complex internet security measures astonished me. He had done everything I had asked for and ingeniously had picked up even more data that only his mind was capable of connecting together at breakneck speed.

His voice actually bubbled at the opportunity to show off how well he had earned his sizeable salary. "I've got several folders here: first is Jack McCarthy's bank statements, second, his telephone and cell phone bills for the past six months, third, his travel itineraries for the past year, fourth, his credit card charges for the past six months, and last, some interesting recent conversations with the Secretary of State. Just don't ask me how I got all this stuff. Where do you want me to start?"

The Admiral was just finishing his third cup of his 'little gray cell energizer', and simply stated, "Any where you'd like, they will probably all come together at the end anyway, but just give us the abridged version, not the whole nine yards."

"You got it," Kevin's voice became more animated, even exhilarated as he plowed into his report. "OK, let's do them in the order that I listed them. With that preamble, he picked up the folder titled, 'Jack McCarthy—Finances'. This guy has been laying out a lot of bucks, not all of which can be accounted for. When we toss out things like verifiable routine expenses, we are left with these doozers— first—one check in August and a second in September, each for $7500.00 each made out to 'The Irish Benevolent Society', which everybody knows is a front for the IRA. By backtracking on the signatures of the endorsers of those checks, we find that they were cashed on the same day they were written by the co-owners of the 'Touch of Erin Bar and Grill" in Boston, also a well-known IRA front. By obtaining those two gentlemen's bank statements, we see that the funds were not deposited, leaving a bundle of $15,000.00 cash lying about loose. Second—in September he wrote a check for $9000.00 made out to cash, which he had the bank convert into big denomination English pounds. Third– in early October he wrote three more checks for $9000.00 each, which his bank converted into three individual packets of well circulated British twenty, fifty, and on hundred pound notes."

"His banker in Boston was a college classmate of mine and she gave some insight into his financial dealings. He usually insists on crisp, new, large denomination bills when he asks for cash. To get the $27,000.00 in small used bills took her two days and the delay did not sit well with him. If he's planning to take the money out of the country with him, he's making sure that he stays below the $10,000.00 level he would have to declare. That would necessitate three trips, but he seems to be facing some kind of a deadline. To show my appreciation for her input, I sent her a five pound box of See's chocolates. Short break—I need a cheese Danish, and a cup of fresh hot 'joe'."

During this part of Kevin's presentation, the Director said absolutely nothing, which was unusual for him, as he was fond of asking pointed questions at any point in a program, to the consternation of the presenter. My colleagues, who regularly briefed him, had long since learned to anticipate these interruptions and not be flustered by them. I noticed that the twenty-five cup coffee urn was already half empty-most of it now swishswing around in the Admiral's stomach. I doubly appreciative of Kevin's thoroughness, and the Admiral's ability to absorb all the data on the first bounce.

"Kevin continued, "there is one outstanding check for $5000.00 written just last week, also made out to cash, that I can't account for at this time."

The Director seemed surprised that Kevin had admitted that he was not omniscient.

Kevin then asked, "Any questions? That's the short report on his finances."

I was ready to jump in with a few questions, but Admiral Billig beat me to the punch with a forceful comment, "None at this time, we'll wait until your finished, and then have at you."

"OK, next, his telephone activity." Kevin's voice was still cheery and excited, as his pride in his work had not abated. "This guy must own stock in the telephone company the way he runs up charges. It took a little more time to dig into this aspect, and again, don't ask me how it was done. You don't want to know. As you can see, there are four land lines into his home – one for routine local transactions, one unlisted number for his private use, one to his computer, and one to his fax machine. We'll concentrate on the unlisted line, and the computer hook-up. I was able to 'hack' into his E-mail bin, and retrieve every incoming and outgoing E-mail for the past year. He'd have a stroke if he knew how easy it was to bypass his security system without him ever realizing it. The fax machine wasn't used to any extent, so I think we can forget it. There are only local calls made and received on his listed number, and I think we can pass over them also."

At the apparent brush-off of the listed and fax lines, my eyebrows arched. I thought to myself, "This isn't like Kevin to take anything for granted."

He must have noticed my eyebrows, because he interrupted his presentation, and looked directly at me with a twinkle in his eyes, "Not to worry. I passed myself off as a telephone company surveyor doing a satisfaction check on the service, and talked to his secretary, his valet, the cook, housekeeper, and chauffer. I'm satisfied that the important stuff is on the unlisted number, his computer and his cell phone."

I thought to myself that we were so lucky that Kevin was on our side. Throughout all of this, the expression on the Admiral's face hadn't changed. He was playing the sponge, and soaking up everything.

"OK, moving right along." The level of excitement in Kevin's voice was geometrically increasing, the further he went into his presentation. "Nearly everything on his unlisted line was long distance, and there were recurrent U.S. and overseas numbers that frequently popped up. Of significance are lengthy calls to the 'Shamrock Pub' in Belfast, his daughter's home phone and to an import-export company in New York that I've been able to identify it as a front for a Mafia type organization. I expect to have more on their dealings in the next forty-eight hours. When we went into his cell phone records, we came up with three numbers of significance, the 'Touch of Erin Bar and Grill' in Boston, and the home numbers of the co-owners of the grill. His chauffer tells me that he prefers to use his cell phone in his limo, and always closes the plate glass divider between the front and rear seats whenever he calls from the limo. Time for a bagel break."

It still amazed me what the Admiral let him get away with. The amount of cream cheese and orange marmalade that he layered on each half of his bagel attested to the appetite his work was generating.

After wiping the crumbs off his chin, he continued, "Now to the travel folder. Everything in here is important. Fortunately, he charges all his big expenses to his five credit cards, spreading the charges out, so that they won't be too noticeable. This sly old fox never charges consecutive plane tickets to the same card, but he does charge all his restaurant bills to his Diner's card. He recently made two trips, one to Shannon, Ireland, and one to Glasgow, Scotland. Each of these trips mesh with the days that SgtMajor McGregor spotted him in Paddy's place. We have no charges for flights between Belfast, Shannon, and Glasgow. We presume that he paid cash for those tickets to hide his movements. His flight and passport control records confirm that his round trip, to and from Shannon originated at Kennedy, but he returned home via Chicago. He flew United Air Lines to and from Europe. On the way out, he took the US Airways shuttle from Logan to New York, and flew Continental from O'Hare back to Logan. Both of these short trips were in coach, which is unusual in that he prefers first class on all flights. Looks like he was trying to cover his tracks as best he could, but he is a rank amateur in that game. The other trip, to and from Glasgow, was on American Air Lines and originated at Dulles and terminated at LaGuardia. Like his other transatlantic flight, this one was also on a full first class fare ticket, nothing too good for our boy. As before, his connecting flight from Logan to Dulles was coach on TWA and his return trip from LaGuardia to Logan was on Delta, also coach."

"Now, here's an interesting fact to consider. He took a two day layover in Chicago and checked into the Palmer House. Likewise, there was a two day layover in New York with a stay at the Waldorf-Astoria. His hotel bills do not show any phones calls, so he must have used payphones, because nothing shows up on his calling card. His Diner's Club card shows that he had hefty charges at Morton's restaurant in Chicago, and Ruth's Chris restaurant in New York. The size of the bills tells me that he had at least two guests at each eatery. We can tie several recent long distance calls from his cell phone to specific numbers in Chicago and New York. I'll tap my contacts at the phone company to find out who was on the other end of these calls."

"Now, for the 'kicker,'" Kevin muttered as he opened the last of his folders which contained only two sheets of green paper. "It looks like there is new additional color code to deal with. The term '*Green Grass*' has started to pop up. The Secretary keeps asking her father if he has arranged to have the grass cut and he keeps telling her that he can't arrange for the mowing until she tells him when, in November, she wants the grass cut. What can be so important about getting the grass cut in November, and why does Jack have to make the arrangements? The incongruity here is that she has a regular lawn service for her property. This just started in the last week and that's all I have at present, but we're working on it. I've given it Top Priority, so I expect answers within two days."

"That's it," he said with a sigh of relief, leaned back in his chair, and poured himself yet another cup of coffee from the now almost empty urn and scoffed up the last Danish. He could still pack away the groceries like a pro footballer.

The Admiral stood up, slapped the table and proclaimed, "Well done, both of you, Bravo Zulu. Now we've got lots of meat to chew on. OK lads, take a ten minute break, and then we'll see about shuffling all the cards into a semblance of order."

The three of us immediately headed for the restroom to unload all the coffee we had consumed. Kevin and I had to go out in the hall beyond Miss Eagleton's desk, while the Admiral, of course, had his own private 'necessary' in his office. As we sailed past her desk, Miss Eagleton had an all knowing smirk on her face. The ten minute break actually lasted fourteen minutes, as we waited for Miss Eagleton to replaced the breakfast goodies with a platter of sandwiches and a twelve-pack of diet cola, following which we were locked in again.

The Admiral's face was clouded and his voice somber as we started again. "Let's see what we've got— we've narrowed the gray areas down a bit—

WHO— the President, the Vice President, the Speaker of the House, and a mystery player, I think the Prince of Wales and the Pope are diversions.

WHAT— sounds like wholesale murder

WHERE— in the western Pacific ocean, in downtown Belfast and Jerusalem, and somewhere here in the states, probably here in the District

HOW— a SAM[ii] strike, a terrorist bombing, probably a suicide attack, and what is beginning to sound like a paid 'hit'

WHEN— in a narrow time frame around Thanksgiving

WHY— that's the $64,000.00 dollar question. We have reasonable explanations for the North Koreans, the IRA, and the Arabs to go crazy, but there doesn't seem to be any connection between them. Also, why is the traffic involving <u>local</u>

[ii] SAM= Surface to Air Missile

foreign agencies, when the action is obviously going to take place thousands of miles away from here. Maybe, when we identify the 'Green Grass' connection, the fog will clear. Let's hope so."

A period of intense brain storming ensued, that was interrupted when Miss Eagleton entered the room and apologized for the intrusion, "I'm sorry Admiral, but we just got a red priority message from Yokosuka and I thought you should see it immediately." As she laid the dispatch case on the table, she glanced over at the Admiral's phone bank and gave us an aside, "I was in the Secretary of State's office this week, and noticed that she has a color coded phone bank almost like yours, sir, red, white and blue, but she has a green one also. She was talking to Senator Willis on the green phone while I was in her office. It sounded like she was warning him to back off something she was pushing in the Senate. Her tone of voice was anything but diplomatic."

The silence in the room was deafening after she departed. The three of us just sat there with our mouths open, dumbfounded at the bombshell that has just exploded in the room. The implication was staggering.

The Admiral recovered first, and thundered, "It can't be, but if in fact, Senator Willis, the President Pro-Tem of the Senate is 'Green Grass', and he was out of the picture, the next person in the line of succession to the Presidency is," and here he took a deep breathe, "the Secretary of State! It all makes sense now and, unbelievable as it seems, we have to proceed on the assumption that Madam Secretary is orchestrating her inauguration as the next President, with lots of help from her father and interests outside the country. What a can of worms we have just opened!"

"The timing and urgency to get things rolling in such a tight time frame is so that no one has a chance to be inaugurated before her turn comes up. How diabolical and how clever! OK team, back to the drawing board. Let's complete the picture and put all the pieces into their proper places as fast as possible. We reconvene at 1800 hours this evening."

As Kevin and I were leaving, Admiral Billig was reading the message that Miss Eagleton had delivered before her bombshell. "Wait a minute," he said, "The heat just got turned up even higher." His facial expression was darkened as he put out the word, "The boys in the Yokosuka 'spook' cave just found out that the *Red Vengeance* has made a successful submarine SAM launch and knocked down a drone target over the Yellow Sea."

CHAPTER 11

Secretary of State Maureen McCarthy Kavanaugh was born, raised and educated in the shadows of the State Capitol in Boston. Her father was native born, but her great-grandfather and grandfather had emigrated from Northern Ireland. All were faithful marchers in the annual St. Patrick's Day Parade and all had held various prominent offices in the Friendly Sons of St. Patrick. Young Maureen McCarthy also took part in those parades, at first in her baby buggy pushed by a proud grandfather, later in her stroller pushed by an even prouder father and eventually marching in the parades between the family patriarchs, each holding one of her hands. With the passing of her grandfather, she continued marching in the parades on her father's right. As an adult and a force in local politics, she perennially had a place at the head of the parade and once participated as the Grand Marshall. Throughout her formative years, both her grandfather and father were vocal and prominent supporters of the IRA and were warmly welcomed into Irish pubs and back rooms, where plans to raise money for the 'cause' were hatched. With the assets of a very successful construction business as backing, both men were heavy contributors to every fund raising event.

During her grade and high school years, the McCarthy family were rabid Boston Red Sox fans, attending almost every home game in their front row box directly behind home plate and frequently traveling with boosters to the home of their arch rivals, the New York Yankees. Young Maureen became such an avid devotee of the game that her most favorite toy was not a Barbie doll, relishing instead her baseball glove. Since she had no brothers, her father was more than eager and proud to play catch with her, teach her how to bat and especially how to pitch. In the summers, she played sandlot baseball with the boys. She remained fond of using baseball terms in her speeches long after her playing days were over.

Miss McCarthy excelled in high school sports, lettering in girl's softball, volley-ball, swimming and track and was noted for her very high level of competition. She was a firm believer in Vince Lombardi's dictum, "Wining isn't everything, it's the only thing". She never won a popularity contest like homecoming queen, Senior Prom sweetheart or class President, but her academic performance was recognized by her being chosen as the Valedictorian of her graduating class, and voted "the girl most likely to succeed". Those honors were looked upon as 'sour grapes' by her peers, as nearly all of her classmate's fathers, who worked for her father, advised their children that it would not be 'prudent' to deny her these honors. Under her sweetly smiling picture in her class year book, the adjectives "smart" and "ambitious" were printed over her own quote, "I'm going to be the first woman in space."

She attended college on an athletic scholarship and continued to excel in swimming, but her 'dream of dreams' was to play hardball with the men. While she never realized the dream (this was in the days before Title IX), she did talk the baseball coach into letting her (begrudgingly) pitch batting practice for the varsity baseballers. Her specialty was a 'duster' and she greatly relished seeing the future professionals on the team 'hit the dirt' to avoid her high and inside fast ball. After much cajoling, the coach (again begrudgingly) allowed her to play in an intra-squad game. The crowning embarrassment came when she tried to score from third base on an outfield fly ball. After tagging up, she barreled towards home plate with every intention of bowling over the burly catcher protecting the plate. The ensuing collision knocked her cold and she had to be assisted from the field, cursing and swearing that she would never ever suffer such a humiliation again. Her hardball playing days were over!

Her academic success continued, as she graduated Magma Cum Laude. By this time, the honor of being the first woman in space had gone to a lady Russian Cosmonaut, so she shifted her aspirations from outer space to the legal arena. The quote under her college yearbook picture said, "I'm going to be the first woman to sit on the Supreme Court," a clear omen of what was to come. Her classmates described her as 'brilliant' and a 'driver', another omen of her developing personality. Her marriage to pre-law classmate Michael Kavanaugh was the social high light of the season and the McCarthy and Kavanaugh families were overjoyed the next year with the birth of twins, Michael Jr. and Kristin. Everything pointed to a rosy future for the young family.

Her accomplishments in law school further embellished the characteristics that her classmates had recognized. She avidly pursued her legal studies with a zeal that could only be described as 'tireless'. In mock trials, she never lost a case and ran rough-shod over her more timid colleagues. Agatha Christie once described Miss Marpole as having a 'mind like a bacon slicer'. If Agatha had lived to see Madam Secretary, she would have surely described her as having a tongue 'like a cat-o-nine tails'. Graduating again with honors, the terms 'very goal oriented' and 'egocentric' appeared in many of her professor's letters of recommendation. As her dream to be a space traveler was over-taken by events, so was her dream to be the first woman to sit on the Supreme Court thwarted by Justice Sandra O'Connor. Undaunted by another setback, she set a new goal for herself, to be the first woman President of the United States, as she joked, "by hook or by crook". This presumptuous statement was printed in bold faced type under her picture in her law school year book.

Because of her special interest in and high grades in criminal law courses, she had no problem getting appointed as a Deputy District Attorney in Boston. The facts of who she was and that she "aced" the bar exam on the first try, helped in securing this job in the tender young years of her legal career. Her relentless prosecution of criminal cases earned her a new nickname—"The Dragon Lady". She handily won her first attempt in the political arena by becoming the youngest person to be elected Boston's District Attorney. In that office, her ratio of court wins vs. losses, in cases she prosecuted herself, was a record 95%, further enhancing her reputation as the 'Dragon Lady'.

The next rung on her personal ladder to the White House was not secured without an expensive price tag. Her husband, by now, a highly respected and successful corporate attorney, had finally had enough of being referred to as "Mr. Dragon Lady". Rather than go through what would have been a highly publicized and messy divorce, that would have had a negative effect on her upcoming campaign for Governor, they settled for a negotiated separation of households. Since both were independently wealthy, they went their separate ways quietly. The other price tag was more costly. Her children, Michael and Kristin, who had been cared for and trained by a succession of governesses and tutors, sent off to boarding schools and then to West Coast colleges, had grown up with out really getting to know their mother. Their relationships with their father was more befitting of parent and children. The result was that they loved their father but tolerated their mother. The parental separation drove a final wedge between mother and children. Her dry-eyed reaction to the dissolution of her family was, "Well, that's the way it goes."

Her campaign for Governor of Massachusetts was a throw back to the days of the Boss Tweed machine controlled elections. The new Boss Tweed was her father, who through his extensive lists of wealthy friends, business associates and labor union officials guaranteed a 'war chest' that seemed to have no end. The media blitz, bought with funds from this 'war-chest' was the hallmark of her campaign. The success of the campaign rewarded her with a landslide victory, which she interpreted as a mandate to continue her vigorous anti-crime crusade. Indeed, many of the press pundits and political cartoonists had a 'field day' in labeling the new Governor as the re-incarnation of Judge Roy Bean, the 'hanging judge' of the Old West. She lived up to that reputation by denying a record number of requests for executive clemency in her first, and only, term in office. The press and the opposition party, frequently depicted her politics as "far to the right of Barry Goldwater and alongside Atilla the Hun".

As her term of office was coming to a close, she was presented with a golden opportunity for her giant step to the Oval Office. The President was finishing his second term, so she did not have to run against an incumbent. The primaries were one of the fiercest, hottest, and in many respects, the dirtiest in recent history, dwarfing the scandals of the late nineteen nineties. She found herself in a pitched battle with Governor Randolph Alexander of California, a Vietnam war hero, and E. Parker Collins, a computer genius boy wonder whom the business community backed heavily. Other less influential aspirants had been swept away like feathers in a gale during the early primaries. Her father (still aka Boss Tweed) was a tireless campaigner for his darling daughter, raising funds and twisting arms in her behalf. He called in markers, amassed in over a half a century of wheeling and dealing, from all over the country. The markers were repaid not only by financial support, but also with votes in the primaries to select delegates to the National Convention committed to her. He made numerous trips to Northern Ireland between the end of the primaries and the convention, which oddly coincided with massive, and probably illegal, contributions to her campaign coffers.

Going into the convention, all three contenders were still in the hunt, but no one was guaranteed enough votes to win the nomination on the first ballot. Her campaign manager predicted that she would be the top vote getter on the first ballot and sweep to victory on the second ballot. Many convention delegates felt that her smugness was overconfidence, bordering on condescension, with little respect for the voters who held her future in their hands. Her two opponents were totally nonpulsed by her bombastic speeches and not the least bit intimidated by the poll results that her campaign manager was constantly spewing forth (all in her favor of course). They quietly, but effectively, were chipping away at her ultra right wing politics, and slamming sledge hammer blows at her indifference to the nation and her obsession with her own personal agenda.

The first hint of trouble arose during the first ballot, when Governor Alexander started to garner many uncommitted delegates, whom she had felt were in her purse. This minor windfall was not enough to win the nomination, but it did put him slightly ahead of the Dragon Lady. Mr. Collins was in a distant third place, a clear demonstration that money wasn't always everything. "Not to worry," said her father, as he scurried from one state caucus to the next in a furious attempt to call in more markers from delegates who were supporting Mr. Collins. Similarly, her campaign manager descended into both smoke filled and clean air back rooms of various hotel suites to promise the sun, moon, and stars to the influential delegation leaders who could swing their state's votes. The day of the second ballot dawned with Madam Governor already rehearsing her acceptance speech for later in the day.

Just before the second ballot started, the wheels of her well oiled machine started to come off. Mr. Collins made an unscheduled and unanticipated appearance at the podium, stepped up to the microphone and withdrew from the election, giving an impassioned endorsement to her opponent. The look on Madam Governor's face was evil as evil could be, and her grimace was not lost on the delegates as the TV cameras zeroed in on her, projecting her expression of pure hatred on all the king sized monitors and screens in the auditorium. The balloting started and her wheels came off completely. The now released delegates flocked to her opponent in droves. What had seemed to be a lead pipe cinch victory turned into a rout, as many of her delegates were only committed fully for the first ballot and now jumped on her opponent's bandwagon. Her concession speech was delivered in a vitriolic manner. She neither pledged her support to the winner nor did she make the customary motion to make the vote unanimous. As she stepped away from the podium, to only a mild round of applause, she was heard to mutter to herself, "I'll be back, you can be damn well sure of that." When asked, in subsequent interview if she would accept a nomination to run as the Vice-Presidential candidate, her curt and cold response was, "I never run for second place."

The convention eventually chose Representative Michael Flaherty, a veteran of the Gulf War, as their Vice-Presidential candidate. Even before the acceptance speeches had begun, the pundits and power-brokers were already hard at work to mend fences and bring the opposing camps back into the fold. There were many open wounds to heal, as the party image had been tarnished by the viciousness of the campaign. Fortunately Mr. Collins was as gracious in defeat as he was successful in the financial world, leaving only the Dragon lady to be placated. A deal was finally struck. In return for a promise of an appointment as Secretary of State, she agreed, somewhat reluctantly, to fade from the scene and not do anything to damage the campaign of Candidate Alexander.

The Presidential campaign, during which she was conspicuously absent, and the November election swept Randolph Alexander into the White House, and in the formation of his Cabinet, he honored the olive branch that had been offered and nominated Madam Governor to become the Secretary of State. It was not a 'done thing' as there were several Senators, on both sides of the aisle, who were not overjoyed at the thought of the Dragon Lady administrating foreign policy, but vigorous lobbying by the Vice-President and the movers and shakers who had engineered her appointment prevailed, and she was confirmed. She immediately set up shop in the State Department building, dubbing her office "The Dragon's Den". True to her word, she kept a low profile, and did not rock the boat.

When the next Presidential campaign came on the scene, Madam Secretary marshalled her forces and announced that she would campaign against the President for their party's nomination. She was surprised and disappointed when she found out that her father had no more markers to call in on her behalf and the family fortune had been seriously depleted during her previous campaign. Much to her chagrin she was on her own! Staying out of the floodlights of media attention had seriously eroded what was left of her popularity, to the extent that she withdrew from the campaign after a series of early primary defeats. She had learned another bitter lesson— unless an incumbent President had fallen publicly on his sword, his party would nominate him for a second term, regardless of what the polls showed. This time around, the party was not plagued by a costly and vicious campaign and President Alexander easily won re-election for a second term.

World affairs started to change during the first year of the President's second term and serious problems that would divide public opinion arose, problems that would widen the smoldering chasm between the White House and the State department. Her animosity toward the man, who had thwarted her most ambitious dream of a 1600 Pennsylvania Avenue address, resurfaced. Three major issues arose which placed Madam Secretary in direct opposition to the administration. North Korea, buoyed by the enactment of the permanent favorite nation trade agreement with Communist China, was pushing for equal status. The President, whose father had died at Heartbreak Ridge, was unalterably opposed to this attempt, while Madam Secretary saw this as a venue to exact revenge for her political defeats. In Europe, the IRA was making a determined bid to permanently drive the English out of Northern Ireland. Madam Secretary's family, and financial ties to the IRA, placed her in direct conflict with the Vice-President, who abhorred all forms of terrorism and was adamant in not giving in to terrorist demands. In the Near and Middle East, the Secretary of State had become a frequent visitor to Arab nations and was an outspoken supporter of the PLO quest for 'liberation' of Muslim territories from the State of Israel. Here she ran afoul of the Speaker of the House, who, in addition to being Jewish, was also a veteran of Desert Storm. These three major issues, as well as several minor problems within the Organization of American States governments resulted in a battle of ideologies between the Executive and Legislative branches, and the State Department. Harmonious relations between the U.S. and other OAS governments were being disrupted by her 'gun barrel' diplomacy, reminiscent of the Elian Gonzales debacle. Speculation had arisen that her days as Secretary of State were numbered.

As resentment and jealousy escalated into hatred, Madam Secretary became obsessed with the idea of occupying the Oval office, and if she could not get the job at the ballot boxes, she would get it by using the age-old ploy of rejected politicians— by the removal of those standing in her way. The gods of fate, unwittingly and suddenly, presented her with a combination of unprecedented circumstances, that could make this possible and she, and her father, eagerly sought to exploit the opportunity to its fullest.

CHAPTER 12

October 30 (continued)

Kevin and I were still sifting through the background data on the Secretary of State when 1800 hours came and went without the Admiral making an appearance. It was most unusual for him to be late, especially at a meting that he, himself, had called. He tore into the office at exactly 1805, out of breath, and went right to his chair without so much as an apology or an explanation. He had correctly presumed that we would have gotten a fast food supper before the meeting, so he had brought a twelve-pack of diet soft drinks to slake our thirst. He never offered caffeine-free drinks, so that everyone would stay awake and alert. He caught his breath and sat down, and after each of us had selected a beverage, he opened the meeting with what he had learned since we adjourned a few hours ago.

"SubRon 7 reports that *Red Vengeance* has fired three successful sub-SAMs[iii] this week and had returned to port. He presumes that she has finished her 'shake down' training, and is now preparing to deploy. A Los Angeles class boat has been ordered from Yokosuka into the Yellow Sea to track her, and

---

iii Sub-SAM= Subsurface to Air Missile

another boat, out of Guam, will be assigned to keep an eye on the North Korean 'fishing' boat currently off the north shore of Guam, close to Anderson Air Force Base. Satellite and airplane fly-overs indicate that this particular 'fishing' boat has an impressive array of communication and radar antennae that her predecessors didn't. Nobody believes that she is fishing for fish. The Pacific is definitely heating up. The Admiral nodded his head telling me, "It's your turn now."

"Admiral, my stuff is not as concrete as yours, but it is still significant. SgtMajor had reported to MI6 that our friend McCarthy showed up again at Paddy's last week, without any advance warning as far as can be determined right now. The passport control desk at Belfast airport did not record his entry, so he is either traveling on a false passport or he entered the country in an unorthodox manner. This is so out of character for him. A review of the surveillance films at the passport desk did not show him as having passed through however, MI6 is now going through the passenger lists for all flights into Belfast that day, to see where he came from, and what alias he is using. Oh, by an odd coincidence, the three Gilhooley brothers were waiting for him at Paddy's. I'll have better intelligence as soon as MI6 gets back to me."

"Things in Jerusalem are still a little fuzzy yet. Mossad confirms that the '*White Lightning*' traffic in and out of Damascus has increased and they have narrowed the players down to one particular cell that specializes in 'surgical' strikes, mostly attributed to an operative known only as "The Chameleon". This cat is a lone wolf, a master of disguise and ruthless, with over one hundred kills that they know of, but can't prove. Isn't he a nice playmate. Because of the scheduled appearance of the Speaker of the House at the Israeli Medical Society, the Brigadier has placed the Crown Plaza hotel, where the meeting will be held, under tight security status and they are in the process of re-vetting the hotel staff, as well as doing in-depth background checks on all recent hires. They are also screening all the medical people who are scheduled to attend and/or work the meeting to make certain that the Chameleon will not be working with a deep mole within the Medical Society, or have arranged for a back-up. Mossad has not ruled out the possibility that the Arabs might be using the 'Chameleon' as a decoy and assigned the job to another assassin, even a woman, in spite of the Muslim macho masculine image. The Brigadier doesn't want any last minute surprises because he doesn't photograph well with egg on his face. They'll also get back to me after they fill in a few more pieces of the puzzle."

It was Kevin's turn. This time his voice was not as exuberant as it usually was. "Jack is on the move again. Belatedly, and I apologize for this, we discovered that he made round trip reservations from JFK to Paris for his grandson and granddaughter. The date of their arrival in France was the day before the incognito McCarthy showed up in Belfast. It didn't take any fancy work to track down telephone calls to the grandchildren setting up their trips or to uncover their flights into Paris. Nothing suspicious there. Oh, by the way, I solved the riddle of the riddle of the missing three nine thousand British pound note packages. It looks like he was using his grandchildren as couriers of cash without them knowing what was going on. When we re-reviewed, with magnification, the films of them coming out of customs, guess who shows up? Jack, who greets them like a lovey-dovey grandfather. They each pass him a sealed plain brown envelope, which rapidly disappears into his briefcase, but not fast enough to hide the fact that he had a similar envelope already in his possession. I'll bet that each one of those envelopes found its way into a Gilhooley brother's pocket."

"With the transfer of funds completed, he's off and running. Follow-up on the grand children revealed nothing to indicate that they weren't on anything but a grand-daddy paid for pure vacation. There're out of the picture now."

Kevin took in a very deep breath and continued, "Before you ask me, no, I don't how or when he did the trans-Atlantic bit nor do I know how he got from Paris to Belfast. He did an excellent job of covering his tracks this time. A professional must have set it up for him and it worked by fooling us until he was spotted by SgtMajor in Belfast. Admiral, again I apologize for letting him fall through the cracks, but I promise you that we'll fill in the missing pieces as soon as possible, starting with a 24 hour tail that will look like his shadow, once he is back in the country."

The Admiral's expression said it all, 'My son, what happened?" I kept my face a blank, but thought to myself, "So, Kevin, you're human after all."

While Kevin and I were showing that we weren't as infallible as we thought we were, the boss had leaned back in his chair, clasped his hands behind his head and stared at the ceiling. When Kevin had finished his 'mea culpa', he sat forward and slapped his hands on the table. "You know," he almost shouted, "What we have here is Maureen's simple, but complicated route to the Oval Office. What an oxymoronic very hot potato has been dropped into our collective laps. Just think, —to succeed in business or sports, you have to eliminate your competition. The simple part of the scenario is, 'remove the people standing in the way of her trip to the White House'. The complicated part is 'how to do it in a way that nobody realizes what is happening and happening so fast, that nothing can stop the steamroller once it starts moving. The extraordinary part is how the gods have laid this 'once in a life-time' opportunity in Mrs. Kavanaugh's lap."

"See how it all fits in:
- –Access- the competition is widely scattered around the world, some in areas where terrorist attacks are a way of life, which spreads the forces protecting them pretty thin.
- –Vulnerability- as for the President in Air Force One over an ocean, what a target; as for the V.P. and the Speaker, they'll be in areas where the Secret Service has to share their responsibilities with security forces who live and fight against fanatical terrorists, almost as a way of life. I sure hope that the cooperation, understanding and unity of purpose between the security forces involved will be on a level that has never before been reached. As far as the Senator is concerned, who's going to

pay much attention to a Senator who has chosen to retire and go home. We'll have to shoulder the responsibility of protecting him.

–Timing- the dirty deeds must be accomplished almost simultaneously to prevent a rapid appointment of replacements. With Congress in recess, what a windfall! I'll bet that when we mesh the time tables for the assassinations of the President, the V.P. and the Speaker, we'll find a narrow window of opportunity into which the demise of the Senator can also take place.

–Incentives- the proverbial carrot on a stick dangled in front of the North Koreans, the IRA, and the PLO: in one fell swoop to eliminate their arch enemies and replace ALL of them with ONE person, who is sympathico to all their causes, <u>how diabolical!</u>"

The Admiral sat up straight in his chair and almost shouted, "It looks like Mrs. Kavanaugh has written a manual titled 'How to turn a series of seemingly unrelated occurrences into the fulfillment of ones life's dream'. It boggles the mind to realize that it could really happen. I've got to see the President, like an hour ago."

The Admiral reconnected his red hot line to the Oval office and it took a few exasprating minutes to cut through the protective screening that makes sure that only people with a real need to talk to the President directly, get put through to him. Once the Commander-in-Chief was on the phone, the Admiral requested that they use the scrambler. I could almost see the President's usual jovial smile being replaced a dark cloud of suspicion. The bottom line was that a meeting, between just the President and the Admiral, was set up for later that night. After he hung up, he turned back to us, "OK, what's happened, has happened. Let's clean up the mess and get things back on track. I'll get back to you after I brief the President. Good evening."

CHAPTER 13

It was close to 2200 (10:00 PM) when Admiral Billig presented himself at the White House, where he was quickly processed by the Secret Service duty section and escorted directly to the Oval Office. A soft knock on the door was answered with a cheery, "It's open, come on in." On entering the office, the Admiral was greatly warmly by President Alexander, who had been watching TV in his favorite lazy boy recliner. "Vince," he said, "It's been a long time hasn't it?" (the President was one of the few people who dared call the Admiral by his first name, a throw back to the days when they were shipmates and they were Vince and Randy). "You shouldn't be such a stranger. After all, all work and no play turns a man into an Ebenezer Scrooge. Well, what brings you here in the middle of the night? I hope it's really important, because now I'm missing a 'West Wing' rerun. I always watch them to learn how not to do this job."

The Admiral chuckled and answered, "Mr. President, you know me better than that. This time of night is not for socializing and the setting doesn't lend itself to telling 'sea stories'."

The Admiral then flirted with the president's somewhat short temper by asking if they were alone, i.e. no hidden tape recorders whirling, no bugs listening in or the like. The President scowled at the question, but quickly assured his friend that they were totally by themselves and pointed to a large soft sofa, indicating that they should make themselves comfortable and get down to business.

The President never forgot that his first year aboard ship, after graduating from Submarine School, was almost as traumatic as his 'plebe' year at Annapolis. He had to earn his dolphins, which required that he become qualified as a diving officer, then as Officer of the Deck underway, learn how to be a benevolent division officer and to carry out his daily assigned tasks within the Weapons department. His immediate superior and taskmaster was Lt. Vincent Billig, the Weapons Officer. LT(jg) Alexander was fortunate, although he didn't know it at the time, to be assigned to Lt. Billig's department. During this arduous time, Lt. Billig was constantly snapping at LT (jg) Alexander's heels, to spur him on towards becoming 'Qualified in Submarines'. It all bore fruit when the frazzled JG finished the qualification process in record time and won the right to wear his gold dolphins. The second proudest man at the 'pinning', after the boat's skipper, was Lt. Billig. The two men became very close friends from that day on. Later in his career life onboard a 'boomer', during deterrent patrols, became too quiet for LCDR Alexander, so he got himself a law degree and transferred to the JAG (Judge Advocate General) Corps, where the rest of his naval career was spent. During the course of the next fifteen years, their paths frequently crossed until Captain Alexander succumbed to the lure of a life in politics and retired from active service. The next time their paths crossed was when President Alexander tapped retired Vice Admiral Billig to take over as head of the Institute.

Once the men were comfortably seated, the Admiral lit a Tabacalero Filipino cigar (he was the only person to whom that courtesy was allowed in the Oval Office) and got right to the point. "Mr. President, we have very strong indications that there is a plot afoot to overthrow the government by the almost simultaneous assassinations of yourself, the VicePresident, the Speaker of the House, and the President-Pro-Tem of the Senate."

The Admiral paused and closely watched a gamut of emotions that sweep across the Commander-in-Chief's face. They were surprise, shock, disbelief, exasperation and finally anger as he rapidly contemplated the plot and its consequences. The only sound from the President was an audible gasp, followed by the sucking of wind past his clenched teeth.

It was now his turn to read the Admiral's face to be sure that he had really heard what he had just heard. "Vince, if it had been anyone but you, my first reaction would have been that you didn't know what you were talking about and had finally gone over the edge. I mentally started a short list of people to replace you at the Institute, but then reason took over and I realized that you would have never made such a drastic statement unless you were damn well sure of the facts and yourself. So, old friend, before we go any further, let's splice the main brace and give me one of those horrible things you call cigars."

Both men went over to the bar that was cleverly concealed in a filing cabinet labeled "Top Secret" and the President poured them both a tall rum and coke, using his special 150 proof Bacardi. They returned to the comfort of the sofa, and the CinC lit up the first cigar he had smoked in years, and for the first time in recent memory, the Oval office became a smoke filled room "OK" he sighed, "Lay it on me."

The Admiral began by stating, "First of all, only four people know about this, you, me, my right arm Glenn Stark and Kevin Jablonski, my chief cryptographer and analyst, who you know better as the 'Hacker'. In addition to my oral brief, I'm handing you the only written copy of the record for you to read at your leisure. The three of us carry all the details in our brains. It was Kevin, who tumbled to the seemingly unrelated messages he was decoding, as easy as pie I might add, and Glenn who pieced all the parts into what eventually became this briefing. I must admit that I was as incredulous as you were, until I finally recognized the magnitude of the plot."

The Admiral then proceeded to present chapter, bible, and verse of all the facts, the interpretation of those facts and the undeniable conclusions that had evolved. The briefing included flimsies of communications from Washington to North Korea, Northern Ireland and Syria, as well as flimsies of reports by

Naval intelligence on the goings on in the Western Pacific, by MI6 regarding the IRA activities and by Mossad dealing with Muslim investigations. At the conclusion of the briefing, the room was thick with cigar smoke and the old buddies had down-graded their grog to traditional 80 proof Bacardi.

Throughout the lengthy presentation, the President had sat in stony silence, not once interrupting the flow of information. At the end of the briefing, they both sat back for several minutes of soul-searching. Someone with hyper-acute hearing could have sworn that it was possible to hear their brains processing data at warp speed.

The President stood up and put his cigar, which had gone out long ago, into an ashtray and strolled slowly to his office window that looked out to the Washington Monument. When he turned back to the Admiral, it appeared that he had suddenly aged twenty years. With a sigh of resignation he said, "OK, from the beginning again, and this time put some flesh on the skeleton you've just hauled out of the closet and give me the proof for your conclusions."

Again, in the proper order and sequence, the Admiral laid it out, starting with the inklings, then the confirmatory details and finally the probable scenarios that were projected to take place around the 17th of November. The silence in the room was deafening.

After what seemed like an eternity, but was only about five minutes, the President asked, "You done Vince"? Upon receiving an affirmative nod from his guest, he continued, "It is the most dastardly and preposterous story I've ever listened to. It's utterly inconceivable that Maureen Kavanaugh could have ever contemplated doing this, but the more I recall her actions of the past year, it makes sense. But I wish I could be one hundred percent sure of it. Vince, as a lawyer, I have to tell you that, while you've built a very convincing case, the preponderance of the evidence is circumstantial and filled with inferences that a good defense attorney would have a better than fifty per-cent chance of shooting down. Can you get me something concrete and damning that will tie her into this in such a way that it can't be repudiated?"

The Admiral put down his glass and his cigar and bluntly stated, 'Yes, there is. Do you remember back in 1942, when Nimitz's boys were unsure of where the next Japanese naval thrust was going to hit, a smarty, CDR Rochefort, came up with the idea of having Midway send a plain language request to Hawaii for water (which of course was false), and then monitor the Japanese reaction. The ensuing message traffic confirmed that it was Midway that was going to be hit. Let's try a variation of that theme. Get the Secretary of State in here in the morning and tell her in strict confidence, for her ears only, that you might not be able to make the trip to Japan as scheduled, and that she might have go in your place. Be very specific in admonishing her that she was not, I repeat not, to discuss this possibility with anyone until you confirmed it the next day. I'll have my people read everything that goes out to the usual suspects to see if she leaks it. The ploy worked once and it should work again. As far as we can tell, she hasn't the faintest idea that we have exposed her plan. Mr. President. If it comes to pass that I am proved wrong, you'll have my resignation and a letter of apology within twenty-four hours."

It didn't take the President more than a few minutes to reach a decision, "Vince, I'll do it. I have to get this situation completely resolved for my piece of mind, as soon as possible. We will meet again tomorrow evening to let me know what you've shaken out of the trees."

Good nights were exchanged along with meaningless wishes for a good night's sleep. No one was going to get anything close to a good night's sleep this night. On returning to his car, the Admiral activated his cell phone and contacted Kevin and me to meet with him a little after midnight in his office.

CHAPTER 14

ASHBURN
October 31

Kevin and I were again seated at the conference table at 0015. The ever attentive Miss Eagleton had provided a large pot of hot, high octane black coffee to keep us on our toes and a bowl of assorted nuts on the table for our gastric satisfaction. We were then treated to a second earth shattering event within twenty-four hours. Midnight came and went, and for the first time the Admiral was not only late for a meeting he had called, but possibly not even coming. We figured that the reason was that he was probably up to his neck in alligators over at the Oval office. Neither of us had the guts to leave, so sure enough, at 0030 the Admiral entered the office. He looked like he had aged ten years since we last saw him.

"Rough night?," I dared to venture, to which he replied in the testiest tone of voice I had ever heard him use, "A gross understatement."

He plopped heavily into his chair, filled a mug with hot, black coffee and gave us the short version of what had taken place in the Oval office. "Everything is on hold for twenty-four hours. The President was incredulous, obstinate, and full of denial, but finally agreed to one last confirmatory step, which will stay between me and him for the time being. He wants to give the Dragon Lady the benefit of the doubt, but at the same time give her enough rope to hang herself. Glenn, starting first thing in the morning, I want you to arrange to have the Dragon Lady followed everywhere, and I mean everywhere, she goes from the minute she leaves her house. Put a woman agent in the surveillance team to follow her even into the ladies' room. Keep the tail on her until further notice. Get pictures of anything suspicious, get close enough to her to eavesdrop on her conversations if you can, and have the team equipped to take any and all steps to gather iron-clad evidence to hang her high. Kevin, work your magic. Hack into her computer and see if you can come up with the 'colors' in her E-mail. Get a copy of her appointments for the past six months, I'm sure they're in a 'save' box somewhere. This may be lot to ask for on short notice, but see if there were any calls from the State Department to any of the prime suspects recently. Also, get a copy of the 'Visitor and V.I.P. Sign In Register' that's kept in the State Department lobby. It will take a lot of your ingenuity to get past their security, but it would be very interesting to see if any, and how many of the suspects have paid her a visit,. Now, what do you two have for me?"

I passed, seeing that I didn't have any new items for the general good, but Kevin was loaded for bear. He had obviously been working hard to plug the gaps that he had previously confessed to have missed. "In my best inquiring reporter voice, I called the McCarthy residence, and asked if I could have a few minutes of Mr. McCarthy's time for an interview regarding the approaching elections. His valet was very cooperative and talkative, and full of little juicy tidbits."

"No — the boss is away. He went to Paris a week ago for a
    short vacation with his grandchildren
Yes — I was surprised, because I didn't know about the
    trip until he instructed me to pack his bag for a ten
    day's stay.

Yes — we expect him back home tomorrow." "Make that today," Kevin corrected himself after a quick look at his wristwatch. "His chauffeur will pick him up at JFK in mid-afternoon.

No — I don't know what airline he's flying, you might ask his chauffeur in the morning, but I can tell you that he is expected to arrive at 3:30 PM"

Kevin went on, "I've already checked with JFK and United has the only flight from Paris arriving at that time. I propose that we—

— put a tail on the chauffer as soon as he leaves the estate in the morning
— put an agent, who can recognize Jack on sight, in with the boarding party to find out from the flight attendants what name he is using
— station another agent, with a concealed mini-camera, with the passport officers, and when McCarthy passes through, get pictures of the pages covering this trip We might just be able to discover the forger, if he leaves a few of his trademarks about.
— put McCarthy himself under 24 hour surveillance, similar to what you ordered for his daughter, from the minute he leaves the jet way."

"I'll pull up his telephone calling card and his credit card folders again, I'll bet that he used his own over there, rather than getting new ones or using fakes. They'd be a little too risky to cover up if they bounced."

"Also, I think I've solved the riddle of his cash transactions:
— the two $7500.00 checks to the Irish Benevolent Society were probably a down payment for services ordered
— the bundles of big British pound notes were either IRA expense money or good faith money
— the last three $9000.00 packets of old bills were probably a 'balloon' payment that was requested on short notice. His grand children were probably used as unsuspecting couriers. I think that we can forget

about them at this point
— the small $5000.00 withdrawal is still unaccounted for, but I'm working on it."

"This leads me to believe that "D Day" is getting close. Later today I'll start to reconstruct his trail, presuming that he is still a creature of some habits and still enjoys his creature comforts. I'll bet the trail will look something like this: His chauffer drives him to JFK; he flies to Paris; he takes the 'chunnel' train to London and a local train to an Irish Sea seaport for a ferry ride to Belfast. I'll ask Glenn to work with MI6 to flesh out the UK picture. Maybe I'll get real lucky and find out where he sacked out, but I won't promise that, there wasn't much time left for sleeping. Anyhow, I'll try."

The Admiral was quick to approve our plans without any changes, which told me that he was really tired and wanted to get to his bed. After all, he was going to have a heavy day too. He closed the session by saying, "We'll wait until 1700 this afternoon for our next get together. By then, the President should have made up his mind once and for all, and we'll take it from there. The last thing we want to witness is another 'date that will go down in infamy'. That's it for now gentlemen, get as much sleep as you can. It may a long time before any of us gets another good night's sleep. And, don't worry, I'll be on time next time!"

CHAPTER 15

It was unbelievable how fast 1700 had arrived and we were again seated at the conference table. Neither Kevin nor I had shaved today, but Admiral was in his usual casual office attire and cleanly shaved. Miss Eagleton had confided to us that he had locked himself in his 'sanctum' all night and threatened to make her 'walk the plank' if she disturbed him. He left his office early in the morning and didn't reappear until mid afternoon when he sent out for a three piece Kentucky Fried Chicken box lunch, and instructed her to be sure that there was a pot of strong, hot coffee for our meeting. Knowing him, we postulated that he was in his "Hercule Poirot" mode, driving his little gray cells to the max to come up with a plan of action.

The session was called to order by the Admiral's simple statement, "Glenn, you start."

The ball was in my court, and I knew I didn't dare bobble it. This time I used notes to ensure that I didn't leave anything out. "Per your instructions, Admiral, our 'tail' team picked up Madame Secretary as soon as she left her home this morning. The full report of where she went, whom she met, and what she did fills three pages, I have a print-out for you peruse at your leisure. Most of it is routine and boring. The high lights are: a visit to the White House, from there a quick trip to the Ritz-Carlton, where she made a pay phone telephone call and she's been in her office at the State Department ever since. We could not get a read on the conversation because it was too short and we couldn't get close enough to overhear her. Let me tell you about that phone call. The Dragon Lady is one slick chick. She marches into the hotel and heads straight for a bank of three pay phones, well removed from the lobby. Obviously she knew right where she was going. She marked time until all the phones were clear and then she pulled two 'out of order' signs from her purse and hung them on the outer phones. She hunched over the dial of the middle phone, preventing us from seeing what number she dialed, but we pretty much know who she was calling, don't we? She then turned to face the foot traffic that was passing and when she was sure that she was alone, she cupped her hand over her mouth and the mouth piece frustrating our lip reader. She spoke so softly that the audio monitor couldn't hear her either. The call was less than one minute in duration. After she hung up, she retrieved the 'out of order' signs, and left the hotel. Judging from her actions, she has probably done this routine several times. We'll be ready for her the next time. Kevin is running a trace on the number she dialed to confirm our suspicions."

I then made a feeble attempt of humor, "Nothing out of the ordinary took place in the Ladies Room," which fell flat on its face as the Admiral growled, "Stick to the meat."

I shrugged my shoulders and continued, "Switching topics, MI6 in London and SgtMajor McGregor in Belfast filled in some of the holes in Jack's recent travels, but I don't want to steal Kevin's thunder, I defer to him at this point."

Kevin picked up the ball and taking in a deep breathe he started, "First, the Dragon Lady–her E-mail shows numerous references in the past six months to *'Red Storm'* in messages to the North Korean Trade Commission and *'White Lightning'* in those to the Syrian Embassy, but nothing in her incoming traffic. Second, – her appointments—she has had an unusual number of visits from various North Korean and Arab nation officials. She has also recorded more visits to Arab nation embassies than the combined total to every other embassy or consulate. Three—phone calls nothing out of the ordinary recently. Four—visitors to the State Department—they should install a special entrance for members of the North Korean Trade Commission. Various officials from the Commission have beat a steady path to State, calling on everyone of importance in the Far East section. I'll come back to her later, on to Jack McCarthy."

"Our 'Sneaky Pete' operation at Kennedy went off like clock-work, one– the flight attendants identified our Jack as a 'Mr. McCormack', two– the picture in 'his' passport that we got at Immigration was his, but he was traveling under the alias of a 'John McCormack of New York City'. Then we got a bonus. While he was waiting in the customs line, one of our best 'sticky fingers' agents lifted his documents wallet and photographed every page of 'his' passport, and everything else he was carrying in it. He even got it back into his pocket without Jack missing it. Shrewd, by using his own first name and the 'McC' from his last name, he reduced the risks of giving himself away by inadvertently answering up to 'John', 'Jack' or 'Mac'. He was also carrying a drivers license, Medicare card, Social Security card, and a Carte Blanche credit card all with the name of John McCormack. Hidden in a 'secret' pocket in the wallet was his own ATM card. We did a follow-up, and surprisingly, the passport was for real and issued to a 'John McCormack' at the New York address listed. Now, the hooker, the real John McCormack died two weeks ago. Another funny twist, John McCormack actually worked for the import/export company in question, so I guess that's how they were able to get a hold of the stuff and recycle it for use by our boy. Oh, by the way, while the picture in the passport was our Jack, the signature was totally illegible, definitely not his. It could have been written by a chimp. Back to you, buddy."

"Got it," I said. "On the day in question, MI6 was able to ascertain that McCormack did not fly directly into or from Belfast, nor did he fly either out of or back into Gatwick or Heathrow. Checking on alternative methods of transportation, his trail was picked up in Liverpool, when he was listed on the passenger roster for an over-night ferry trip to Belfast. SgtMajor reported that after he was spotted at Paddy's, he was tailed back to the harbor, where he booked passage back on the ferry to Liverpool. In London, lucky for us, British Railways was doing a 'spot check' on passengers and a John McCormack did take the "chunnel" to Paris, pick it from there, Kevin."

Kevin was definitely over his depression of the night before, "Another bonus—one of our more enterprising agents donned a chauffeur's suit and casually joined Jack's driver in a coffee shop at JFK. To pass the time I guess they swapped 'chauffeur stories'. Here's a wrinkle I didn't expect. Jack didn't go directly from home to JFK. He took a side trip into New York City and made a stop at his good friends, the shady import/ exporters. Then he went to JFK. Almost as an aside, McCarthy's driver threw in another bonus, he usually travels with everything, including the kitchen sink, but this time he had just a soft bag that just barely fitted into the overhead bin, and a small 'over-the-shoulder' bag. But he did have his usual attaché case. So much for the two carry-ons per person limit."

"I think I can fill in the blank spaces now: Day one,– Jack departs Boston, makes a trip into New York City to pick up his new passport and the supporting documents. I'll bet that the 'front' also made his transatlantic reservations and bought his tickets as a company representative. Now I know where the five grand I couldn't account for wound up, to pay for the false ID credentials. He then goes to JFK. We checked United flights to Europe until we found a John McCormack booked on their Paris flight. Day two,– he arrives at Charles De Gaulle, meets his grand kids, collects the money they carried for him, goes to the "chunnel" terminal and crosses under the English Channel to London. I figured that he wasn't doing the tourist bit, but would keep a low profile while enjoying his creature comforts. By doing a quick computer search of hotels around Heathrow, we found that a Mr. John McCormack of New York City stayed one night at the Hilton London Heathrow facility and paid cash when he checked out the next morning. His room was not reserved in advance, i.e. no paper trail. Day three,– somehow he got to Liverpool, how is not important, and books the overnight ferry to Belfast. Day four,– he shows up at Paddy's, lightens his wallet by $27,000.00, probably had a pub lunch and a pint (on the house), completes the plot to murder the V.P., and goes back to the harbor where he boards another overnight ferry back to Liverpool. Day five,– back on British soil, he retraces his steps to London and back on to Paris. Again presuming that he wasn't in town to go to the Follies, I had a colleague of mine in the Surete run a guest check of Paris airport hotels, and sure enough, he had an overnight stay at the Hilton Paris Roussy, where else? Again, no paper trail and he pays the bill in Euros. Day six,– today, he flies back to JFK, where his chauffeur meets him and where we put our tail back on him. I'll bet that he was wishing that the Concorde was still flying. He then goes directly home and probably straight to bed. His ATM transactions have not been posted yet, but when they come in, I'll be surprised if they don't show some hefty withdrawals in France, England, and Belfast."

Feeling quite proud of himself, Kevin added, "I do have one item of a follow-up nature to report. Jack's calls to Chicago were to another import/export company that does a lot of business in Canada. They are not squeaky clean, operating just barely on this side of the line between legal and illegal, but they have a super high-powered legal department that keeps them out of court most of the time. There haven't been any calls to them lately, so I think Jack completed his business with them on the first go around, time will tell."

By now the Admiral was actually smiling again, "Well done, Bravo Zulu to both of you. My faith in you has been restored. Let me know ASAP [as soon as possible] when either of you have something new. He looked at his watch and noted that he had about an hour before his next scheduled meeting with the President. He said that he wanted to be alone to gather his thoughts for the meeting, so we were dismissed.

CHAPTER 16

It was early evening when Admiral Billig was again knocking on the door of the Oval Office. A gruff, "Come in," greeted him. The President, who was at his desk having an animated conversation on his 'regular' business phone, motioned to his friend to take a seat on the conference sofa. This time the President was ready for his visitor, for on the coffee table in front of the sofa, a bottle of Chardonnay was chilling in ice and a large bowl of freshly popped popcorn was waiting for them. The odor of cigar smoke still hung in the air, so it was not surprising that ash trays were conspicuous by their absence.

The President ended his phone conversation and came immediately to the sofa muttering, "Junior Senators can be a pain in the butt, especially when they have an over inflated opinion of their own importance." He poured two glasses of wine, passed one to his friend, grabbed a handful of popcorn and plopped onto the sofa. There was no smile on his face as he addressed the Admiral, "Vince, your face tells me that you don't have good news for me, not that I'm surprised, but I had hoped that things would not get to this point. Lay it on me."

After a long sip of wine, the Admiral took several pieces of paper from his pocket and began his tale of woe. "This morning I had a tight tail attached to the Secretary of State from the time she left her home. After she left you, she wasn't gone ten minutes before she made a call from a public phone in the Ritz-Carlton hotel. The phone was immediately placed 'out of order' as soon as she hung up. Subsequently, the 'Hacker' was able to electronically trace the call to what was supposed to be a secure line in the North Korean Trade Commission office. All of these proceedings were recorded on film with time and date identification. Her finger prints were also lifted from the phone itself. This message was picked up later and decoded, it was sent within an hour of her leaving this office."

He handed the first piece of paper to the President, whose scowl had gotten increasingly blacker as he read it. It was the decrypt of an encoded "urgent-priority" message from the head of the Trade Commission to the Foreign Secretary in Pyongnang. It read, "<u>Urgent</u>, DL reports possible changes to "*Red Storm*" travel plans that may result in her replacing "*Red*," confirmation to follow."

The president's only comment was, "Damn!".

Without comment, he was handed the second piece of paper. This was a copy of a decoded "FLASH-PRIORITY" message from North Korean Naval Headquarters to the Commanding Officer of the submarine base where *Red Vengeance* was being prepared to deploy. It read, "Time table for commencement of "*Red Storm*" on hold, pending confirmation of possible changes to current itinerary. Proceed with preparations for deployment, but do not establish an exact under-way time as yet."

President Alexander had a look of utter amazement on his face, as he spoke through clenched teeth and tight lips, "How in Hell's name did you get all this?"

The reply was, "Our Naval intelligence staff at Yokosuka cracked the North Korean naval code a long time ago, and just like the Brits read German enigma transmissions in real time during WWII, so have they been reading the Communist's traffic. So far, the Reds haven't tumbled to the fact that their code has been compromised."

A brief period of silence followed as the President re-read the messages, closed his eyes, sank back into the sofa's soft cushions and retreated into quiet solitary meditation.

When he again opened his eyes and sat forward, Admiral Billig said softly, "What is your pleasure, Mr. President?"

The answer was, "Well, Vince, I've been giving this a lot of thought and conjured up several scenarios. Let me share them with you and then we'll discuss them. As I see it, if we break the chain, anywhere, the whole plot falls apart. Obviously, the simple solution would be to 'can' Maureen right now. But, I could cancel my trip to the Far East summit and send someone else, not Maureen, to the meeting. Another option would be for me to cancel my stopover in Guam at the last minute and fly directly to Japan over the Northern Pacific route via Alaska."

"I could give in to the Secret Service and have Mike Flaherty stay in town. I could always send the elder George Bush to the wedding in Dublin. Bill Clinton would jump at the chance to have another taxpayer sponsored boondoggle, but I couldn't do that to the Irish. Also, I could come up with something special for Sid Rosen to do for me while I was away, that would require him to decline the invitation to go to Jerusalem. It would also be easy to find a reason for Bryan Willis to go to Australia and New Zealand on a fact finding mission and make sure he stays 'down under' until this all blows over. He is very popular in both countries and would be warmly received."

Parenthetically he added, "You aren't aware of this, but Bryan's among the top three persons I'm considering to replace the Dragon Lady. That tidbit is for your ears only. I've just started to break down his decision to retire from the political scene. After the untimely and unexpected death of his wife earlier this year, he decided against seeking another term in the Senate and announced plans to go home and write his memoirs. I'll bet a lot of his colleagues are sweating bullets at the prospect of what skeletons he could shake loose. Those are my thoughts, what do you think?"

The Admiral stated that he would like to play the 'devils' advocate. "A lot of skullduggery, plotting, counterplotting and major felonies have been proposed by people who are used to this type of 'diplomacy', and who have pretty much had their way in getting away with murder, literally, without so much as a slap on the wrist. Call me a vindictive son of a bitch, if you wish, but here we have a golden opportunity to deal these scum bags such a decisive defeat that they will think long and hard before they try anything like this again."

"Fortunately, none of the players, except Madam Secretary and her father, know the full game plan. Everybody else is concerned only with their own agendas. Unfortunately, the zealots and fanatics we are dealing with are just crazy enough to go ahead, on their own, with their plans as a show of defiance and derision towards us. Once the lion smells blood, blood will flow. Even if we take Maureen out of the picture, it could lead to the Secretary of the Treasury taking this office. With all due respect to Felix Molder, he is an accomplished banker and financier, but he has never held any office requiring him to make executive decisions on any matters, except fiscal. Also, he is thick as flies with Maureen Kavanaugh, and it could very well come to pass that he would nominate her as his Vice-President. He wouldn't know it, but he'd be signing his own death warrant if he did."

"Sending someone else to the summit in your place is not really an option. No one else could speak for us as convincingly as you. You have to go regardless. Changing your flight plans at the last minute sounds good and would probably work, but it would set off all kinds of bells and whistles and cause panic when the air traffic controllers are tasked to adjust to an unplanned deviation to Air Force One's flight plan. Just think of the flap a major change like that would cause the Secret Service. It would be next to impossible to arrange for an adequate fighter escort for AF One on such short notice and a lone aircraft, or one with an insufficient escort in the northern latitudes would be an easy target for a determined enemy."

"Ordering the Vice-President and the Speaker of the House to cancel their plans would cause lots of 'heart burn', 'sore toes', and 'bent psyches' in Dublin and Jerusalem. Also, you would have to concoct really convincing reasons that would not set off red flares in the investigative reporting department of the Washington Post. Sending Senator Johnson 'down under' really doesn't take him out of danger. The way these kooks operate, arranging an 'accident' anywhere on short notice would be a piece of cake. Think what his assassination in either country would do to our relations with them!"

"No, Mr. President, band-aids won't work, you have to cut the cancer out."

The President then popped the last handful of popcorn into his mouth and took a sip of wine to help wash it down. "What you heard me say earlier was the politician and diplomat in me talking. Now, I'll tell what the former prosecuting attorney in me would say. Let's start kicking some butt, can you do it?".

A smile, slowly worked its way across the Admiral's face. His answer was simply, "Can do."

Randolph Alexander stood up directly in front of his friend and almost shouted, "You sly old fox, you had already figured out what I was going to say and you came in here today with a plan in your hip pocket, didn't you? You read my mind without betraying an inkling of what your little gray cells were inventing, didn't you?"

Admiral Billig remained seated and benignly replied, "Mr. President, have I ever let you down?"

The President sat down again and faced the Admiral with a frown on his face, "Vince, you said 'can do', not 'I'm sure it can be arranged', or 'I think it's possible'. You obviously have you ducks in a row, but I have to ask again, "Can we really kick butt?"

The answer came shooting back, an emphatic "<u>Can Do!</u>".

A smile started to replace the President's frown, as he asked once more, "Is that your final answer?"

The Admiral stood up, came to attention, and even more emphatically said, "<u>Most definitely, Can Do!</u>"

The President was now excited at the thought of really 'kicking butt' and prodded the Admiral to reveal what he had in mind. Turning serious once more, Admiral Billig flatly stated, "Mr. President, if you turn me loose, you don't need to know nor should you know what steps will be taken to squash this cabal.

If anything does go wrong, no one will be able to implicate you. But, I'll need your unqualified support to get the wheels moving. I'll guarantee you that these nutsy-cuckoos will be hit so hard and so fast, that they'll never know what hit them. It will be done in a manner that can never be traced back to this office. Do we have a deal?"

The President responded immediately, "Make it so, do what you need to do".

The Admiral then warmed to the anti-conspiracy taking place and laid out the opening moves in his plan. "First of all, get the Dragon Lady back in here tomorrow morning and tell her that it won't be necessary to alter your Far East plans, but she has to keep it to herself so that no one but her would ever know that changes were ever considered. I think we should have one more meeting some time tomorrow to put the project to bed."

He then gave the President the third piece of paper he had brought with him, a short 'shopping list' of things he would need from the CIC[iv] to expedite the execution of his plans. The President glanced briefly at the list and laid it face down on his desk without comment.

By now the wine was gone and the popcorn bowl was empty. The two jovial conspirators shook hands and exchanged knowing smiles over the prospect of being in the hunt again.

As the Admiral was getting into his car he thought, "It's a good thing the President didn't take a good look at the list while I was still there. I'd still be there for breakfast justifying what I was asking him to arrange for me."

---

iv *CIC= Commander-in-Chief*

CHAPTER 17

November 1

The next morning found the three of us each trying to tie up loose ends in our respective areas of responsibility. The Admiral was on the phone with a conference call to the senior naval officers in the Western Pacific. The list included Commander, Naval Forces Marianas, Commander, Naval Forces Japan, Commander Seventh Fleet and Commander Submarine Squadron Seven. Without going into details, he hinted that the Commander-in-Chief was about to task him with orchestrating counter measures to a suspected attack on the President during his up-coming trip to Japan. He then astonished his colleagues with his 'shopping' list, as he called it,–three nuclear powered submarines, one being a *Seawolf* class, one electronic warfare chopper, and one over age KC-10 flying gas station that the 7th fleet was retiring from service. He, in return, got a short briefing on the latest intelligence gathering from Yokosuka There was nothing new of significant importance. The Admiral then alerted them that there would probably be fresh activity in the next few hours and to pass everything to him as fast as it was decoded. He hung up the phone and nodded to me to brief him on Madame Secretary's day.

Taking a deep breathe, I began, "This morning's activity was almost a carbon copy of yesterday. After leaving home, she went directly to the White House. From there she again went to the Ritz-Carlton Hotel, where she again used her favorite public telephone. Presuming that she would repeat yesterday's routine, we bugged all three phones. Her call was to the same number as the day before. Her message was typical of Maureen, "The old fart in the White House changed his mind again. DL confirms that *"Red Storm"* is back on schedule, act accordingly."

The unflattering reference to the President caused the Admiral to raise his eyebrows, He said nothing, but smoke was starting to come out his ears. A wave of his hand told me to continue. "We also have time dated photographs documenting her use of the phone in question along with a clear set of her fingerprints lifted from the hand set that was wiped clean just before she used it. To be sure that we got hers, and only her fingerprints on the hand set, we had agents, with gloves, using all three phones until the lookout at the front door reported her arrival. The rest of her morning was spent at the State Department, where she had one visitor of significance, the head of the North Korean Trade Commission who paid her an unscheduled call within a short time of their telephone conversation. Within an hour of his departure from her office, we intercepted another 'Urgent' message from the Commission to the Foreign Office in the North Korean capital. Once decoded it read, "DL confirms <u>no</u> changes in *"Red Storm"* travel plans. Original schedule operable."

Kevin tightened his surveillance of McCarthy and, working his electronic magic, had learned that Jack had made numerous ATM withdrawals in England, Ireland and France, just as he had expected, to cover all his expenses and probably transfuse his grandchildren's travel accounts, because we knew that they hadn't exceeded the allowable amount of money to be taken out of the country without declaring it. The tail on Jack had nothing that was worth repeating. Apparently the whirlwind trip to Europe had finally taken its toll and he was staying at home, probably in bed.

Kevin had also been busy, getting a 'handle' on Senator Willis's daily routines. "There is both good news and bad news. The bad news is that unprotected, he is a relatively easy target to 'hit'. The good news is that he is easy to protect. The 'kicker' would be to protect him against all contingencies without being too obvious about it. He is back in his home state now, where he has been stumping for his replacement in the Senate. The way he moves, he presents problems in keeping a tight tail on him but, at the same time, he's a difficult moving target. He is expected back in Washington soon after the national elections and as soon as he steps off the plane at Reagan National one of our agents will put a 'loose' tail on him for the time being."

The major event in the afternoon was a high priority call from Yokosuka. As the Admiral had predicted, message traffic in North Korea had picked up. From the date and time groups on the messages, it was evident that a message from the trade commission in the morning had triggered off all sorts of activity in the Yellow Sea.

A message from North Korean Naval headquarters to Captain Kim Dac Hyun, the skipper of *Red Vengeance* read, "No change in original "*Red Storm*" time table, report readiness for deployment."

The answer from Captain Hyun to Naval Headquarters read, "Normal preparations for underway completed. Special weapons load to be completed in thirty hours. All crew onboard, shore leaves cancelled. Will be ready in all respects to deploy in forty hours."

The reply from Naval Headquarters to Captain Hyun read, "Well done. Action date now confirmed for pre-dawn hours of 18 November local time. Deploy no later than November 14."

Another message from Naval Headquarters to the C.O. of the' fishing trawler' off Guam stated. "Action date of 18 November local time confirmed, agent ashore will confirm "*Red Storm*" departure from Anderson base."

We had a brief meeting in the Admiral's office late in the afternoon to bring him 'up to speed' on our roles in the day's activities. His only comment was, "It's all falling into place. If the President delivers what I asked from him, we'll be set to roll in the morning." And with that, he departed. Kevin and I were left to enjoy quiet suppers, which we both felt would be our last quiet moments for a long time.

The next meeting of the 'architects of butt kicking' took place in the early evening. The President was standing in the middle of the Oval Office, dressed in formal attire, ready to head out to a State dinner when the Admiral was announced. Once the two men were alone, the Admiral began his report immediately, recognizing that the meeting would be short. He handed the Commander-in-Chief copies of two of the afternoon's intercepts–the one where Mrs. Kavanaugh had spilled the beans (without the slur) and the one giving sailing orders to *Red Vengeance*. The Admiral did not feel that is was necessary to bother the President with details of the other intercepts.

The President read the messages with a sad expression on his face. The stark reality of the scenarios that were soon to unfold was weighing heavily upon him, but his resolve to see it through was unwavering. He then handed the Admiral the papers that were previously requested of him and asked bluntly, "Anything else, Vincent?"

The reply was quick, having been well prepared and practiced, "Mr. President, it is of the utmost importance that the Vice-President and the Speaker of the House not be informed of what is afoot. Between the Secret Service and MI6, the 'Veep' will be more than adequately protected. The Speaker already has an Institute team covering his every move. Mossad will take over once he boards the El Al jet at JFK. What these men don't know won't hurt them and actually allow them to behave as if nothing was out of the ordinary."

"The situation regarding Senator Willis is a little different. We will be putting him under protective surveillance as soon as he gets back from his electioneering trip. It will be impossible to put a tight cover on his security without tipping our hand. It would make our job easier if you would call him in here and leak to him that he is on the 'short' list to be the next Secretary of State. While leaking this, get across to him that the information is for his ears only. Then tell him a little white lie, let him believe that a few of the really bad felons he had helped incarcerate when he was an Attorney General are out on parole, which they have violated by dropping out of sight. Remind him that they had sworn to 'get even', and that you are greatly concerned for his safety. Then inform him that he will be getting protection from some of our special agents and that he will be contacted by Kevin Jablonski to make all the arrangements. I've tasked the 'Hacker" with the assignment to foil their plans for him. Now, Mr. President, you can go off to your dinner, eat heartily."

President Alexander let a sigh of relief escape from his lips and whispered, "It will be done. Vincent, roll the dice," and out the door he shot.

CHAPTER 18

After the Admiral had left the Oval office, but before he departed the White House grounds, he was on his cell phone to the Chief of Naval Operations requesting an urgent meeting with him that night. Fortunately, it was a night without any social engagements for the Navy's top sailor so he was able to tell the Admiral to come right over to his quarters in the Washington Navy Yard. Within twenty minutes of leaving the President, the Admiral was ringing the doorbell at the CNO's residence.

Admiral Mark Kiley, who was several years behind Vincent Billig at Annapolis, greeted him warmly and they immediately went into the CNO's study. In his southern accent Admiral Kiley softly said, "Now, now, Vincent, take it easy, what's so important that we had to meet on such short notice?"

Politely declining an offer of a highball, the retired Admiral launched into his presentation at 'all ahead flank' speed. "First of all Mark, I'm acting under direct orders from the President. Read this, it's the authorization he gave me earlier this evening."

Putting on his reading glasses, the CNO read the document and raised his eyebrows almost to his receding hairline in amazement. "Whooie," he whistled, "What in the name of Neptune is happening? I don't ever remember a civilian, even a retired Admiral, except for the Secretary of the Navy or the Secretary of Defense, getting a directive superceding the CNO in naval matters. While I don't doubt you or the President, I've got to check this out before we go any further."

Admiral Billig was not surprised at his friend's reaction. If their situations were reversed, he would have done the same thing. "Of course, you do," he agreed, "here's the telephone number where the CIC can be reached right now. He's expecting your call. Please use your secure line."

The CNO dialed the number he was given and was surprised that he had the President himself on the line right after the first ring. "Good evening, Mr. President, this is CNO," and that's as far as he got as he suddenly became the recipient of a short, and to the point, confirmation of the written orders he was holding. "Certainly, Mr. President, I fully understand your position, I will cooperate completely."

The expression on his face suggested that he had just swallowed a dose of castor oil. "Boy, Vincent, you sure do know how to get a man's attention." The look of distress slowly faded as he put the phone down. "I don't know about you, but I need a drink." With a tall scotch and soda in his hand, the CNO sat down at his desk and motioned his visitor to a chair alongside his. "What can I do for you?"

Admiral Billig then made one of his famous bullet style presentations:

"The North Korean government has committed to an attack on the U.S. of the magnitude of Pearl Harbor, but not in the same manner. This time we are forewarned and in a position to thwart the proposed attack!"

"ComSeventhFlt and ComSubRon Seven have played vital roles in discovering the plot, but they have been sworn to secrecy by the President, which is why you haven't gotten wind of it until now."

"I'm going to need operational and tactical control of several elements of the Seventh fleet for a short period of time."

"It will facilitate matters if you would kindly cut me a set of orders for my temporary recall to active duty, let's say for three weeks, starting tomorrow, non-pay of course."

"Finally, I'd like the exclusive use of your private jet for the next three weeks. I promise that you'll get it back without any holes in it."

At that point, the CNO's jaw dropped open in sheer shock, "Vincent, what the hell are you going to do—start WW III? Damn, you aren't asking for much. Maybe next you will ask for my job?"

It was now Vincent's turn to cool down the CNO. "Now, now Mark, take it easy. I don't want your job. All I'm asking for is to borrow your authority to augment my task."

After Admiral Kiley had replaced his jaw and clamped down hard on his teeth, Admiral Billig continued, "Everything about this operation is on a need to know basis, with the extent of a person's need to know based on the level of cooperation needed from that person, and the commitment by operational units essential to do the job. I promise you that when this is all over the President will fill you in on the details, if you haven't figured them out for yourself, which I suspect that you will."

Admiral Kiley responded, "Vincent, you're asking for the sun, moon, stars and a few planets, but I've always respected your judgment and I'm well aware of the vital service you provide the government in your present capacity."

The CNO's mood was definitely softening, "When do you want your orders?"

"Mark," Admiral Billig continued, "I'm really going to put you on the spot. I plan to be on your plane heading west by 1030, at the latest, tomorrow morning. I'd appreciate it if you could get the orders delivered to me personally at my office, by at least a Commander on your staff,—can do?"

"Will do," said the CNO with a mild hint of frustration in his voice, "anything else?" "No-no," assured Admiral Billig, "you will never regret my intrusion into your authority, I promise you. And now, I must be on my way. Like Santa Claus, I've got more chimneys to scoot down tonight, thank you, thank you, thank you."

The two officers shook hands and Admiral Billig was on his way.

His next cell phone call was to the Commandant of the Marine Corps who also was conveniently at home and free. It took only ten minutes to get to the Marine Barracks from the Navy Yard. Neither of the men knew each other personally, but they were well aware of the reputation that the other man had earned and held mutual respect for each other. During the short drive, Admiral Billig silently thanked his lucky stars that the President and the Marine General had worked together in a few hairy joint Navy and Marine operations. He also prayed that the General, famous for his short temper, would not go ballistic. After he had parked his car in front of the CMC's quarters, the Admiral sat in the quiet darkness for a few minutes and steeled himself for the upcoming meeting. The Commandant had the reputation of being a curmudgeon, who hated being blind sided, and he would, literally, tear apart anyone who dared to do it. Tonight, he was about to be broad sided by a freight train.

The doorbell was answered by the General Kendall Golden's wife, who greeted the Admiral like a long lost, dear friend. She was famous for her talents as a grand hostess as she frequently had to offset her husband's gruffness with her charm. She led their late night visitor to the General's den, said, "Good night," sweetly and closed the door behind him.

True to his reputation as a crusty old warhorse, General Golden greeted Admiral Billig with his shields up and fully powered. "What's up Admiral," he rasped, "isn't it highly irregular to do urgent business at this hour, and in my home rather than the Pentagon?"

The Admiral used his most disarming tone of voice saying, "General, I appreciate you seeing me in the privacy of your home because the President felt that this meeting should be far away from the Pentagon."

At the mention of the President, the General instinctively added a force field to the shields he already had in place. The expression on his face literally shouted, "This can't be happening to me! Where the hell did this guy come from, what the hell is he up to?"

Admiral Billig read the General's expression and body language for what they were– defense mechanisms and hastened to relieve the tension that had suddenly mushroomed in the den. Reaching into his pocket, he drew out the piece of paper that had completely unnerved the CNO and shuddered to think of what was in store for him. "Before we go any further, you'd better read this."

The General literally grabbed the paper from the Admiral's hand and immediately started to read Admiral Billig's commission. The further he read, the redder his face got, approaching apoplectic levels by the time he was finished. "Who the hell do you think you are that you can waltz into my home and, for all practical purposes inform me that all of a sudden, I'm working for you," he thundered.

In the kitchen, his wife shook her head and said to herself, "It's going to be one of his mega-nights, I hope he doesn't have a stroke," and started to brew a pot of industrial strength coffee for the long night ahead.

Back in the den, the Admiral was a little taken back at the ferocity in the General's voice, It was worse than he had expected, so he immediately started to defuse the situation and calm down the man glaring at him like he was Satan personified. Abandoning his usual method of presentation, Admiral Billig used his 'oil on troubled waters' approach, which he had learned the hard way was the best method to cool a raging tiger.

"It's not as bad as you're reading into it General," he spoke softly, "all the President, (the magic word) and I would like from the Marines is to borrow your executive jet for a few days, starting tomorrow for Glenn Stark, my Chief investigator, to make a quick trip to London and Jerusalem and back again. The urgency of the situation is such that using civilian or even scheduled Air Force resources will not give us the latitude in scheduling flights necessary to the expeditious completion of our tasking."

The General looked incredulous, "Is that all you want, for a while there I was expecting you to ask to borrow Fleet Marine Force Pacific to go on a rampage." In a milder tone, but still a loud voice, General Golden added, "What's so hush-hush and hurry up about this? My people are going to wonder, and ask questions why they are suddenly being seconded to an unknown civilian? I doubt if anybody at their pay grades even heard of your Institute."

"General" the Admiral continued, "it won't make any difference to Glenn if they ignore him completely. They must be well used to doing things like this for other departments of the Government besides Defense, aren't they?"

"Yes, you're right," the General's voice was definitely lowering down to ear-drum shattering levels, "I'll get right on it first thing in the morning and call your office when all the arrangements are complete. I presume that he will want to fly out of Andrews Air Force Base?"

"That will be fine," replied the Admiral, a little disappointed that the wheels wouldn't start turning right away but he was savvy enough to know when not to push his luck. "And one last favor, I'd appreciate it if you could have your helo pick Stark and myself up at the Leesburg airport at 0900 tomorrow."

As he was asking for the aerial taxi service, the Admiral braced himself for a gale force explosion. But it was in just his usual tone of gruffness that the General growled, "Why not?"

The entire confrontation, for that was what it was, lasted only twenty minutes, during which time, both men stood face to face. The Admiral said a silent prayer of thanks that the General had not insisted in calling the President, that would have been a catastrophe. Sensing that it was time to leave before the General could raise any other issues, Admiral Billig thanked General Golden for his courtesy and withdrew. Additionally, he felt a touch of pity for the General's wife, who was going to have to live with a raging bull that night. But she must be used to his temper outbursts by now.

Once seated in his car, the Admiral heaved a huge sign of relief and felt himself fortunate to have all his body parts attached in their appropriate locations. His final call of the night was to his secretary (who was always on call) sweetly asking that she get in touch with Stark and Jablonski for a meeting in his office at 0600 the next day and to tell Stark to bring his traveling gear and his red diplomatic passport.

CHAPTER 19

ASHBURN
November 2

To be hard at work at 0600 was nothing new to the Admiral, who always said that he got his best work done before people started bugging him. But to a psuedo-swinger like me it was the middle of the night. It took the better part of a half hour to get all my body parts working and three cups of strong, black Kona coffee to arouse my little gray cells before attempting to drive to the Institute. I imagined that Kevin also had a hard time trying to explain to his wife why he was deserting her at that time of day when their four, three and two year olds needed morning parental care. I met Kevin in the express elevator to the 'bridge' and he didn't look any better then I felt.

As we headed towards the Admiral's office, the ever present Miss Eagleton had a Cheshire cat smile and a bright twinkle in her eyes. "Brace yourselves," she warned, "you're in for a big surprise." On entering the 'sanctum' shock, more than surprise, was what we felt.

There was the Admiral, bright eyed and bushy tailed, all decked out in a meticulous set of summer khakis, complete with his six rows of colorful ribbons and freshly shined stars. We had never seen him in uniform or without a tie when he was working. He was like a child relishing a birthday present. Discretion told us not to ask questions, he would tell us later. Instinctively, we both snapped to attention, saluted and congratulated him on the transformation.

In quick order, he gave us a run down of his most recent trip to the White House and his late night confrontations with two of the biggest egos with soft toes in the military hierarchy. As he talked, he passed out copies of the marching orders he had received from the President and my authorizations for dealing with our respective allies.

The document concerning the Admiral read as follows:

From: The President of the United States
To: Those Commanders, whom it has been determined. will have a 'need to know'.
Subj: Special Mission
1. This document has the weight of an Executive Order, a security classification of top top Secret and carries a FLASH priority.
2. Admiral Billig is under direct orders from the Commander-in-Chief to carry out a secret mission of immediate urgency pertaining to the security of the government of the United States.
3. All commanders, who read these orders, will provide Admiral Billg with any, and all, personnel and physical assets he deems necessary to complete his mission.
4. Those commanders, who are not tasked to provide personnel or physical sup-port, will consider these orders to be 'For your eyes and information only'.
5. This document will not, repeat will not, be reproduced by any form of copier, or from memory, and will not be discussed with <u>anyone</u>, repeat <u>anyone</u>!
6. Those commanders tasked with providing personnel and/or physical assets necessary to the completion of

this mission will do so without delay or question. All orders to personnel involved will be issued in person, verbally with no official record of such assignment being entered into service jackets or unit operating schedules. To all intents and purposes, those personnel and/or assets are to be listed as carrying out their normal and usual assignments. The last sentence of paragraph 4 applies with even more emphasis on the need for secrecy.

Signed, on the date and time listed above:
Randolph Alexander
President of the United States, Commander-in-Chief of U.S. Military Forces.

The documents delivered to me, while not as intimidating, carried the same weight, security classification and urgency. The first was to be hand delivered to Sir Malcolm, and the second to Brigadier Templeman. In essence they both said:

1. Glenn Stark is under direct commission by the President of the United States to act on behalf of, and for the President in matters of mutual concern between November 15 and November 30, 2006. This commission will expire on December 1, 2006.
2. It is requested that Mr. Stark be allowed to participate in the preparations for events that will concern the Vice-President of the United States (and the Speaker of the House of Representatives of the United States). All courtesies extended to him will be greatly appreciated.

Signed by the President.

Kevin and I looked at each other with complete amazement. In a voice that betrayed a new level of appreciation for my boss, my only comment was, "Oh, boy! The CNO must have gone completely bonkers when he read your commission." Kevin's comment was a little more earthy, "I'll bet the CMC had to go change his skivvies before you two got down to serious talking."

The Admiral was the epitome of understatement, "It all went down like a swallow of neat Kentucky moonshine."

A twinkle returned to the old sailor's eyes when Miss Eagleton announced that there was a Commander from the CNO's staff here to see him. The Commander was ushered in and ignored Kevin and I as he strode over to the Admiral, gave him a brisk salute and handed him a sealed Official Correspondence envelope, and waited in silence while the Admiral read its contents. The Admiral signed a receipt and handed it to the Commander, who again saluted smartly, did an about face, and marched out of the office. Not a word had been spoken.

The Admiral was bubbling with excitement as he shared with us what he had just been given, "I won't bore you with the 'boiler plate'. I've just been recalled to active duty, listen to this."

"Effective this date, you are recalled to temporary active duty, with the rank of Admiral, 0-10, in non-pay status for a period of time necessary to complete your assigned mission. On completion of the mission, return to your Home of Record and consider yourself released from temporary active duty. Notify this office of that date. Travel expenses will be shared by the Department of the Navy and the Institute for Intelligence Analysis."

There was a small envelope containing a hand written note pasted to the orders saying, "Vincent, I thought you might need some extra horse power when you jump into the lion's den. I purposely left the orders open-ended in case you run into problems and need extra time. I know that you won't have time to get to the uniform shop, so I've included a spare set of my collar devices."

The envelope contained a set of a full Admiral's four stars. The Admiral was caught completely off guard, a rare event, but he recovered quickly, and let a broad smile of ecstasy cross his face as he turned to us, and said, "Pin them on me, boys."

I don't think that Kevin or I will ever experience the pride and satisfaction that we felt when we each replaced one set the Admiral' three star collar devices with his new four stars. Unnoticed by us, Miss Eagleton had quietly entered the room and had tears of joy streaming down her face as she witnessed the brief ceremony. The last line of the note stated, "My jet will be waiting for you at Andrews."

The Admiral was actually beaming, "Good old Mark, with his knack of 'greasing the skids', it's easy to see why he's the Chief of Naval Operations. I owe him more than a few."

He had no sooner given us his good news when Miss Eagleton buzzed him to tell him that the Commandant of the Marine Corps was calling him.

"Good morning General," he literally purred into the phone. He listened, without interruption, for a full two minutes and again purred into the phone, "Thank you, General, you'll never regret assisting the President (there was that magic word again)."

With a look of angelic beauty on his face, he stated, "That was General Golden" (as if we didn't know) "He's been kind enough to cut through innumerable layers of red tape and provide us, actually you Glenn, with his private jet and crew for as long as you need it. He is also dispatching one of the White House choppers to Godfrey Field in Leesburg to ferry Glenn and me to Andrews Air Force base. Glenn, you're going to London and Israel again, as if you hadn't guessed, when Miss Eagleton told you to bring your bag. By the way, I presume you brought your red passport. I'll be heading to the Pacific and Far East again."

"Kevin, just because you didn't get a Presidential directive, doesn't mean that you're left out. The next time that Senator Willis checks in with his office, he'll be told that the President wants to see him ASAP. He's expected back in town in the afternoon of the day after the national elections, so he'll probably see the President on Thursday morning, the 9th, or Friday morning the 10th at the latest. His tail can tell you when he goes to the White House, so you can contact his office for an appointment right after he finishes with the President. If his staff gives you any hassle, just say that he's expecting you to call for an appointment. Your job will be to sell him on the need for personal protection, based on what the President will tell him, not what we know is in store for him. I'll trust you with the nitty-gritty details."

Kevin's only thought to himself was, "Thanks a lot, sir."

The Admiral then buzzed Miss Eagleton to have his limousine out in front in ten minutes, wished Kevin luck, and dragged me out the door with him. As we passed Miss Eagleton's desk, he told her to contact Andrews Base Operations to have the Navy pilot file a flight plan to Guam and the Marine pilot a flight plan to London, with continuation on to Jerusalem.

The short hop to Andrews was without incident or conversation as we ignored the scenery of the capital as we swept over it and poured over the documents that pertained to the meetings we were going to attend. On touching down at Andrews, we were met by an Air Police car with flashing red lights, but no siren, that escorted us to a remote corner of the field where our executive jets were waiting, engines warmed up and ready to take off. One was emblazoned "United States Navy" in blue lettering, the other "United States Marine Corps" in green lettering. The crews of both jets were in line formation in front of their planes, standing at ease. As soon as the car stopped and the Admiral emerged, they came to attention and snapped him a salute befitting his new rank. The admiral's crisp return salute would have pleased both CNO and CMC. He hadn't forgotten how after all the years. Waiting for us was the base commander, who warmly greeted the Admiral and nodded to me. After the Admiral had signed an inch thick set of forms, we were directed to board our taxis. The Navy crew treated the Admiral like a god, the Marines tolerated me.

Within ten minutes of landing on the base, the Admiral was rolling down the runway. As soon as his plane had lifted off, mine started to roll and I was on my way back to merry old England.

CHAPTER 20

November 2

After the Admiral and Glenn had left the office on their way to Andrews, Kevin returned to his office and enjoyed a mug of steaming decaf coffee and a 'sticky' bun before pulling out his file on Senator Willis. He wanted to have a reasonable picture of the man whose life he was going to save.

The Senator was sixty-five years old and was a decorated green beret during the Vietnam conflict. After leaving the Army, he graduated from law school and had pursued a successful legal career as a deputy district attorney, then a district attorney and finally Attorney General for the Commonwealth of Kentucky. During those years, he had made many enemies among the felons he had gotten convicted, several of whom had sworn that they would get even, once released from prison. His reputation as a 'straight shooter', an eloquent orator and a 'true' Southern gentleman helped him to be elected to four consecutive terms as a United States Senator. During his third and fourth terms, he was the Senior Senator from Kentucky, and his colleagues had honored him with the office of President Pro-Tem of the Senate during his current term.

He was considered a 'shoo-in' for a fifth term until his

beloved wife of forty years died suddenly from a massive heart attack earlier in the year. She was the light of his life and her loss, as he expressed it, 'caused the spark to flicker out'. Without her at his side to encourage him through the difficult times, and to always be there as a sounding board for the difficult decisions he had to make every day, the excitement of life in the Senate disappeared and he announced that he would not seek another term. Despite the pleading and cajoling of his peers to reconsider his retirement, he remained steadfast in his decision and was already negotiating for a palatial home adjacent to the Wailea golf course in the Kahala section of Honolulu to, as he put it, "get as far away as I can from Washing-ton, winter, and snow." As his last hurrah, he had campaigned tirelessly for his party's candidate to succeed him. He returned to Virginia the day after the election to continue winding up his affairs in preparation to his relocation to Hawaii.

Satisfied with the knowledge he had stored in his memory, Kevin took the short drive to nearby Potomac Falls to get an idea of the house where the anticipated attack on the Senator's life would probably take place. Senator Willis lived at the top of Lowe's Island Boulevard in the Cypress Point development. The Willises had built a huge home, with a view of the nearby Potomac river and overlooking the private Lowe's Island golf club. He and his wife were members of the club and a regular twosome on the course. The house was plainly visible from the street and had a good fifteen to twenty feet of manicured lawn and low shrubbery surrounding it. There were numerous entrances to the house through doors, the three car garage and large floor to ceiling picture plate glass windows. All the utilities were underground and a quick inspection of the house's security system brought a smile to Kevin's face as he appreciated the sophistication of the system. On the surface, the house looked defendable, without making conspicuous additions to what was already in place. He was mentally working out the details on the return trip to Ashburn. Back in his office, he contacted the Senator's office and found out that the Senator was not expected to return to Washington until the 8th. The

Senator had no appointments scheduled until meeting with the President on the morning of the 10th, followed by a round of golf in the mid afternoon, weather permitting.

Kevin's thoughts were, "Great, I've got more than enough time to finalize the plans I'll present to him after he meets with the President."

Working from memory, he drew a sketch of the house, the grounds and the roadways in the area, looking all the while like a draftsman. The finished product was a feasible, yet simple, defense system for the Senator's protection. His next task was to figure out what he would need to provide personal security for his charge. Towards the end of the day, he had his secretary call the Senator's secretary to arrange an appointment to see the Senator on the afternoon of November 10. There were no problems, as his secretary was obliging and gave him an appointment time for after the Senator returned from seeing the President in the morning. The 'Hacker' rubbed his hands together, smiled broadly, and said to himself, "So far, so good."

By the end of the week, Kevin had pretty much designed the defenses that he felt would adequately serve his purposes. Several homes in the area already had early Christmas decorations in place, making it easy to blend his refinements into the festive background and not call attention to the specialized lights and sensors required to do the job. Basically, his plan was to surround the house with a lattice work of lasers that would provide 360 degrees of motion sensors which would pin point any intrusions. They would be hidden among the low voltage colored Christmas lights placed in the shrubs and trees rounding the property. The beauty of Kevin's design was that it had its own power source and the monitoring station was no larger than the usual entertainment center. It was portable, easy to install in a small amount of space and required only one person to operate the whole system.

As he put the finishing touches to his masterpiece, Kevin mused, "That was the easy part, now I have to sell it to the Senator. I sure hope the President scares the living daylights out of him." By the time election day had rolled around, Kevin had accumulated the electronics he would install and was ready to go to work.

November 10

The agent assigned to keep a close watch on the Senator reported that the Senator had arrived at Reagan airport late on Wednesday and was now under continuous "protective" surveillance. Kevin spent the morning polishing the presentation he was about to make. It was going to be a complicated presentation, designed to hide the real reasons why the enhanced protection was required.

The Senator's office in the Dirksen building was a scene of orchestrated chaos, as his staff were in the process of packing him out. There were sealed cartons, half full cartons, empty cartons and stacks of books and memorabilia, collected over a quarter of a century, waiting to be moved into storage until the Senator bought a new house. With the Senate in recess, there were no committee meetings or 'back room' conferences to interfere with the moving process.

Kevin was ushered into the Senator's office as soon as he arrived. With sleeves rolled up, the Senator was busy stripping the walls of his plaques, citations and autographed pictures of himself with every President since Ronald Reagan. The Senator was an imposing man, just under six feet tall, and one hundred seventy pounds of fit and trim body. His full head of white hair and full beard, carefully barbered, gave him the appearance of a real live Kentucky colonel. His rich southern accent, complemented by his wife's, had make the couple very popular invitees to the capital's social events. The warmth of his smile and greeting belied the sorrow he still felt since his wife's death, and the sad realization that he was closing the door on his life's work.

"Mr. Jablonski, it's a pleasure to meet you at last. Admiral Billig speaks highly of you, both about your talents and dedication. I must admit my head has been spinning since my session with President Alexander this morning. I'm a little confused as to what the Admiral and you have in your heads. Mind you, the

President stressed that I was only being considered for the post of Secretary of State at this time and that it was of paramount importance that no one else be informed concerning my possible appointment. Then, all of a sudden, I learn that there were three others who knew about this morning's meeting, and who were already taking steps to protect me from a possible threat to my life that I never knew existed nor thought about. I guess that was why the President was so adamant that I talk with you as soon as possible. Are you going to enlighten me?"

Because it is well known that the walls in Washington have eyes and ears, Kevin suggested that they go for a late lunch at a old fashioned kosher deli that served the best corned beef sandwich in town. As they were walking to the deli, Kevin was thinking, "Oh great, this should be easy. The President did a good job in laying the groundwork."

After going through the buffet line, they took seats in a back corner booth, Kevin's favorite, because it got frequent sweepings for bugs, the most recent being by a team of experts, who left the deli as they were getting their food. Kevin gave the Senator enough time to discover that the corned beef was living up to its reputation before he launched into his presentation.

"Senator, the only other people, beside the President, who know about the possibility of your being the next Secretary of State are me, the Admiral, and the Admiral's right hand, Glenn Stark That is the complete list, and it won't get any longer."

"There are several steps to be taken to insure that you are protected, until as Secretary of State, you rate Secret Service protection:

Your home security system will be upgraded with the most modern and efficient early warning system known to man.

I will be the point of contact between you, the Admiral and the President.

You will be provided with a new type of secure communications device that is so new it will take months for a hacker to crack into it.

To guard against a car bombing, we suggest that all your travel, starting this afternoon, be via one of our 'special' limos with one of our agents as your driver. We will also arrange for a 'house sitter' for you to guard against a bomb being attached to your home when you are not there and to be your 'gentleman's gentleman while you are at home. We don't want you to ever be alone for the time being.

We're going to ask you to forego golf for a while, the cold weather is reason enough for that. and we're going to ask you to start wearing a new design, light weight, bullet proof vest.

We would like you to keep out of crowds, especially restaurants, after this lunch is over, and to arrange any meetings you might have to attend to take place in your office.

Body guards, whom you will not recognize, will accompany you everywhere, even into the john."

"Your job, Senator, will be to carry on as if you are still heading for Hawaii and too busy with your preparations to take on any new responsibilities. Do exactly what you are planning to do, just don't deviate from the plans without notifying me."

By this time the sandwiches, desserts and beverages had been consumed. Throughout the entire lunch, the Senator wore the blank expression that was his trademark when he listened to those testifying before his various Senate committees. He was notorious for keeping those in front of him completely in the dark as to the impression they were making upon him. And now, Kevin was experiencing that same feeling of uncertainty as to whether, or not, he was getting through to him.

When a short period of silence signaled that Kevin's presentation was over, the Senator started in, "I see, I must admit that I'm even more confused as to what is really going down. You made an excellent point for your concern about my safe being, but behind all the verbage I detect something more ominous. My first reaction was that I was a green beret and should be able to take care of myself, but then I realized that that was thirty years ago and the jungle within the beltway is a world apart from the jungle of 'Nam'. You also convinced me that you know what you are talking about and have done a lot of professional planning for my benefit. I'd be a fool, which I've been accused of being by those seated on the other side of the aisle, if I didn't take your advice. OK, I'm in your hands and I'll try my best to not make your job any harder than it is."

Kevin emitted a long sigh of relief, and silently thanked as many deities as he could think of for the Senator's quick understanding of the situation and his promise of co-operation. The short walk back to the Senate office building was filled with light banter. Kevin did spot, only because he knew him, the inconspicuous bodyguard who was already on the job.

As they entered the building and passed through the security check point, Senator Willis gave Kevin a bonus, "You know, I've got a pretty damn good security system already installed at my place. In fact, Maureen Kavanaugh was so impressed with it that she had the same one installed in her home."

Kevin's verbal response was, "I'm familiar with it and know it's good, but is doesn't hurt to be super secure." But his silent thought was, "Great, it'll be a piece of cake for me to crack Maureen's if it ever comes to that."

At the door to the Senator's office Kevin took his leave, "Thank you, Senator, we won't let you down."

He reached into his pocket and produced a less than hand-sized communication device which had completely fooled the metal detector. As he shook the Senator's hand, the device was passed to him along with its instruction sheet. Glancing at it, the Senator started to say, "Good bye young man," but Kevin had turned away and was already swallowed up in the corridor traffic.

CHAPTER 21

LONDON
November 2

While Kevin was attending to details concerning Senator Willis, my flight across the Pond, as the Brits called the Atlantic, was choppy but more than comfortable. The latest version of the C-20 aircraft had all the amenities of a private limousine. After takeoff, and prior to taking a nap, I reviewed the itinerary of the Vice-President's upcoming whirlwind tour to the Emerald Isle.

He would be leaving Washington on November 16th, arriving in Dublin early in the morning of the 17th to represent the United States at the mid-morning wedding of the Prime Minister's daughter. After the reception, he would make the short trip from Dublin the Belfast for an early evening reunion dinner with several family relations. He would leave Belfast later in the evening for the return trip to the Capital, arriving in the early hours of Saturday the 18th. The two hours nap I had on the plane left me wide awake and 'raring to go'. I arrived in England at 2200 hours Greenwich time, but only 1700 hours body time.

Once in English air space, air traffic control gave us a direct course to Mildenhall RAF aerodrome north of London. Sir Malcolm had arranged our meeting to be held there to make maximum use of the time that I would be spending in the U.K. By eliminating the commute time from Heathrow into London and back, we had an extra two hours for our discussions. The sensitive nature of our agenda was also a factor in avoiding the 'glass fish bowl' environment of Heathrow. Over night accommodations had been arranged for me and the Marine flight crew at the Base Bachelor Officers Quarters.

We were met in the conference room by British Immigration authorities who processed us expeditiously, my red diplomatic passport being a big help. Once that formality was completed, my air crew adjourned to the base pub and I was ready to get down to work. Waiting, with Sir Malcolm, for us to finish the protocol of my entrance into Great Britain was SgtMajor McGregor, clad in 'mufti' as befitted the informality of the meeting. The compulsory pleasantries were exchanged, and as soon as the steward who served us tea and scones had departed, the briefing started.

I presented my Presidential commission to Sir Malcolm, whose comment on returning the document to me was, "Hrumph, a bit cheeky, but typical for a colonial." I made like I didn't hear it.

Sir Malcom started by detailing the arrangements that were concerned with the multi-national cooperative efforts:

"Once Air Force Two is in Irish air space, it will get an RAF fighter escort. The Irish government is as eager as we are to ensure that no accident should befall your Vice-President while he was in their country, so they were more than glad to allow the RAF to operate in their air space on this occasion."

"Since the wedding is a State Affair, many foreign dignitaries are expected and security is going to be on a very high level."

I thought to myself, "There is safety in numbers so everything should go off without incident, at least on the formal part of the agenda."

Sir Malcolm continued, "For the flight from Dublin to Belfast, the RAF will again escort Air Force Two with four helicopter gun ships riding 'shot gun'."

"Once on Northern Ireland's turf, plain clothed MI6 agents will augment your Secret Service personnel. The Vice-President will be covered like a blanket once he exits the door of Air Force Two until he reenters the plane for his return home."

"RAF fighters will then again escort him out of English and Irish air space."

"The local constabulary in Belfast has already completed enhanced security in the Belfast Hilton, which the Vice-President is not expected to leave at all during his short stay, thereby further limiting his exposure to a terrorist attack."

"His family members, who will be joining him in a private hotel dining room, have been cleared by MI6 security teams and the guest list has been finalized. No one, but those on that final list would be allowed into the reunion banquet."

"Only senior waiters and support staff, who have been carefully 'vetted', will serve the meal and beverages during the social hour."

"The possibility of wholesale food poisoning was considered, and while it is a throw-back to less civilized times, we will be using food tasters, with the appropriate medical support close at hand."

Sir Malcolm paused to see if I had any questions at this point. When I offered none, SgtMajor took over to enumerate the results of his continued surveillance of Paddy's place and the usual suspects. He used his best parade ground voice for his presentation.

"Thank you, Sir Malcolm. Mr. Stark, I think you'll see that we have anticipated and planned for every contingency that we could imagine. The security arrangements for the trip from the airport to the hotel and back to the airport will be exactly the same as we would provide if the Queen herself was in the car. The route, that the motorcade will take, will not be chosen by the Chief Constable, riding in the escort vehicle, until your Vice-President is in the bullet proof limousine."

"Once the route is selected, an army of uniformed and armed

constables will be deployed along the route. Plain clothed officers will also be scattered all over the area."

"The motorcade will be preceded by a mine detector vehicle, and if anything that even looks like it might be an explosive devise is detected, the motorcade will be switched to one of several alternative routes."

SgtMajor then opened up a blown-up street map of Belfast, and proceeded, using a pointer to draw my attention to important details, "What you see on the map are all the possible routes, each one color coded. I don't have any idea which one will be selected. The final route will be selected by the Chief Constable, based on weather, traffic and crowds."

He paused, and when I didn't open my mouth, he folded up the map, and went to an update on the Gilhooley brothers. "As you already know, these lads are well known as explosives experts par excellance, having been well trained by the Royal Army before they joined the IRA. They have been lying low for the past few months, but I'm not surprised that they're in the game. Your Vice-President is very mobile and rarely presents himself as a 'sitting duck' target. By reviewing tapes your Secret Service supplied to us, we have determined that the only time he will be fully exposed and stationary will be just as he is taking his leave of his family before heading back to the airport. Because this window of opportunity will be short, the only sure way to 'get' him is with a bomb big enough to wipe out everybody surrounding him at the time. Pretty disgusting, isn't it, but the Gilhooleys are suspected of scores of such attacks. I stress 'suspected'. There just happens to a sewage collecting opening right at the curb where limos usually drop off and pick up their passengers. It serves the purpose of ensuring that the water doesn't backup over the feet of their passengers. We feel that it is there where the attempt will be made, we're working on how to upset the plans as we talk."

"Other types of attacks that are possible, but not probable include:

"Firing an anti-tank missile into the limousine while it is en-route to or from the airport. To offset that possibility, the police motorcycle escort will use an overlapping concentric pattern, which will provide a continuous screen around the limo. At the hotel V.I.P arrival and departure area riot police, in full gear, will provide a similar curtain."

"A helicopter launched missile attack will be countered by our helo guns ships, who will have orders to shoot first and ask questions later, but this type of attack is very unlikely, because the Gilhooleys are strictly ground operators."

"A direct close range attack is unlikely for two reasons, the Gilhooleys never dirty their hands directly and the numbers of Secret Service and MI6 agents will keep your Vice-President completely surrounded to the extent that no stranger will get that close."

"Only one representative of each media will be allowed to do a short interview in the hotel lobby upon his arrival. No photographs will be allowed. The media will scream 'harassment', but they can scream all they want, we won't buckle."

"Paddy has been busy collecting snorkeling gear and wet suits, and Sean has been conducting business with a big supplier of under world munitions. We're not sure yet what he's getting, but it all comes in small wax paper packages that shout PLASTIQUE. The Gilhholeys have no transport of their own and they sure as hell are not going to use one of Paddy's cars or trucks. We expect them to either steal a vehicle when they make their move, or more likely have someone else steal one, and deliver it to them at Paddy's place."

"Each of the 'usual suspects' is being shadowed by a three person team of Royal Marines, in mufti of course, including a few of the prettiest lasses in the Corps. Who would suspect a pretty lass of being a trained killer?"

He concluded his brief on a somber note, "Mr. Stark, can I give you a 100% guarantee that there will be no surprises, of course I can't. We're dealing here with fanatics and fanatics are the most unstable type of terrorist. An organized crime 'hit' man doesn't deviate from his particular 'modus operandi'. To reduce the possibility of a 'surprise' being staged, there will be a company strength detachment of Royal Marines protecting your Vice-President at all the critical times. I'm confident that we'll give him back to you in the same condition as when he arrives."

Sir Malcom seconded the SgtMajor's confidence and expressed his complete confidence in the preparations for the 'coming attraction'. The preparations were so well thought out and inclusive, that I had only a few questions, mostly of a technical or diplomatic nature, which were quickly answered to my complete satisfaction. I could have left my commission in my pocket. With business completed, we adjourned to the BOQ bar for a 'swift pint', following which I retreated to the very posh suite that had been reserved for me. It was going to be short night, because we had an early departure time in the morning for the next leg of my trip to Israel.

CHAPTER 22

GUAM
November 2

After leaving Andrews Air Force Base, the CNO's C-20 aircraft headed west towards Hawaii, with a brief refueling stop at Miramar Naval Air Station just north of San Diego. Twelve hours after leaving Washington, the Admiral was landing at Hickam Air Force Base on the island of Oahu, where he had a brief meeting with the Commander, Pacific, and Commander, Pacific Fleet, who were obliging enough to join him in the base operations office while the C-20 was being refueled again and readied for the long eight hour flight across the Mid-Pacific Ocean to Guam. Admiral Billig was joined on this final leg of his trip by Rear Admiral Phillip Morgiewicz, Commander Submarine Force, Pacific. During the flight, Admiral Billig briefed Admiral Morgiewicz on the submarine support he would need from ComSubRonSeven for the upcoming operation. They touched down at Anderson Air Force Base on Guam shortly after 0100 hours Sgt Major two days after leaving Andrews. They were met by Rear Admiral Tonelson, Commander, Naval Forces Marianas, who accompanied them to the Senior Officers BOQ.

He brought both his guests up to date on what was planned for the next day's meeting. Admiral Drapcho and Captain Simpson had flown in from Japan earlier in the evening and were with Admiral Kiesel on board his Seventh Fleet flagship in Apra Harbor. Both Admirals then retired to their VIP suites at the Naval Station to be well rested for their meeting later in the morning.

November 4

At exactly 0900, the following high ranking Naval officers were assembled with Admiral Billig in the conference room of the Commander, Naval Forces Marianas headquarters, located on what was called, 'The Top of the Mar'—Admirals Kiesel, Tonelson, Morgiewicz, Drapcho, and Admiral (Selectee) Simpson. In the outer reception room of the conference room was a Submarine Captain, who jumped to attention as the 'brass' passed through. The obligatory Naval protocols were quickly completed and, over their first cups of coffee, his colleagues read Admiral Billig's orders from the President and his orders of recall to active duty.. Eyebrows were raised, questioning glances were exchanged and deep breaths inhaled before the customary congratulations on his promotion were extended to Admiral Billig. The temperature in the room had cooled noticeably, as the assembled officers waited for the second of Admiral Billig's shoes to drop.

Admiral Billig then launched into his presentation, wielding the authority of his four stars as if he had worn them for several years, rather than several days. He began by assuring everyone that CNO, CMC, ComPac, and ComPacFlt had all been informed about his Presidential commission and that all were giving him their full cooperation.

His first question was addressed to the Seventh Fleet Commander, "Tom, where do stand on the KC-10 and the electronics warfare chopper?"

Admiral Kiesel took one swallow of coffee before he replied, "We just pulled a KC-10 off the line. It's currently at the Atsugi

Naval Air Station, near Tokyo, undergoing decommissioning stripping. You can have it next week. Regarding the chopper, the *Carl Vinson* battle group is conducting exercises north of here. The Air Group Commander can supply you with one rigged to do drone control flying anytime you need it."

Admiral Billig rubbed his hands together and broke out into a wide grin. "Fine, I would like all external markings removed from the KC-10 and have it equipped for remote control flight capability for use as a drone. I would like it delivered here no later than the 14th. Please arrange the flight plan to have it arrive here well after dark. The fewer the people who know of its arrival, the better. The crew that delivers it can return to Atsugi as soon as they turn it over to Air Force personnel. Tom, contact the *Vinson* battle group commander, the C.O. of *Vinson*, and the Air Group Commander to expect a visit from me in the next few days. I'll make all the arrangements from here. You've done well!"

Admiral Kiesel's response was a simple, "Will do."

Turning to Admiral Tonelson, Admiral Billig's tone softened a bit, "Jim, you and I need to have a meeting with the Commanding Officer of Anderson AFB [Air Force Base] to bring him up to speed on what services I will need from him. Please see if you can set it up for tomorrow morning. You and I will get together this evening to finalize what we are going to ask for and you can clue me in on the best way to approach him. I've never met him and don't know much about him. Next, I want the visual, electronic, and photographic surveillance on the North Korean trawler milling about off Anderson stepped up. Pay specific attention to any differences it might have from her predecessors in her physical appearance and her communications activity."

Since none of the action was going to take place close to Japan, Admiral Drapcho did not need any further instruction. His role was to continue to supply up to date intelligence to all the players and to keep relations with Japan calm and serene during the next few weeks before Thanksgiving..

After a brief question and answer period, Admirals Drapcho,

Tonelson, and Kiesel departed to start carrying out their assignments, leaving the three submarine Admirals to continue the conference, which would now deal with the undersea operations of the upcoming events.

Admiral Billig cut right to the chase, "On the way out here, Admiral Morgiewicz went over my 'shopping list' and he and I agree on all the major points. What I need is— One submarine to be detailed to stick to the 'spy' trawler, keeping her under constant surveillance and to tail it for one hundred miles when she sails away. Our boat is to make sure the trawler is aware of her presence but to make no hostile moves towards the trawler unless provoked. If provoked, her Commanding Officer will be authorized to take immediate offensive action to wipe the trawler from the surface of the ocean, as the German U-boat captains were fond of saying, "Spurlos versunkt."(sunk without a trace); another submarine to be on station in the Yellow Sea, no later than November 10, to tail the *Red Vengeance* once she leaves port until they come within sonar range of the third boat I'm going to ask for."

"I need the most modern submarine in SubRonSeven, commanded by an officer of impeccable loyalty and dedication to duty, who would not blink twice if ordered to 'pull the trigger'."

Admiral Morgiewicz looked at ComSubRon 7, who immediately stated that he could provide all three of the boats. He was quite positive in giving these three boats and their C.O.s his whole hearted endorsement as 'just what the Admiral wanted'. Convinced that the 'ball' was in good hands, Admiral Morgiewicz departed saying, "You don't need me here, Dick will fill you in about his recommendations. I'm going down to the tender to do some of my own paperwork that I brought with me. Vince, when you're ready to go back to Pearl, give me a growl."

Admiral (Selectee) Simpson started right in, "Cdr. Frank McDade's boat, the USS *Scranton* will 'baby sit' the trawler. Cdr. McDade is thoroughly professional and trustworthy. His wardroom and crew love their boat, the skipper and the Silent Service. They've done this kind of exercise before and, as far as being able to respond to any hostile action taken against them, they wouldn't hesitate to respond in kind. The *USS San Francisco* is my choice to track *Red Vengeance*. She has done several monitoring patrols into North Korean waters in the Yellow Sea and has recorded a complete sonar book on *Red Vengeance*."

Admiral Billig nodded, signifying his concurrence with these recommendations, and wondered what the next recommendation was going to be.

A grin that could only be described as 'the cat who ate the canary' spread across SubRonSeven's face. He figured, based on his previous meeting with Admiral Billig and the super hush-hush nature of the current situation, that something big was in the wind, so he had put his best boat and its skipper on a short leash, available for any short fused scenario. His stated, in no uncertain voice, "I have just the man and boat for you. I just happened to have brought Captain Savage and his service jacket with me." He handed the jacket to the Admiral and poured himself a cup of coffee while the Admiral scanned through the thick file.

Captain Bart Savage, a 1986 graduate of Annapolis, had been deep selected for both Commander and Captain based on his exemplary career. A great uncle had died in the attack on Pearl Harbor and one of his grandfathers was killed in the battle of the Chosin Reservoir in Korea in 1951. His father had been a 'guest' at the 'Hanoi Hilton' after being shot down on a mission over the Mekong delta. Captain Savage had graduated with honors in the top five per-cent of his class and was selected as a second string All American footballer in his first class year. His team mates had dubbed him "Bee" Savage for his ferocity as a defensive tackle. His year book picture carried the caption, "a lean, mean fighting machine". Upon graduation, he immediately volunteered for submarine school at New London and during his first sea tour on a 'boomer' (ballistic missile submarine) had earned his dolphins in record time. Subsequent tours in various shipboard departments prepared him for command of a fast attack boat and his deep selection for the four stripes of a Captain had earned him the honor of being given command of the *USS Sea Lion*, the newest of the *Seawolf* class nuclear powered submarines. He and his crew were 'plank owners', the first crew to be assigned to a new ship. They had worked the boat up during builder's trials and acceptance trials, and had proudly 'manned the side' as her ensign, colors and commissioning pennant were hoisted to crackle defiantly in the breeze. She was now making her first West-Pac deployment and was currently completing voyage rehab along side the sub tender in Apra harbor. She was available for immediate duty.

Admiral Billig allowed a wistful smile to cross his face as he briefly thought back to his tour as a 'plank owner' of a *Los Angeles* class boat. Submariners have always been considered a 'breed apart' and the men of the *Sea Lion* were no different. She had the latest and most modern sonar gear, fire control array, efficient and safest nuclear power plant, guided missile weaponry, wire guided torpedoes and she was the quietest boat ever constructed. The leading sonar petty officer was once asked how good the new sonar was, to which his salty reply was, "I can hear a whale fart at ten thousand yards," such was his pride in the equipment.

As with most first crews, men and machine had bonded right from the start and the rapport between officers, chiefs, and enlisted men couldn't be better. It was not unusual, in such circumstances, for an atmosphere of informality to arise, though not at the expense of discipline or neglect of the Code of Conduct or Navy Regulations. Aboard ship and underway first names were often used, Savage's being "Cap'n".

The Admiral asked only one question, "Is there a second choice?" to which the answer was a definite, "No others close." The Admiral broke out in a broad smile as he said, "I presume that this man, who can walk on water, is in the other room. Let's get him in here and see what he looks like in person."

Capt. Savage, in the flesh, looked like he had just stepped out of a Hollywood casting department to play the role of a submarine commander. He was the personification of Rock Hudson in 'Ice Station Zebra'. He was the type of man to whom everybody turns when he enters a room. His smile and voice radiated warmth and joviality, but the set of his mouth and his steel gray eyes warned that he was not to be taken lightly or summarily dismissed as 'just another ring knocker' (Naval Academy graduate).

Admiral Billig got right to the point, "Captain, would you be able to 'pull the trigger' without hesitation, if an acct of aggression were about to be committed against the U.S.?"

The grin on Captain Savage's faded and his eyes became as hard steel and you could almost sense the Captain coming to attention. His face was all business as he answered, "Yes sir, no problem!"

The Admiral's next question was posed with an admonition to take enough time to consider all sides of the question before he answered, "OK, Captain, <u>you</u> can 'pull the trigger', but will there be any 'heart burn' among any of your crew if you do have to 'pull the trigger'?"

What could only be described as an evil grin slowly spread across "Bee" Savage's face. It took less than thirty seconds for his answer, "Admiral, I have the best crew in the force, this is what we train for, the men will relish the opportunity to wax an enemy." When asked if became necessary to fire a 'fish' in anger, would he actually push the button, the *Sea Lion's* CO answered emphatically, 'No sir, I'd give that honor to the Chief of the Boat. He also lost a grandfather in Korea and has been itching for a pay back ever since he got out of boot camp."

The Admiral then handed his Presidential commission to Captain Savage, who read the document without blinking an eyelid. Never before, and probably never again, would he see anything like it. His comment was, "I feel just like Captain James T. Kirk of the starship *Enterprise* reading the Prime Directive."

The Admiral's last question was simply, "Understand?," to which he got an equally simple answer, "Understood!"

The Admiral then reminded Capt. Savage that from here on in, the actions of he and his crew would come under the National Securities Act and that no one, repeat no one, was ever to tell the story of the upcoming 'exercise'. He was instructed to make his boat 'ready for sea' in all respects, to insure that his full crew was aboard and to get a full weapons load. They would be going to sea sometime in mid November for a 'training exercise' in the waters northwest of Guam and would return to port only on the orders of SubRonSeven, who would also give them their final sailing orders immediately before getting under way. Also, under no circumstances would there be any official written record of the 'exercise'.

The Admiral thanked Capt. Savage for his 'volunteering', and for his strength and fortitude and dedication to the nation and the service. The skipper of the *Sea Lion* walked on air back to his boat. Just as the knights of King Arthur's roundtable were given quests, he had been given his. He would not go forth riding a magnificent pure bred stallion, but in a magnificent lethal steel charger of the ocean depths.

The Admiral smiled at CSR7, and said simply, "Done, now let's do it right. You've got the ball, the game is going to be played on your home court. I want *San Francisco* on *Red Vengeance* from the moment she leaves her pier. We have a good idea where she will take her shot, but we take nothing for granted. Once *Sea Lion* tags her, she sticks to her like glue, ready to take a 'snap' shot, if it comes to that. I want the *Scranton* on which ever trawler is on station from November 13. I want her to monitor all her communications, in and out. I'll bet that the trawler will be one of their most sophisticated 'spy' ships. After she makes her last transmission, I expect her to high-tail it out of the action zone. At that point I want McDade to let her know that he has her in his sights and that she is to make no attempt to re-enter the zone. Oh yes, block all her communications after her last transmission, you'll recognize it when it hits the air. When it's all over, *Sea Lion* is to transmit 'Bohica', the code word for a successful 'exercise', directly to Air Force One, copy to me. I'll inform everybody else."

Admiral Billig thanked Admiral (Selectee) Simpson for his wholehearted cooperation and the level of enthusiasm for the upcoming operation. SubRonSeven then returned to the tender to confer with the three submarine commanders who would carry out Admiral Billig's instructions.

Admiral Billig paused at the door of Admiral Tonelson's office as he took his leave, "Jim, thank you for all the arrangements. You've got lots of work to do, so I'll leave you to it. I'm going to take a breather and get back to you this evening."

CHAPTER 23

ISRAEL
November 5

It was shortly after 0700 and the air crew and I were enjoying a traditional full English breakfast in the BOQ dining room, when a Royal Air Force petty officer approached our table, gave the plane Commander a smart, heel clicking, hand jerking salute and handed him a sealed envelope. Being uncovered, it was not appropriate for the Marine Lt. Colonel to return the salute, so the best that he could do was a mumbled, "Thanks a lot," as he struggled to get to his feet. Completely non-pulsed the petty officer saluted again, did an about face and marched out of the dining room. A frown crossed the pilot's face as he read the memorandum he had been handed.

Turning to me, he said, "Sir, looks like we have a glitch. It seems that the Israelis and the Arabs are having another one of their to dos, and Ben Gurion airport has been closed for the time being. We are directed to re-route to an Israeli air base between Tel Aviv and Jerusalem."

Before I could ask the question, he answered it, "There will be just a minor alteration to the flight plan, mainly when we cross into Israeli air space. They will advise us about the landing when we are making our final approach. The flying time will be the same, about five hours, depending on the winds. With the three hour time differential factored in, if we have wheels up at 0900 as scheduled, we should be there at tea time, or what ever they call it there."

I took a quick glance at my watch and asked if we could take off any earlier. The answer was a definite, "Yes, sir. We're ready to go right now. If we eat a little faster we can be in the air by 0815."

"Good," I said through a mouthful of sausage, "make it so." True to his word, the pilot was saying, "Wheels up" at 0810. We were on our way.

The flight from England to Israel, over the heart of Europe, was comfortable and without incident. The view of the ground was remarkable in how the topography changed as we passed over one country and entered the next. I spent the time reading the latest updates from Mossad and reviewed my notes on my earlier visit. A careful screening of events scheduled to take place in Jerusalem in the latter part of November revealed no specific event that would trigger a terrorist attack, other than the visit of the Speaker of the House to the Israeli Medical Society annual meeting. The Pope was no longer considered the prime target.

By a process of elimination, the most likely terrorist group that could launch an attack upon a specific individual target was one whose fanatic leadership hated everything Jewish first and anything related to Americans second. This group had one of the most elusive and deadly agents that Mossad had ever dealt with in the person known only by the code name, 'Chameleon'. This person had never been photographed and no one knew, with any certainty the person's sex. It was felt that the 'Chameleon' was most probably male and a master of disguise.

Security at the Crown Plaza Hotel, where the Speaker would be staying, and where the dinner he was to speak at would be held, was being beefed up. Security at the Hadassah Medical Center, located near the hotel, was also being reinforced for the anticipated visit by Dr. Rosen to their renown Pediatric service. Dr. Rosen was a Board Certified Pediatrician who, even though a full time politician, still kept his medical license current and up to date relative to completing his CME (Continuing Medical Education) requirements. As he often said, "What if I lose an election? I am always only two years away from having to go back to work for a living."

When we still had about fifty miles of the Mediterranean to cross before entering Israeli air space, we suddenly acquired an escort of two Israeli jet fighters who shepherded us to our alternate landing site. When we were on final approach, the jets peeled away and a helicopter gun ship became our escort until we touched down. My thoughts were, "Boy oh boy, I don't know what is going on down here, but it has to be real big."

Immediately after touch down, a jeep displaying a FOLLOW ME sign pulled onto the taxi strip in front of our C-20 and lead us to a remote part of the airfield, out of sight of the tower, where we were directed into a large hanger. There were no other planes in the hanger, only a couple of Mercedes limos and a truckload of heavily armed soldiers. Brigadier Templeman emerged from the closest limo followed by Becky Zelman, who in turn was followed by two officers, and their gear, from the other limo. The Brigadier moved very quickly and met me at the top of the C-20's steps. The traditional Eastern greeting of hugs and kisses were exchanged and I was gently pushed back into the plane. The plane was then pulled to a remote corner of the hanger and surrounded by twelve soldiers in full battle gear. The air crew had been greeted, in traditional Western style, by the two Mossad officers and all five were huddling in the cramped cockpit.

The Brigadier quickly answered the look of bewilderment on my face, "You don't need to know the nitty-gritty but at this particular time it is not advisable for you, or your crew, to set foot on Israeli ground. By conducting our business inside your plane, no one can say that you ever set foot in Israel and without immigration processing your passports, no one can refute the statement. Becky and my associates have all the material we need for the briefing here with us. So, let's make ourselves comfortable in your lounge, and we'll bring you up to date."

The Brigadier and I took seats at the rear of the lounge and I handed him his copy of my presidential commission. On reading it, he broke out in a laugh, chuckling, "Spoken like a true politician."

Becky and the other two officers selected seats near the front bulkhead of the compartment. It was obvious, from the number of audio-visual aids and VCR tapes that were piled up on the lounge's small table, that an in-depth briefing was going to take place.

The Brigadier explained, "Glenn, we had planned to give you an on-site full dress rehearsal of the greeting Speaker Rosen will get when he arrives, but the current circumstances dictate otherwise. So, we'll do the next best thing, run through a virtual reality condensed version."

"To start, we will arrange with EL AL to have Mossad security teams in every cabin of the jet Speaker Rosen travels on to Israel and back to New York. At each terminal, he will be the only passenger in the VIP lounge The other people in the lounge will be our security team disguised as first class passengers and your Secret Service escort. Once all the real passengers are aboard, he will be escorted into the first class cabin. When he is buckled in, no one from the rear cabins will be allowed into the first class space. No one in the first class cabin will be allowed to go into any other space. The change in the normal operating procedures will be explained as a test run for enhanced security against skyjacking. I'm sure that your Secret Service will be able to complement our strategy to the degree that Speaker Rosen will be totally unaware of the special care he will get. The reason that we will use the same precautions on his return trip is, that while the chances of an attempt on his life at that point in his travels will be greatly reduced, it is always better to be safe than sorry."

"We will arrange with Alitalia to have the Pope's plane arrive at the airport at about the same time as Dr. Rosen's. Both planes will get the same sort of escort that you had when you entered our air space today. Once each plane pulls up to its gate, our arrival teams will board each jet and escort the honored guests to the pilot's compartments, where they will remain until all the other passengers have deplaned. Then the jets will be moved into a secure hanger, similar to this one."

"His Holiness will be greeted by our religious leaders. Speaker Rosen will be greeted by senior Medical Society staff and officials of our government. Please explain to Doctor Rosen that, for security reasons, the Prime Minister will meet him at the hotel."

"Both Speaker Rosen and the Pope will travel in bullet proof limousines. Their personal body guards will travel in security limos, one in front of and one behind the VIP limos. The security procedures, that we will use, will be the ones we had arranged for the Pope. By having Speaker Rosen travel with the Pope's entourage, we hope and pray that nobody will notice the extra limos."

The Brigadier took a healthy swig from a bottle labeled 'Coor's Lite' and continued, "We live and work in an armed camp city and the more uniformed and battle armed soldiers there are in evidence, the less likelihood there is of a specific target being successfully attacked. So there will be lots of uniforms along the route to the hotel. The video you are looking at shows you the route you would have traversed today. It is only one of several possibilities. Today's trip would have served three purposes: 1) to demonstrate to you, for relay to your President and the Speaker, the security steps that will be in force on his arrival and during his trip to the hotel, 2) to serve as a word to the wise that it will be next to impossible to attack his car, even with a suicide bomber, and 3) to serve as a smoke screen by letting any terrorists who might be watching think that the plans are so elaborate, that this must be the route that will be used. The major difference between this scenic sight seeing route that dignitaries are usually treated to and the real route will be used is that the caravan will proceed quickly and directly to the hotel, bypassing the sight seeing."

As we proceeded on our 'virtual' way, he pointed out specific protective measures. "There will be at least four heavily armed soldiers at every street corner. All side streets will be barricaded off well back from the intersections and the barricades will be manned. The side streets themselves will be covered with anti-vehicle obstructions. There will be no large crowds lining the streets and only a minimum number of on lookers from high-rise windows. Mine detection units will sweep the route two minutes in advance of the caravan. Troops in the truck at the rear of the convoy will deploy to take up defensive positions should they be needed, God forbid. Once we reach the Speaker's hotel, the Pope's entourage will continue further on into the city."

Taking a deep breath he continued, "There will be no advance publicity on TV, radio, or in the newspapers concerning Dr. Rosen's visit to our fair city. Thanks to martial law regulations, knowledge of our distinguished guest will be on a need to know basis. Even the Medical Society's announcement of his speech was buried deep in routine press releases. The security procedures we will now outline are specific for your Speaker."

The Brigadier then turned the briefing over to the Senior Mossad officer who had come with him. He started off by reciting the usual announcements of the security level of the brief, which is as far as he got before the Brigadier cut him off and curtly told him, "Just get on with it."

With a blush on his face, he continued, "Our sources tell us that this attack will be what we call a surgical strike, one usually carried out by a small attack team against an isolated target. The team most probably will be only one terrorist, whom we feel sure will be the Chameleon. Our sources also tell us the target will definitely be the American and no others, their reasoning being that the chances of a massive retaliatory attack by our armed forces will be minimal if no Israeli nationals have been harmed."

"We have been informed that the distinguished American is small in stature, so the guards who will surround him will be at least six feet tall, a protective measure against a head shot. We have also been informed that he is fluent in our language, so he will understand any protective orders given to him in either language."

Turning to a topographical map, the second Mossad officer continued the brief by using a pointer to depict the other possible routes from the airport to the hotel. The use of a helo transfer to the hotel was rejected because a missile attack from close range would be almost impossible to stop.

My attention was then directed to a three dimensional mockup of the lobby of the Crown Plaza Hotel, the VIP floor where Dr. Rosen would stay and the banquet room where he would deliver his speech. He then enumerated several of the protective measures that would be employed, "The lobby will be secured by the usual methods to protect the Prime Minister. There will be just one area where a limited number of the press will be allowed to interview Dr. Rosen for a brief time. He will be the only guest on the VIP floor and access to the floor will be granted to only hotel personnel identified by special ID badges that will not be issued until our guest is actually in the hotel. They will be changed every day."

"The floors above and below the VIP floor will be closed to guests and guarded, and all three floors will be constantly swept for explosive devices. No one but the Speaker and his Mossad body guards will be allowed into the VIP suite."

"Only fully vetted food preparation and serving personnel will attend to him."

After taking a sip of water, he returned to his presentation, "The only place where it will be difficult to maintain maximum security is in the banquet room. This is what we have arranged for that occasion. Only accredited members of the Medical Society will be admitted. Members of the press will be concentrated in a sound proof booth with bullet proof windows. Security agents will escort them to and from the booth at all times. The few staff who will serve the head table will go through the same security process as when the Prime Minister attends a banquet and of course, our distinguished guest will be escorted to and from the banquet by security forces."

My attention was then directed to the street display showing possible routes from the hotel to the medical center, back to the hotel and back to the airport The security procedures would be exactly the same as used from the airport to hotel. The next display depicted the hospital's Pediatric ward and the synagogue that held the famous stained glass window that was created for the hospital by Marc Chagall.

In the same monotone voice, he droned on, "Security measures arranged for the hospital include: Only senior hospital staff will greet their visitor in the hospital lobby. The official party will always be accompanied by security personnel. Elevators will not be used. No parents or family members will be allowed in the wards or halls that the visitor will visit and/or traverse. Only head nurses will accompany the official party on wards rounds. The synagogue will be closed to worshippers for that afternoon. The entire visit should take only about one hour, during which the visitor will be gently kept moving, except for a brief prayer in the synagogue."

That completed the first part of the presentation, during which I asked no questions. Cold beer and fresh cucumber and cheese sandwiches for everyone were brought into the plane by stewards at that point.

Once refreshed, the Brigadier asked, "Meet your expectations, Glenn?" I assured him that my expectations were more than met. "Fine" he said, "now Becky will tell you all about the Chameleon."

In contrast to the cryptic military voices that had given the previous parts of the brief, Becky's voice was controlled and soft in tone, "As you know, we didn't know the real appearance of the Chameleon, so we didn't waste time by trying to prevent his/her entrance into Jerusalem. While we have made plans covering all possible attack sites, the most probable spot for a 'surgical hit' is the banquet hall, which still leaves a lot of options to prepare for. We started screening the hotel staff right after your first visit and any one who didn't pass was dismissed. We then zeroed in on all new hires, those re-placing those people who were dismissed and temporaries brought in to augment the banquet staff."

"We eventually concentrated on two possibilities, a maintenance tech and a waiter. There were several peculiarities that aroused our interest in them. This is how we proceded."

"Each of the suspects were placed under constant surveillance while in the hotel, and they proved hard to cover, which aroused our suspicions even more. We ascertained that the addresses listed on the suspects' employment forms were bogus. On reviewing the surveillance reports, we discovered that they were never at work at the same time, so we surmised that they were the same person. When they left the hotel, they always took complicated routes, never repeated, to the same low class boarding house. We then searched the room that was rented and our findings confirmed that we were dealing with only one man."

"These are the interesting things we found: theatrical make-up kits, workman's clothes and waiter's uniforms, western street wear, and traditional Arab garments. This guy never appears in the same clothes twice in a row."

"Surprisingly, we found no cache of arms other than two small caliber handguns and a small amount of ammunition, which pretty much rules out a long range attack. There was some electronic materiel, all still in packing cases that we didn't disturb."

"I'm pretty good at disguises myself, so I'm going to work with the surveillance teams to see what else incriminating that we can dig up. I'll keep you posted."

That completed the presentation and it was my turn to ask my few questions regarding a few technicalities. When there were no more questions to be answered, and no more beer to be drunk, the Brigadier dismissed Becky and his aides.

When we were alone, in a conspiratorial tone of voice, he did a short re-cap, "We've covered a lot of ground, learned a lot and discovered that we still don't know everything, but for sure, we'll be well prepared when Dr. Rosen lands. I hope that he will be open to suggestions and follow orders if push comes to shove."

I interrupted him there, "Don't worry, my President will program him for you. Today's fracas, whatever it is, will be the cover for President Alexander to tell him that he will only be allowed to make the trip if he behaves himself."

"Good, good," replied the Brigadier, "One last point, a moving target is the hardest to hit, so we are planning a forward motion itinerary for our guest. He will be gently prodded into constantly moving from one spot to the next. If we play it right, the only times he will be stationary will be in his suite, in the synagogue and at the banquet. We hope that, by keeping him moving we will force the Chameleon to attack him during the banquet, where we'll have the best chance of stopping him."

I smiled to myself, "Now, where have I heard that plan before?"

The intercom squawked at that point to notify me that the plane was refueled and ready to go. "OK, Glenn," the Brigadier was actually smiling for the first time since he boarded the jet, "So long, it's been good to know you. I'd have enjoyed taking you to my favorite deli for a New York style kosher meal, but the sooner you're out of here, the better. We've taken the liberty of changing your return route. Instead of going to Rheimstad, you are going due West across the Mediterranean, for a refueling stop at Rota. They'll be expecting you. You'll also have the helo overhead until you're fully airborne and the fighters will escort you out of Israeli air space and protect you as far out to sea as they can go without running out of gas. We'll keep in touch."

The customary hugs, kisses and handshakes were replaced by a hearty slap on my back and he was running down the steps. Within five minutes of his feet touching the ground, we were airborne and on the way home. It was pitch dark when we landed in Rota, so common sense dictated that we take an overnight, rather than pushing our luck with an additional nine hour flight across the Atlantic in the dark. We were not on that a tight schedule at that point, so I made an executive decision to sleep in the next morning and cross the ocean in the afternoon.

CHAPTER 24

GUAM
November 5

After Admiral Tonelson had taken care of his usual morning duties, he and Admiral Billig paid a call on Colonel Leonard Gillespie, the Commanding Officer of Anderson AFB. The Colonel was obviously a little edgy, as he had never before received a call from two Admirals at one time, much less a four star Admiral. Befitting this auspicious occasion, he was attired in his best dress uniform and his staff rendered all the appropriate honors to Admiral Billig as he made way to the Colonel's office. Admiral Tonelson made the introductions and, after a very brief period of light conversation, coffee was served and the three officers took seats in very comfortable chairs. Before beginning his presentation, Admiral Billig handed his commission to Colonel Gillespie, who became even more tense, the further he read. To be perfectly sure of what he read, he re-read it slowly, during which time Admiral Billig started to strum his fingers on the arm of his chair. He was eager to get on with the meeting. There was very little color left in Colonel Gillespie's face as he handed the commission back to Admiral Billig and poured himself another cup of coffee. Admiral Tonelson stepped in at that point to assure Colonel Gillespie that he was not going to asked for anything he could not easily provide.

Admiral Billig finally got to have his say, "Colonel, I know that you're up to your eyeballs with preparations for the President's visit, so I'll make this short. On or about November 14, the Navy is going to deliver an unmarked KC-10 here. It will arrive undercover of darkness. Once it lands, I would like it immediately parked in a hangar as far away as possible from the main terminal. It will stay here no longer than the 18th. The flight crew will return to Japan as soon as they turn the aircraft over to your personnel. Please arrange to have no other aircraft housed in the same hangar while it is here. I'll have more details about that in a few days."

Throughout the Admiral Billig's presentation, Admiral Tonelson sat back quietly and watched a gamut of emotions sweep across the Colonel's face. He thought to himself, "You don't know the half of it."

Colonel Gillespie finally got to speak, "Admiral Billig, no problem. Please step over here to the window. I'll put your KC-10 in that hangar that you see at the south end of the field. It's 1.8 miles from the terminal, so that regular traffic and Air Force One will be kept far away from it. What kind of security do you want me to provide?"

Admiral Billig's answer was a short, "None. Just park it in there, lock the door and leave it there until a new Navy crew arrives. I don't want to call any unnecessary attention to it while it's here."

Colonel Gillespie visibly relaxed at the simplicity of the request and asked, "Is there anything else I can do for you?"

"Nothing else at the present time, Colonel," Admiral Billig replied, "I have to go out to the *Vinson* battle group and when I get back we'll get together again to finalize the arrangements. If any questions arise while I'm gone, refer them to Admiral Tonelson. He is authorized to act for me in my absence. OK, we all have work to do. I can be reached at the Navy BOQ for the rest of the day."

With that, the meeting was over, the Admirals drove off and Colonel Gillespie heaved a huge sigh of relief and directed his secretary to start phoning members of his staff to report to his office on the double.

Admiral Billig spent the afternoon doing business, on a very secure communications link, with the Chief of Staff of the *Vinson's* battle group commander, arranging a 'taxi' service to take him out to the carrier in the morning. He even had enough time left over to play nine holes of golf on the base course, the first bit of relaxation he had in the past month.

PHILIPPINE SEA
November 6

It was shortly before noon when the *Vinson's* COD[v] aircraft landed at Anderson and taxied up to the terminal. As the pilot climbed down from the cockpit, Admiral Billig left the terminal and headed for the plane. He was accompanied by Colonel Gillespie, who had provided him with the appropriate flight gear. The jaw of the Lt.-Commander pilot dropped when he saw the four stars on his passenger's collar. All he had been told was, "Fly into Anderson, pick up a passenger and bring him back to the carrier."

The Admiral was amused by the reaction he had caused and moved quickly to put the pilot at ease. After all, he was putting his life into this man's hands. "Take it easy, son, I'm not going to tell you how to fly your plane. I'm going to settle into a seat in the back and won't bother you. I won't even speak unless you want me to talk to you. You give your full attention to getting us back to the *Vinson*."

With that, the Admiral took his leave of the Colonel, climbed into passenger/cargo compartment of the twin engined turboprop plane, buckled himself in, put on his helmet and sat back for the short hop to the carrier.

Within an hour, the Admiral was treated to his first arrested

---

v   *COD= Carrier On Board Delivery*

carrier landing. For the first time in his life, his heart was in his throat. By the time the COD was moved close to the carrier's 'island', it was back in his chest, where it belonged. As he climbed down from the plane, he was greeted with full honors appropriate to the visit of a full Admiral to the ship. Once inside the 'island' he was escorted to the battle group commander's conference room by the ship's Executive Officer. There he was greeted by the Battle Group Commander, the *Vinson's* Commanding Officer, and the Air Group Commander (commonly referred to as 'CAG'). Admiral Billig was welcomed warmly by his hosts, handed a mug of steaming, hot, black coffee and directed to a seat at the Group Commander's right. A steward entered and placed a platter piled high with hot freshly baked apple popovers in front of the officers. Admiral Billig treated himself to two of the goodies, while the other three men read his commission. There were no outward signs of emotion, nor questions when the commission was returned to him. It was as if they were used to having bombshells dropped on them. Admiral Kiesel had obviously forewarned them about what was heading their way when he notified them of the Admiral's impending visit.

It was now time to get down to business. Admiral Billig started by thanking his ship board hosts for his reception, their courtesy, and their full cooperation that he knew he was going to get. The short version of his presentation was, "We anticipate an attack on Air Force One by a North Korean missile toting sub, somewhere between here and Japan. While it won't be successful, we are going to let the attack take place to teach them a lesson."

At that point, the three other Naval officers almost went ballistic in their reactions. "What the hell?" "Are you crazy?" "Does the President know what you're doing?" "Is this a joke?," were only a few of the milder comments shouted from the very red faced and clearly upset Commanders, all of whom had jumped up from their seats and were glowering down on their guest. Out in the nearby pantry, the mess specialist suddenly decided to go inventory his stockroom.

When the initial expressions of incredulity had run their course, Admiral Billing calmly defused the highly flammable situation, "Gentlemen, belay your fears, nothing is going to happen to the President. ComSeven will deliver a decommissioned KC-10 to Guam sometime next week. It is being re-configured to be flown by remote control as we speak. It will be flown along the usual flight pattern from here to Japan, while Air Force One will take a detour to the northeast."

Normal color returned to the faces of the other officers, their respiratory and heart rates slowed appreciably, they again sat down, and tuned into the rest of Admiral Billig's plans

"From *Vinson*, I need an electronics warfare chopper that has the capability to fly the KC-10 by remote control from Guam to its appointment with destiny. Can you provide me with what I need?"

Like the true professionals that they were, the three officers unanimously pledged their full support. CAG was tasked with making all the arrangements and he left at once to start the ball rolling. The carrier's skipper returned to his bridge and Admiral Billig and the Battle Group Commander adjourned to the flag bridge, where they observed the day's flight operations.

After the evening meal, the four senior officers again met in the Battle Group Commander's conference room, where the CAG had the floor. With pride in his voice, he outlined what plans were underway to meet Admiral Billig's requirements, "I've tasked my chopper squadron commander to fly the mission. He will use his personal chopper and his own crew. The crew will start working on adapting their equipment to fly a drone as soon as they get some extra parts. The parts have already been ordered and will be delivered from Atsugi within forty-eight hours. The chopper should be fully operational by ninety-six hours from now. When and where will you need it?"

Admiral Billig took a quick look at his calendar and replied, "The KC-10 will be delivered to Anderson no later than the 14th. I'd like to have your people there when it gets there, so they'll have a couple days to test out the systems before the 18th, the date that we expect the 'you know what' to hit the fan."

CAG simply answered, "Can do. They will be ready to deploy as soon as ComSeven confirms the delivery date of the KC-10. I presume that we'll get further details from you when all the pieces fall into place."

Admiral Billig's immediate response was, "You can bet on it." He was then treated to a first rate movie, more freshly baked pastries, and given a *Vinson* coffee mug and a ball cap with the battle group's logo, complete with a full admiral's 'scrambled eggs' as souvenirs of his trip. He then 'turned in' for a full night of uninterrupted sleep.

GUAM
November 7

Morning found a well rested and well fed Admiral Billig, garbed again in flight gear, ready to return to Guam. The same Lt.-Commander, who had flown him to the ship, was standing by to take him back. Before climbing into the plane, the Admiral noticed a new sign painted over the door.. It read, "Four Star Taxi Service". After a very brief departure ceremony, the Admiral buckled himself into his seat, donned his helmet and the plane was positioned on the catapult. The take off again found his heart in his throat and he silently prayed that he would never have this experience again. He was definitely more at home in the ocean's depths rather than the wild blue yonder.

The return flight to Guam was uneventful. Admiral Billig spent the balance of the day reviewing with Colonel Gillespie what further support he would need from the Air Force. Basically, what was required was space for the chopper to be parked close to the hangar where the KC-10 would be hidden, accommodations for the crew of the chopper, and whatever technical support was needed to ensure that the KC-10 would be ready to fly on time. Colonel Gillespie readily understood what he needed to do and assured the Admiral that there would be no 'glitches'.

HAWAII
November 8

After another night's restful sleep, Admiral Billig boarded CNO's jet and crossed the date line on his return trip to Hawaii, where it was still November 7. This bonus day was spent meeting with Admirals Robinson and Morgiewicz to bring them 'up-to-speed' on what had been accomplished since their last meeting on Guam. Admiral Robinson would brief Commander, Pacific when he returned to his office. Admiral. Billig's second Wednesday of the week was spent in the comfort of the CNO's executive jet as it returned him to Washington, where he arrived early on November 9.

CHAPTER 25

ASHBURN
November 12

The Admiral and I had been back from our whirlwind trips for ninety-six hours, during which time we both took well deserved rests to erase the effects of jet-lag, as well as pure physical and mental exhaustion. Since I had returned home earlier than the Admiral, Kevin and I spent the 'down' time completing our plans to protect Senator Willis. Cindy Lou and I even were able to attend a Veteran's Day concert of the Virginia Grand Military Band, a fitting prelude to today's meeting. As soon as I was back ~~SgtMajor~~ I had called General Golden to inform him that I no longer had need of his jet, to which I got a gruff, "About time, your boss will have the gas bill on his desk tomorrow!"

The Admiral had met briefly with the CNO to report on the plans that the Pacific fleet were working on, and spent almost a full evening up-dating the President, who was perfectly at ease with the situation as it now stood. Madam Dragon Lady was keeping a low profile, so the pot was just simmering.

Even though it was Sunday morning, all three of us were in the Admiral's office, no rest for the wicked. When Kevin and I passed the ever present Miss Eagleton's desk, she smiled sweetly and purred, "You're in luck, he's fully rested and in a good mood." The first thing we noticed when we went into his office was that there were no nibbles or liquid refreshments in evidence, this was going to be a very serious session.

The main, and only, item on the agenda was an in-depth review of what each of us had accomplished since our last meeting and what plans had been made to counteract the events that Madam Secretary and her father had arranged for the coming weekend. I reported that MI6 and Mossad, in the persons of SgtMajor MacGregor and Becky Zelman, were fully prepared to carry out the counter terrorist plans that I now laid out for the Admiral. I added that they had given me full assurances the Vice-President and the Speaker would not be harmed. Kevin added that the Senator's safety was well in hand and that the Senator was being fully cooperative.

The Admiral was basking in the power that the extra star had given him and gleefully reported that the Navy was fully cooperating with him, "I've been given temporary tactical command of all the assets I had requested. The *San Francisco* has already sailed, and is on station in the Yellow Sea to tail the *Red Vengeance* when she deploys."

At this point Miss Eagleton interrupted us with a FLASH PRIORITY message from Yokosuka. Intelligence. They had intercepted a one word message from Captain Hyun to North Korean Naval Headquarters—-"Underway". Admiral Billig immediately picked up the red phone and, in less than a minute, was giving the President a quick update on what was the prelude to the coming weekend. I could easily imagine the gamut of emotions that President Alexander was experiencing—relief that the waiting was over, – concern for the lives of himself and the others who would play the starring roles in the scenarios, – confidence that everything would be resolved in our favor, and finally thankfulness that he was surrounded by top-notch and fully dedicated supporters! The conversation ended with the Admiral assuring him that all our prayers had been answered, and agreeing to meet him at the White House early in the evening.

The Admiral then gave Kevin and me our marching orders, and wrapped up the meeting, "OK gents, we've gone as far as we can go at this point. We have to rely on our A-Teams to hand us a total victory. I think I now know how Chester Nimitz felt on the eve of the Battle of Midway. We both knew what was coming, where it's coming from, and what the enemy's objective is and we both sent out our best to meet the enemy. The big difference is that this time, <u>WE</u> have all the big guns. I'm heading back to Guam to run the show out there."

As Kevin and I were leaving his office, he was telling Miss Eagleton, "Contact CNO's pilot and tell him to prepare a return trip to the Pacific early tomorrow morning." Show time was definitely upon us!

———•◆•———

It was shortly after 1800 hours when the Admiral was ushered into the Oval Office. No formalities were appropriate to the meeting, so as soon as both men were again seated on the conference sofa Admiral Billig began, "Mr. President, everything is falling nicely into place. The protective measures for ALL the intended victims of Madam Secretary's coup have been finalized. There will be no fatalities, at least, on our side. I'm heading back to Guam in the morning to assume command of the forces that will protect you. I have one last request. The cover for the KC-10 flight will be that the Navy is going to conduct a simulated missile attack on it from a deeply submerged submarine. The exact location of that exercise will be highly classified and listed as 'north of Guam'. I will notify all the concerned parties, including the Air Traffic Controllers about the 'exercise'. Upon your arrival in Guam, have the pilot of Air Force One file an emended flight plan for your trip to Yokota AFB that will take you slightly north northeast of the direct route to Japan to avoid the 'exercise' site. With the ground work that I will lay, there should be no ruffled feathers or heart burn. I'll be at Anderson when you arrive and we can put the finishing touches on the plans before you exit your plane."

The President absorbed all the details by just nodding his

head in understanding and agreement as each step was outlined. When Admiral Billig concluded his recital, the President let out a long sigh of relief, "Vinnie, you don't know how much the country and I are indebted to you. It is a travesty that no one out side of the four of us will ever realize the extent and seriousness of the plot and the far reaching consequences that would have ensued if it had been successful, nor appreciate all the hard work that went into the plans to thwart it. I don't know how, but some way I will repay you. God speed you on your flight tomorrow. I'm looking forward to seeing you in Guam."

The meeting was over. To all intents and purposes, the script was completed and put to bed. The curtain was about to go up on an epic saga that was to be played on a world- wide stage.

CHAPTER 26

VIRGINIA
November 15-17

Kevin arrived at his office, early on Wednesday, November 15 and turned on his computer for the latest surveillance report on Jack McCarthy. "Hmmmm," he mused, "He's off and running again." On the previous day, he had made another cell phone call to his underworld contact in Chicago, bought a commuter air ticket for the 16th from Logan to Reagan National, and called his daughter to tell her that he would be in D.C. for a few days and wanted to stay at her home rather than a hotel.

He had also withdrawn forty thousand dollars from his bank account. An E-mail message from Kevin's 'contact' at his bank reported that McCarthy was converting the forty thousand dollars into new thousand dollar bills, which had recently been reissued by Treasury Department. Because it was a limited issue for these big bills, his banker had to request help from all their branches in the Boston area to fill the order. Not only was this a departure from Jack's usual way of handling cash, it would also draw attention to whomever tried to pass the bills.

"Hmmmm," Kevin mused, "Large denomination bills, what's he up to? He certainly isn't going to take that many large denomination bills out of the country. Using them in Belfast would draw all kinds of attention to anyone passing them. So, who in this country would ask for those bills? About their only advantage is that they don't take up too much space. Well, we'll soon see."

Kevin next contacted the surveillance team in Boston, alerting them that McCarthy would soon be on the move, instructing them that every move he made from here on in was to be video recorded, and they were to notify him as soon as he left Logan. Kevin then called the team who would pick him up at Reagan, putting them on stand-by alert and instructing them that they were also to record all his movements on tape, with special attention to whomever he might meet and to identify them as soon as possible. Kevin continued to muse, "The pot is now on the front burner and the heat is turned up."

BOSTON/WASHINGTON
November 16

The call from the Boston team came in at 9:15 AM on the sixteenth. Jack had boarded a United commuter departing Logan at 9:00 AM with a scheduled arrival at Reagan at 10:30 AM. He was traveling light, with just a brief case and a carry-on overnight bag. One of the Boston team was able to board the same flight, and even managed to get the seat alongside him. Kevin smiled, "How's that for a close tail."

The DC team picked him up as soon as he entered the arrivals lounge from the jet way. The first thing they checked was that he still had the same briefcase and bag in his possession. While one of the local team followed McCarthy, his team-mate spoke briefly with the Boston agent who had accompanied Jack, who reported that Jack had made no contacts with any of the other passengers. McCarthy was then tailed to the curb, where he boarded a taxi that took him directly to McCormick and Schmick's seafood restaurant on "K" street in downtown Washington. On entering the restaurant, the hostess directed him to a booth in the back of the restaurant where two men, dressed in business suits, were waiting for him.

The DC team immediately put in a call for a 'back-up' team to latch onto the new players, who were code named "Mutt and Jeff" because of their height differences. While the three conspirators enjoyed a hearty lunch, their watchers ate sparingly, keeping them under constant visual contact, and taking only a few photographs of the dining room, just like the other tourists. Several of the pictures documented McCarthy removing two thick envelopes from his briefcase and passing one to each of his lunch companions. The back up team had arrived, including a petite young lady dressed in a waitress's uniform. Her assignment was to casually pass by Jack's table frequently to eavesdrop on the conversations. Unfortunately, whenever anyone approached their table, McCarthy and his companions turned their attention to serious eating of their meal.

As soon as the three men had left the restaurant, the 'waitress' unobtrusively picked up the water glasses that Mutt and Jeff had used and took them and several digital photos taken of them to the FBI for fingerprint and mug shot identification. It only took about an hour for the FBI to identify them as a high priced Midwest 'hit' team, who were suspected of at least a dozen assassinations of high profile targets. There had never been enough proof to get even an indictment. Jack had definitely bought his own 'A-Team'.

Mutt and Jeff were tailed to the Hilton hotel on Connecticut Avenue, where they spent the rest of the day in their room, probably watching sports on TV. Their room number was called into Kevin, who immediately put his patented computer hacking to work. From the hotel records, he got their names, probably aliases and a credit card number that was traced to an elderly man, bed-ridden in a Waukegan Illinois convalescent hospital. The only true facts in the hotel record were the check-in date of 11/4 and the license plate number of a rental car, which was traced to an agency at Reagan National airport. The rental car contract revealed a different alias that was back tracked to a Joliet Illinois widower, who was currently vacationing in Europe. The plot was definitely thickening, and taking on all the aspects of a big time mob contract 'hit'.

Kevin immediately contacted the team at Senator Willis's home to see if the mobsters or their car had been spotted in the vicinity. This was followed up with fax pictures of the two suspects. The team, at the Senator's home, confirmed that the suspects had slowly walked up one side and down the other side of the street at least twice in the past two days, and their car had made one slow pass in the evening.

"Could they have been casing the joint," Kevin mused to himself facetiously.

Kevin then called me with the news and we mutually decided that it was time for me to augment the Senator's protectors and for Kevin to take the controls of the security system. I took my carefully concealed nine millimeter pistol from its case, checked that it was in perfect working condition, loaded it and put a few spare clips in my pocket. I couldn't remember exactly when I had last fired the gun in anger, so I prayed that all the range firing had kept my aim sharp and true.

Kevin and I were driven to Virginia in an unmarked CIA van. Our compatriots were 'experts' in 'sanitizing' a messy scene and on loan to us from the CIA. The Admiral had called in one of his 'quid pro quo' IOUs. Their equipment was capable of cleaning up everything from a simple shooting to a bomb blast. They parked the van well away from the Senator's home and settled back to do what they were used to doing, waiting until they were needed. Kevin and I walked slowly towards the Senator's home, trying to look like ordinary citizens out stretching their legs, but scanning the neighborhood for any unexpected items that would affect our plans. To our relief, we found none. Using the gear that Kevin had installed, the two agents in the house identified us as 'friendlies' and we entered through a partially hidden patio door. As instructed, the Senator was keeping out of sight.

A quick pow-wow put the final touches on the battle plan. The Senator's personal body guard would put a sleeping potion in his supper that would cause him to have a deep sleep and awaken with no recollection of the events about to take place. I would be the point man and play Matt Dillon. Kevin would take over the electronics console for the rest of the night, freeing our remaining agent to back up where needed. This scenario was definitely more to my liking than waiting by the phone for a report of the action.

November 17

It was after midnight when Mutt and Jeff checked out of their hotel. Once in their car, they began a circuitous route into Virginia, frequently doubling back on their track to ensure that they were not being tailed. Even though they felt perfectly safe, years of habit were hard to break and their modus operandi had always kept them out of court and jail. Because their destination was known, a very loose tail was employed by our agents. The traffic on Route 66 was still heavy enough to close up the tail and keep the 'hit' car in sight. After turning west on route 7 and heading towards Leesburg, the first tail car radioed ahead to another tail car waiting at the Cascades exit. Because of the complexity of the street pattern in the Cascades, the tail had to move in as close as they dared to see where they would park their car. They finally parked their car a few short blocks from their target, oddly enough in plain view of the CIA van. Once they were on foot, I was notified that action was imminent.

Mutt and Jeff took their time covering the short distance from their car to the Senator's house, and only started their penetration when they were sure that no other citizens were out and about. Their main concern was a person taking the household canine for a late night walk. As expected, they then knocked out the electrical and phone connections to the house. Kevin's laser field and the video cameras picked them up as soon as they entered the protective shield around the house and their efforts to get into the house unobserved were in vain, because all of Kevin's electronic devises were still powered by long-life batteries.

The front door was quickly picked open and the hoods, with drawn guns, entered the darkened hallway. As soon as they closed the door, they were greeted by a hidden voice, "Stand still, drop your guns, and raise your hands!"

The gunmen reacted by firing several silenced shots in the direction of the voice, which, of course, was a tape recorder. I had a large advantage by having a night scope on my pistol, and wearing night goggles. They were clearly visible to me and my return fire of one head and one chest shot into each assailant proved that I still had the "touch". Mutt and Jeff were dead before they hit the floor.

External power was restored and a call sent out for the 'sanitation' team. In a very dignified and professional manner, they packed Mutt and Jeff into body bags, cleaned up the mess in the hallway, and recovered the hood's bullets from the wall. They even plastered over the holes and repainted the wall. Their work was accomplished quickly and almost noiselessly, and within forty-five minutes of their arrival, the hallway, where all the action had taken place, was restored to its normal appearance. The Senator would never know what had gone down. Within an hour after they had left their rented car, Mutt and Jeff were being taken for their last ride to oblivion. Like Jimmy Hoffa, they were never seen or heard from again. Before they were bundled up, the dead were relieved of their clothing, their guns, the envelopes that McCarthy had given them, the car keys, and two airplane tickets for a 8:00 AM flight to O'Hare, which they were going to miss.

While being almost sure that it was over, the Senator's body guards did not relax their vigilance in case a 'back-up hit team' was in the picture. As it turned out, there was no such team, but the protective measures were kept in place until the Admiral had determined that there was no longer a threat.

Post action comments:

The Senator slept like a baby through the action and never tumbled to what had gone on. He was later told that the parole jumpers had been recaptured and the threat was over.

Ballistics confirmed that Mutt and Jeff's weapons had been used in a number of murders of which they were suspected, letting the FBI close several cases finally. Their clothing, (except those articles with bullet holes or blood spatters) was stripped of all identifying tags and laundry marks and donated to the Good Will Thrift Shop. The rental car was taken to the economy lot at Reagan National, where it was eventually recovered by the owner.

Each of the $1000.00 dollar bills ended up in the Salvation Army's Christmas buckets throughout the metropolitan Washington area. You might say that the last acts of their lives of crime were atonements for their past nefarious deeds.

CHAPTER 27

JERUSALEM
November 17

Following Derek's last visit to Israel, Brigadier Templeman had given Becky Zelman a totally free hand in devising the final plan to thwart the Chameleon's mission. She, and her team, had proved conclusively that the waiter, the maintenance tech and the Chameleon were one and the same. A second search of his hotel room was conducted with some enlightening discoveries. He had constructed a small metallic box measuring 24"x18"x 3". The supports for the sides and top were strong steel, while the sides, top, and bottom were lighter weight metal. All together the box weighed only about twenty pounds. Inside the box was a transistorized mini-electrical generator, capable of producing seven hundred volts of power. There was also a sophisticated electronic receiving devise attached to the generator which, when activated, would turn the generator on and transmit the current to the box. A Mossad electronic expert had analyzed the circuitry and determined the frequency of the signal that was pre-set into the activator. The resulting shock would be an electrifying experience to anyone holding the box or standing on it.

When Becky had read that report, she almost jumped for joy. The file on Dr. Rosen had made specific reference to him being of small stature, probably requiring a platform to stand on when stepping up to the podium for his speech. Now they knew how the dirty deed was to be attempted. The Mossad electronic genius fabricated an electronic jamming device that, when it was engaged, would block the signal from the activator to the generator. The Mossad agent would be stationed in the audio-visual control booth in the dining room and neutralize the electrocution device from there.

On the morning of November 17th the Chameleon, in his maintenance man disguise, left his room carrying a large valise that could only be the murder weapon. A subsequent search of the room showed that it had been stripped of all evidence of his ever having lived there.

This day was going to be the day. On arriving at the hotel, the Chameleon joined the electricians who were setting up the audio-visual equipment, lighting and the sound system. It was easy for him to mingle in with the workers and to replace the hotel's step platform that the guest speaker would use that evening with his own special box.

After completing his task, the Chameleon changed his disguise and reappeared as the waiter. Now outfitted in the traditional white jacket and black bow tie, he casually leaned against the wall of the hallway just outside the doors to the biggest banquet room in the plushest hotel in Jerusalem. He was indistinguishable from the other waiters in the small army of waiters, waitresses and bus boys waiting for the head caterer to open the doors to admit them to complete preparing the tables that would soon be occupied by the crowd of Jewish physicians attending the closing event of their annual symposium. As his own personal finishing touch, the Chameleon checked the triggering device in his pants pocket. He had carefully locked it in the OFF position and cushioned it with handkerchiefs to insure that it could not be accidentally activated should anybody bump him or jostle him.

The doors slowly swung open and the wave of white coated

servers rushed into the banquet hall to fill water goblets, arrange the table decorations and position serving trays. The Chameleon slowly worked his way towards the podium and, bending over to retrieve a dropped napkin, ascertained that the metallic step platform was exactly in the place where he wanted it to be. Everything was in place for the electrifying conclusion to the guest speaker's speech.

As he went about his waiter duties, he was totally unaware that he, himself, was being very closely watched by Becky. Her name tag identified her as the Crown Plaza's Public Relations Officer and her disguise as a photographer gave her the freedom to roam the room without evoking suspicion. The state of the art camcorder that she carried was capable of taking high resolution pictures but it also happened to have two special attachments. One was a very bright flash gun that could temporarily blind the person whose picture was being taken and the other was a single shot automatic pistol aligned with the centering reticule of the camera. If any dire emergency arose threatening Doctor Rosen, she had the capability to end it promptly.

The banquet attendees started to filter in for the evening meal. When they had all taken their assigned seats, the emcee asked the diners to rise and greet the dignitaries who would sit at the head table. Applause greeted the dignitaries as they took their places. The loudest applause greeted Dr. Rosen, who was the last to take his place. The sumptuous meal went like clock work. The chilled salad, the steaming hot soup and the delectable main course were expertly served, and the food was devoured with a relish that caused the maitre-d and the head executive chef to bubble with joy. Throughout the meal, the Chameleon managed to pass the podium frequently to make sure that the step/platform was still in place. He paid no attention to the pretty photographer, who was never very far away from him.

Desert had been served and the maitre-d motioned for the serving staff to leave the room, except for a small number to serve after-dinner liquors. The Chameleon had made sure that he would be one of those to stay in the room and his total attention was directed towards the man seated alongside the podium. His thoughts centered upon how pleased Allah would be with him and how great his reward in Heaven would be, once he had disposed of the hated infidel.

It was 9:00 PM (4:00 PM in Washington) when Dr Rosen was introduced, stood and approached the podium. He smiled broadly, emitting the aura of self-confidence that had taken him so far in his political career. While another standing ovation was taking place, he mounted the metallic step, giving the audience a clear view of his face. In the audio-visual cubicle, the Mossad electronics expert activated the jamming mechanism. The other head table dignitaries pushed their chairs back and angled them so that they could see Dr. Rosen's face as he spoke. This left a convenient safe buffer zone between the Chameleon's target and the other dignitaries seated at the head table.

In the back of the room, the Chameleon waited, with the same bored facial expression as the other waiters. He was so intent in focusing his attention on the speaker that he did not realize that Becky had slowly moved into position almost alongside him. He had already uncushioned the trigger device and unlocked it. His hand was firmly on the device, with his finger ready to flick the switch that would send 700 volts into the hated American. He had decided to give a touch of theatrical flare to the demise of Dr. Rosen by letting him complete his speech before he killed him.

Dr. Rosen finished his remarks and was graciously receiving another standing ovation, when the Chameleon flipped the switch. Nothing, absolutely <u>nothing</u> happened! The Chameleon's expression of ecstatic expectation was replaced with a mixture of consternation and rage. He flicked the OFF and ON several times with the same results-nothing. He then locked the trigger in the OFF position and, with a look of pure hatred on his face, watched as the dignitaries surrounded Dr. Rosen to shake his hand. The Chameleon was seething with a feeling of impotence. His orders had been explicit, kill only the American, and no one else. He would have to improvise, but that would have to wait. He was so sure of his original plan that he had not prepared an immediate back-up plan. It was the first time in his infamous career that he had failed. Throughout the time that he was experiencing this gamut of emotions, he never realized that Becky had moved right behind him, with the camera pointed at his head.

Eventually, the banqueters departed and the clean-up crew descended on the room. As he went through the motions of clearing tables, the Chameleon was constantly asking himself, "What had gone wrong?" While he waited impatiently for the room to be cleared, the Chameleon had sneaked out of the banquet hall and rushed to his locker in the employees lounge. In a matter of seconds, the waiter was replaced by the maintenance technician who rushed back into the dining room and headed straight for the podium. He paid no attention to Becky and was also oblivious of the Mossad electronics expert still in the audio-visual control cubicle.

Finally, the room was clear and only dim lighting was left, but it was enough for him to see what he had to do. The metallic step platform had not been moved from the spot where he had placed it. He bent over and removed the top of the box. Nothing was out of place and all the connections were hooked up correctly. He stood up, scratching his head in bewilderment at his complete ignorance of what had gone wrong. As he continued to try to find a solution to his dilemma, the Chameleon had picked up the platform to examine it more closely. As soon as he had the whole rig in his hands, the Mossad electronics expert shut off the jamming field that blocked all the signals to the activating devise. The Chameleon removed the triggering devise from his pocket and flicked the switch one last time.

The resultant lightning bolt was immediately followed by the acrid stench of burning flesh. Becky, who was witness to the final seconds of the Chameleon, approached the podium and gazed, with a look of satisfaction, on the crumpled smoldering remains of the Chameleon. Her thoughts were, "Good, he's already in Hell, and I'll bet there were no virgins on hand to greet him."

The Chameleon had achieved his greatest and final disguise, that of a dead terrorist. She knew that Brigadier Templeman and Glenn Stark would be pleased.

CHAPTER 28

BELFAST
November 17

It was mid-afternoon of the 17th of November when one of the Royal Marines, keeping watch on the Gilhooleys and Paddy, called headquarters, "SgtMajor, the Gilhooleys are loading an unmarked van with mud splattered license plates with what looks like skin diving gear and numerous packing crates of various sizes

SgtMajor broke out in a broad smile, "Aye, just as we expected. Tighten up the surveillance on the Gilhooleys, but keep Paddy on a loose leash."

Late in the afternoon the report came in that Air Force Two had departed Dublin and was expected to arrive in Belfast at 5:00 PM. SgtMajor then called in three of his best men, a sergeant, a corporal and a private and ordered them to pack their van with their gear, that had already been stock-piled in the armory. Joyfully, he announced to his team, "The balloon is going up, it's time for us to earn our pay."

When the van was loaded, SgtMajor and his men drove to the

Belfast Hilton and took up a position that had an unobstructed view of the V.I.P. arrival/ departure area, but far enough away as to not attract the attention of the Vice-President's security detail. The sergeant and the corporal changed into black skin diver's suits, blackened their faces and donned light weight snorkel gear. The four Marines settled down to wait for things to start happening. An hour later the Marines tailing the Gilhooleys called in, "SgtMajor, our 'friends' have parked their van on a semi-deserted street, adjacent to a vacant lot five blocks from he Hilton." To SgtMajor's question regarding a sewer access in the area, the answer was, "The van is parked directly over a man hole cover."

Dusk was just starting to fade into evening, when the motion sensor that had been previously placed close to the sewer grating in front of the Hilton VIP entrance registered activity on the monitor in the Marine's van. SgtMajor immediately barked an order, "Okay lads, off you go!"

The corporal quietly left the van and disappeared into the sewer system through a nearby man hole. Two important parts of his equipment were an infra-red night light lantern and a tracking bug that, once activated, would allow his companions in the van to keep track of his position in the sewers on a large scale map of the drainage system of the area. The corporal arrived at a pre-selected vantage point in the sewer, where he had a clear view of the sewer grating in front of the hotel VIP entrance. He, himself, was well hidden from the person who was sloshing through the ankle deep waters of the sewer towards him. His thoughts were, "This place stinks like Hell, I hope we get this job done real quick."

Seamus Gilhooley came into sight slowly, carefully carrying an object encased in a water-proof satchel. On reaching the grating, he carefully opened the satchel and with deliberate slowness removed a device that could only be a bomb. With painstaking detail he attached the bomb to the grating. The attachments of the device were sturdy and the device itself was cushioned so that it could be neither dislodged nor set off by street traffic. After double checking the placement and securing of the device, he retraced his steps back into the dark recesses of the sewer, thinking to himself, "Sweet dreams, Mr. Vice-President!"

As soon as Seamus took a turn in the sewer that took him out of the corporal's sight, the Marine started to follow him. Once the corporal started to move, his bug was being tracked in the van. As soon the bug's track showed that the corporal had taken a ninety-degree turn in the sewer, the sergeant quickly and quietly departed the van and dropped into the sewer. He paused to make sure that he was alone and then approached the bomb. Skillfully and rapidly, he deactivated the bomb and removed it from the grating. He then proceeded to follow the corporal, repeating softly to himself, "Slow and easy, no short cuts, do it once and correct the first time."

While all this was taking place in the sewer, SgtMajor's van was moved to a new location on a street parallel to the Gilhooley's van, where neither van was visible to the other. The corporal's bug had stopped moving five blocks away from the Hilton, directly under a man hole cover close to the curb. It was through this manhole, via a hole cut in the bottom of the Gilhooley's van, that Seamus left the sewer and re-entered the safety of the van. He quickly removed his sewer stained boots and coveralls and joined his older brother in sitting back comfortably to await for their target to appear.

SgtMajor had left his van and rendezvoused with the Gilhooley's watch dogs. Sean and Seamus did not leave the van, but Liam had taken a casual walk towards the Hilton. He had entered a nearby pub and took a window seat that gave him a clear view of the Hilton VIP entrance. The Marine private, assigned to keep an eye on him, had casually entered the same pub, and 'bellied' up to the bar on a stool facing Gilhooley.

SgtMajor, using a high power telescope and infra-red lighting, was able to make out the numbers and letters on the partially obscured license plate. The details were relayed to base and it was only a matter of minutes to learn that the Gilhooley's van had been reported as stolen earlier in the day. Satisfied that the Gilhooleys were not going anywhere, SgtMajor returned his van to its original location near the Hilton. At that time the sergeant emerged from the sewer and changed back into battle dress. The corporal was left on guard in the sewer to make sure that the bomb did not return to the place where Seamus had positioned it. The Marine driver then negotiated the city streets in a round-about course to take up a new position a long city block from the Gilhooley's van, but hidden from the terrorists by vehicles parked in front of and behind the Marine's van. Like the terrorists, they, too, settled back waiting for the main event to start.

Just after 8:00 PM GMT (3:00 PM EST) the limousine that would take the Vice-President back to the airport approached the hotel. The limousine was the object of intense scrutiny by the beer drinking Liam. He took a cell phone from his pocket and established communications with his brothers. Sean Gilhooley activated several switches on the control panel he operated. As the Vice-President's limo neared the curb and stopped exactly alongside the 'mined' sewer grating, Liam whispered, "Stand by," into the phone. As soon as the limo had come to a stop, the Vice-President and his party left the hotel lobby and headed for the limo. As he usually did, the Vice-President paused just before entering the limo to take his leave from his family members who had just dined with him. Liam then whispered, "Bingo," into his phone and bent over to pick up his napkin, which he had purposely dropped to the floor below window level. Within the van, Sean Gilhooley triumphantly flipped the detonation switch.

The bomb went off with a tremendous blast, sending a plume of fire and smoke high into the evening sky and bits of pieces of vehicle and bodies showered the street, only it was on the street on which the Gilhooley's van was parked. When the sound of the blast had died down, Liam straightened up, surprised that the plate glass window had not shattered, and stared in shock at the still living Vice-President, who was being quickly and unceremoniously shoved into his limo by his Secret Service bodyguards. The driver of the limo burned rubber as the car sped towards the airport, with the motorcycle escorts using flashing red lights and screaming sirens.

Liam then turned in horror to look to where the smoke and fire were contaminating the air. He bolted out the door of the pub and ran as fast as he could towards the rising column of black smoke. The sight of the smoking wreckage was too much for him. He fell to his knees and started to sob convulsively when he realized that his brothers were gone. It was in that position that the Belfast police found him.

In the Marine command van, the Royal Marines, who had pulled off the coup, smiled broadly and congratulated each other. They drove slowly past the smoldering ruins of the van that was now a fiery tomb. The sergeant, who had removed the bomb from the grating in front of the hotel had then repositioned it under the Gilhooley's van and rearmed it. As they were returning to base, after recovering the corporal from the sewer, SgtMajor notified Sir Malcom that everything had gone off as planned. Sir Malcom's only thought was, "Live by the bomb, die by the bomb."

Back at the Shamrock, Paddy frowned as he saw two Royal Marines, dressed in combat fatigues, enter the pub and stride purposefully towards him. An oily smirk started to form on paddy's face as he greeted his unwelcome visitors, "Gentlemen, and to what do we owe the pleasure of,"— was as far as he got.

One of the Marines had drawn his side-arm and was pointing it at the barman, who decided that he didn't want to reach for the shotgun concealed under the bar. The other Marine had spun Paddy around and was handcuffing him as he growled, "Patrick O'Rourke, you're under arrest for conspiring to kill the Vice-President of the United States!"

The silence in the bar was deafening, as the awe struck patrons saw their favorite pub owner being unceremoniously hustled out of his own pub into a waiting police van.

CHAPTER 29

WESTERN PACIFIC
November 13-18

Monday, November 13, the watch section in the intelligence cave on the Yokosuka naval base suddenly snapped to attention as a one word encrypted message sent from *Red Vengeance* to North Korean Naval headquarters was intercepted. Decrypted it read, "Underway". The decrypt was immediately relayed to Admiral Billig (chapter 25) and to Admiral Selectee Simpson, ComSubRonSeven, who had recently moved his headquarters from Yokosuka to the submarine tender, *USS Cable*, moored in Guam's Apra harbor.

Captain Victor McDade, C.O. of the *USS Scranton*, was summoned to the squadron commander's office and given his sailing orders.

"Vic, I want you to take *Scranton* up here," he said, pointing to the letter X on a map of the waters surrounding Guam spread across his desk. "The North Korean trawler that has been snooping around just north of Anderson AFB will be somewhere near there. Once you've made contact, give her a real good look and report anything unusual to me. Then you are to baby-sit her, but don't let her know you're watching her. I expect that sometime early in morning of the 18th she will depart the area. When she does, I want you to surface and scare the crap out of her skipper. Ride herd on her and make sure she heads East, away from here. Bird dog her until I radio you to break off contact and return to port. Any questions?"

Captain McDade shook his head, "No sir, seems straight forward. Should I be ready to sink her?"

"Not unless she fires on you first," was his boss's terse reply, "which I think is highly unlikely. Just the sight of you should be enough for her skipper to want to get as far away from you as fast as he can."

An evil grin spread across Cdr. McDade's face as he acknowledged his orders, "This should be fun. The crew will enjoy the change from the daily routine."

Dusk was falling when *Scranton* cast off and silently headed for the open waters of the Pacific ocean. Once in deep water, the submarine dived and within two hours was on station, able to observe the North Korean trawler that was sailing in a circle just into international waters off the northeast corner of Anderson AFB. Captain McDade made one pass under the trawler and took pictures of its keel. Analysis of those pictures told him that this particular trawler had a special under-water communications dome, an advance Talk Between Ships system. Standing off at a safe distance from the trawler, where her radio antenna could not be seen, *Scranton* sent a short message to SubRonSeven detailing the trawler's new equipment. Then the boat, and its crew, settled into the boring job of keeping a silent watch on the trawler. Once a day, for the next four days, *Scranton* came to periscope depth and fixed the trawler in the optical sights of her attach periscope. If it became necessary to sink her, the trawler didn't stand a chance.

EAST CHINA SEA
November 14

Since departing the Yellow Sea, *USS San Francisco* had no trouble trailing the *Red Vengeance*, whose intrinsic noises, much louder than *San Francisco's* made the task easier. Captain Hyun carried out all the correct maneuvers to determine if he were being tracked; sudden changes in course, speed depth, and sudden turns called 'Crazy Ivans' when they were done by Russian boats. *San Francisco's* experienced crew had matched *Red Vengeance's* every maneuver and remained invisible to the North Korean boat. The red light illumination, used to preserve night vision in the event of an emergency surfacing between sunset and dawn, cast an eerie glow in *San Francisco's* control room.

Captain DeGarmo entered the compartment and joined his X.O. at the plotting table and asked, "X.O., when was the last time our 'friend' up ahead cleared his baffles?"

The exec checked his watch and the plotting board, answering in a skeptical tone, "A little over an hour ago, skipper. Since then his speed, course, and depth haven't changed."

Captain DeGarmo rubbed the stubble on his chin and took in a deep breathe, "Not at all like the guy who ran us ragged keeping up with him the past few days. I wonder what he's up to." Turning to the compartment phone talker, he gave a short order, "Ask sonar if they are picking up anything unusual?"

The answer came back almost immediately, "Sonar reports nothing unusual, sir. She seems to be 'steaming and dreaming.'"

Captain DeGarmo turned to the COB (Chief of the Boat), "Senior Chief, I've got an itch right between my shoulder blades. This guy must be up to SOMETHING, like lulling us into complacency before he pulls some new trick we haven't seen. Pass the word to all on-coming watches to be alert for the slightest indication that he's tagged us. To the X.O. he added, "Hopefully he's convinced that he's out here all by himself and is more concerned in setting up for his grand plan. When will we be in range of *Sea Lion?*"

After a quick check of the projected course and speed, X.O.'s answer was, "In about forty-eight hours, if nothing changes."

"Good, good," replied Captain DeGarmo, "Keep everybody on their toes, I don't want to blow this job when it's so close to being over. I'll be in my cabin."

The X.O. simply nodded his understanding.

GUAM
November 15

Shortly after 0100 hours, *Sea Lion* quietly slipped away from her moorings alongside the *USS Cable*. To anyone, who might have been up at that hour, it appeared that she was heading East but, once out of sight, she 'pulled the plug' and dropped into the still waters of the Pacific ocean. Leveling off at the ordered depth, the navigator plotted a course to take *Sea Lion* around the southern shore of Guam, and then north to a point approximately 500 miles northwest of Guam to wait for *Red Vengeance* and *San Francisco* to arrive on the scene. The waters where the rendezvous would take place was directly under the usual air traffic corridor from Guam to Tokyo. While proceeding, Captain Savage had the crew conduct numerous torpedo attack drills. To preclude the possibility of detection, the boat was operating under 'patrol quiet' conditions.

GUAM
November 16

President Alexander had arrived late in the day for his scheduled meeting with the Governor of Guam on the 17th. The long flight from Andrew's AFB to Anderson AFB was the inaugural flight of the new Air Force One, the latest version of a Boeing 777 executive jet liner. It boasted more amenities and electronic gadgetry than its predecessor. The sick bay alone would have turned the average university hospital trauma center physician green with envy. Admiral Billig, who had earlier arrived in Guam on the CNO's jet, joined the President in the spacious conference room of AF One, where the two men, in strict privacy, reviewed, in exacting detail, the plans for the 18th and put the finishing touches into the plan. Nothing was going to be left to chance. Every possible contingency was covered—-they hoped.

GUAM
November 17

President Alexander spent the day in conferences with the Governor of the Territory of Guam, was escorted on a tour of the island, and was treated to a lavish Pacific rim gastronomic extravaganza at the end of the day.

Admiral Billig met with ComSubRonSeven and the crew of the chopper that would fly the drone KC-10. The Admiral had chosen 'Big Kahuna' as his call sign when he had assumed command of his task force.

Both men retired early in the evening, the President aboard AF One and the Admiral with the crew of the control chopper. Reveille would be very early the next day.

GUAM
November 18

At 0530 hours, AF One slowly taxied onto the main runway of Anderson AFB and the pilots completed their pre-take off check-off sheet. At the same time, Admiral Billig's chopper lifted off the ground and hovered over the KC-10, as the chopper crew brought the big bird to life. Once take off clearance was granted, AF One thundered down the run way. Almost every cabin window was illuminated, the navigation lights burned brilliantly and the magnificent Presidential flying office lifted into the air, and was swallowed into the pre-dawn darkness on its three plus hour flight to Japan. The projected ETA at Yokota AFB was 0800 hours, Tokyo time.

As the 777 passed the terminal on its ascent, an Asian, who was intently waiting for the take-off, keyed the communications instrument he was holding. When his call was connected, he twice said three words, "*Red Storm*" airborne!" With his assignment completed, he turned the communicator off, pocketed it and casually left the terminal, got in a taxi and returned to his hotel in Agana. He never saw the blacked out old KC-10 come down the tarmac and lift off about ten minutes after AF One had departed. He also never saw the huge Navy Helicopter that appeared to be escorting the tanker.

Once through the light cloud cover, and out of sight of land, Air Force One altered its course to the north northeast, while the KC-10 headed north northwest towards Japan. Over the open ocean, the KC-10 climbed to 35,000 feet, the altitude that was assigned to Air Force One, while the chopper hugged the waves, under radar coverage.

THE PHILIPPINE SEA
November 18

Just after midnight, *Sea Lion* arrived at its destination five hundred miles northwest of Guam, where the ocean depth was about fourteen hundred feet, a depth at which recovery of any debris would be extremely difficult and hazardous, with little chance of success. The officer on watch, a young lieutenant, reduced speed to bare minimum to maintain course and depth. The electricity in the control room air was evidence of the level of anticipation of the crew for the up-coming action.

About two hours of quietly lying in wait, the control room phone talker suddenly keyed his microphone and whispered, "Con, aye." Turning to the Lieutenant he passed the word that would trigger the anticipated action, "Sir, sonar reports a contact, designated Bogey One at twenty thousand yards, bearing three-one-five!"

The Lieutenant acknowledged receipt of the message and ordered the messenger of the watch to inform the captain. Captain Savage entered the Control Room almost immediately and announced, "I have the conn," assuming command of the boat from his junior officer.

Thirty seconds later, the phone talker addressed his C.O., "Cap'n, sonar reports ports Bogey One maintaining course three-one-five, speed six knots, depth approximately five hundred fifty feet. Sound signature matches *Red Vengeance*. Designation changed to 'Target One'. CPA[vi] will be five hundred yards to starboard."

A wicked grain spread across Captain Savage's face as he acknowledged the sonar report, "Very well, X.O. station the tracking party! Chief of the Boat, have maneuvering prepare to answer voice bells and set General Quarters!"

"Aye, aye, sir," replied the COB as he keyed the ship's annunciator, "Now hear this, all hands to General Quarters, this is NOT a drill, all hands to General Quarters. Make readiness reports to the Executive Officer in Control. General Quarters, set battle condition torpedo!"

By now Captain Savage has assumed his normal GQ station, right behind the diving officer, where he could see every man in the compartment and read all the important dials and gauges. Adrenalin level in the boat had already been running high and in anticipation of the action, most of the crew were already at their GQ stations. When the Exec reported, "All stations manned and ready," Captain Savage smiled noting that the crew had just set a record in doing so.

As *Sea Lion* was taking position on her enemy, sonar reported another submersible coming down the same track as *Red Vengeance* and quickly identified 'Bogey Two' as the *San Francisco*. When *San Francisco* was in range, as pre-arranged, *Sea Lion* hit her with a short low powered 'ping'. *San Francisco* immediately broke off contact with *Red Vengeance*, went deep below a thermal layer that hid her from *Red Vengeance*'s passive sonar and headed West at a slow speed, leaving only *Sea Lion* and *Red Vengeance* in the area.

On board the North Korean trawler, the radio operator rushed to the bridge with the *"Red Storm"* airborne message, excitedly handing it to his Captain. For his part, the Captain displayed the calm demeanor of a veteran sea captain. Once the radio operator had calmed down, the Captain ordered him to forward the signal

---

vi CPA= *Closest point of approximation*

to *Red Vengeance* on their low frequency under-water phone. After the radio man had departed the bridge, the Captain went out on the exposed wing of the bridge and barked orders to triple the usual number of lookouts, and to pay particular attention to the air west of their position. Within five minutes, one of the lookouts shouted and gestured toward the west where a plane could be seen heading in the direction of Japan. Almost immediately, the radar operator confirmed the sighting and the course and speed of the aircraft. No attention was paid to the Boeing 777 that passed almost directly overhead, presumably going to Hawaii. The Captain replaced his binoculars in their bridge case and ordered the helmsman to set a course due east, and rang up 'All ahead, full speed' to get his ship as far away as possible from the area where the expected action would take place.

The usual placid demeanor of the North Korean Sea Captain suddenly melted away as a look out frantically shouted that a submarine was surfacing behind them. The Captain's fear of a torpedo attack was so great that he ordered the helmsman to start zig-zaging wildly. All this panic maneuvering was wasted, as *Scranton* could have 'had' the trawler anytime she wanted, but was just making sure the trawler kept heading East, away from Guam. Two hours later, Captain McDade received orders to return to Guam.

———•·———

Aboard *Red Vengeance*, Captain Hyun nodded his receipt of the trawler's message. His years of training and cruising the oceans were about to bear fruit. While still maintaining ultra-quiet status, he ordered the boat brought to periscope depth, the air search radar mast raised and the missile room to ready their deadly missile for firing. All they had to do now was wait!

On board *Sea Lion*, the sonar watch reported, "Target One just received an underwater communiqué and is heading toward the surface. Increased sound levels noted." Captain Savage responded, "Very Well. Diving Officer, plane up to one hundred fifty feet and open the range to Target One to one thousand yards. Torpedo room, prepare to fire tubes one and two. Do not open outer doors as yet!"

About one hour after receiving the *"Red Storm"* airborne message, the *Red Vengeance's* air search radar picked up a plane flying at thirty-five thousand feet, on a course for Tokyo, rapidly coming into missile range. Captain Hyun ordered the missile crew to complete the launch sequence. When Captain Hyun determined that his target was almost directly overhead, he ordered, "SHOOT!" and started counting the seconds to impact. Exactly on time, the targeted aircraft disappeared from the radar screen. For the first time since they had left port, smiles started to appear on the faces of the crew. They started bowing to each other and slap each other's shoulders. There was no longer any need for silence, or so they thought. They had killed the hated President of the hated Americans. Captain Hyun was already visualizing the ceremony that would bestow on him his country's highest military honor.

Sea Lion's sonar operator had immediately reported the sounds of the missile silo opening and everyone on *Sea Lion* heard the missile launch. At the same time, Captain Savage ordered, "Open outer doors on tubes one and two!" The sounds of the missile launch smothered the sound of the doors opening. The tracking party reported, "Solution good and in the torpedo computer guidance system." When the muffled sound of the air borne explosion filtered down through the water, Captain Savage quietly, and in the same tone of voice he would used to order a pizza, ordered, "Fire One," and five seconds later, "Fire Two." Without hesitation, the Chief of the Boat pressed the firing button twice. Within seconds sonar reported, "Both fish have acquired Target One, guidance wires cut, both weapons running hot, straight and true."

On the *Red Vengeance*, the sonar operator suddenly screamed, "Torpedoes in the water, incoming!" But it was already too late. The first torpedo hit *Red Vengeance* just forward of the sail and the second just aft of the sail. She was split into three sections that rapidly sank to the ocean's floor. As the sounds of the torpedoes hitting home and the noises of the target breaking up filled the control room of *Sea Lion*, Captain Savage broke out into a smile of satisfaction, knowing that the game was over. He had a fleeting sense of pity for his dead enemy, but he also felt pride for his crew. They had played a major role in saving the life of the President of the United States and made the enemy pay dearly for his failure. The COB expressed it best, as he muttered, "Gotcha" and then silently whispered, "Now you can rest easy, Gramps."

Captain Savage ordered his radio operator to send the code word "Bohica" to Air Force One, with a copy to 'Big Kahuna'. He then activated the ship's intercom system and addressed the crew, "Captain speaking, men—[vii]BRAVO ZULU! I'm proud of all of you and honored to be your skipper. Each of you carried out your individual tasks in this morning's operation in the efficient manner I knew you would. Our mission was successful and we had a big role in preserving the security of our country. I must remind you that everything that has happened since we left Guam is classified 'Top Top Secret' and super hush-hush. You can never discuss the details of this patrol with anybody, not your parents, not your sweetie, not your wife, not your children and especially not your drinking buddy off another boat, NOBODY!! Maybe some day in the future, this patrol may be declassified and you can tell your grandchildren. Until then, keep the past few days to yourself. Again, well done, and for your information our next port of call will be Perth, Australia. Captain out!"

The cheers that arose from every compartment would have pained the ears of any sonar operator within five hundred yards of *Sea Lion*. A very broad grin broke out on Captain Savage's face as he listened to the cheers and gazed on the happy faces of the control room crew. As the cheers died down, he turned to the Chief of the Boat, "Secure from General Quarters." To the Diving Officer he said, "You have the conn." To the Quartermaster he added, "Set a course for Perth, all ahead flank!"

The Quartermaster of the Watch, a Master Chief Petty Officer with over twenty-five years service in the boats, dutifully entered the orders into the special ship's log that he had been

---

vii BRAVO ZULU= WELL DONE

meticulously maintaining since leaving port. He proudly signed the log and presented it to the Captain, who scanned the last page and, just as proudly, added his signature. Captain Savage took the log to his cabin and locked it in his safe, where it would stay until he handed it over to COMSUBPAC when they returned to Hawaii. The Quartermaster then put the regular ship's log on his desk and brought it up to date. This log would show that *Sea Lion* had proceeded directly to Australia after leaving Guam. As far as the Navy was concerned, the event never happened.

While the sub-surface scenario was being played out, the crew in the helicopter, flying almost at sea level a mile behind the KC-10, shut off the remote control guidance system that flown the KC-10 on its last flight. Unlike the 'decoy' set up in the year 2000 by the then President on his visit to Pakistan, this decoy had put no air crew or secret service agents in jeopardy. When they hovered over the spot where the missile had broken the surface of the ocean, the waters started to heave and bubble as the *Sea Lion's* torpedoes struck home. In the semi-darkness of the helo's cabin, a broad shit-eating grin lit up the Admiral's face. When the radio operator handed him the 'Bohica' message, he heaved a huge sigh of relief, tapped the pilot on his shoulder and whispered, "Home James." The chopper returned Admiral Billig to Guam and then headed for its home aboard *Vinson*.

In the cockpit of Air Force One, the pilots had observed a bright yellow flash of light in the direction that they had been expected to fly. The colonel, who had the controls, called the President to report the sighting and to ask for any further orders. The President, himself, answered the phone, received the report and, after a few seconds of thought, told the pilot that it didn't concern them and to now alter course to fly directly to Japan. The pilot dutifully said, "Yes Sir, Mr. President," and banked the heavy plane to come to the new course. Back in his private office, the President was burning a message form that said, "From *Sea Lion* to CIC, 'BOHICA'."

YOKOTA AFB, JAPAN
November 18

The dignitaries, who were on hand to greet President Alexander, had gathered in the VIP lounge of the terminal at Yokota Air Force Base. Among their number were the eldest son of the Japanese Emperor, the Vice-President of South Korea, the U.S. Ambassador to Japan, several other Ambassadors, a company of flag officers from various services, and the Premier of North Korea. They were engaged in polite conversations, when an Air Force Major entered the lounge and announced that Air Force One had been delayed in route and that a new ETA will be announced when it was confirmed.

The North Korean Premier smiled inwardly to himself and thought, "Just like these American fools. They are unable to accept the inevitable and will postpone the fateful announcement until their Air Sea and Rescue force verifies that the President's plane has crashed, rather than just delayed."

At 0820 hours, the doors of the jet way at which Air Force One would dock silently opened to admit three Secret Service agents, who quickly ascertained that there was no danger in the lounge and that it was safe to start the deplaning process. President Alexander strode briskly into the lounge, exhibiting his best confident smile and greeted the Emperor's son. The Premier of North Korea was dumbfounded as he witnessed the impossible arrival of President Alexander. His facial expression, the epitome of the inscrutable Oriental, melted into an expression of horror as he clutched his chest and started gasping for air. He toppled to the floor and lay still.

Indeed, this was the day on which it had been determined that the leader of a powerful nation was to die—only it was wrong leader of the wrong nation who had suddenly passed away!

CHAPTER 30

STATE DEPARTMENT
November 17

It was mid-afternoon when Madame Secretary strode confidently into her office in the State Department building. Her hair was freshly coiffured and she presented a regal appearance, dressed in a meticulously tailored dark blue pants suit. The look of smug satisfaction on her face prompted several of her staff to wonder whom the Dragon Lady had feasted on for lunch. On entering her private office, she checked her Geochron, which told her that it was early evening in Europe, night in the Near East, and very early morning in the Western Pacific Ocean, where it was already the 18th of the month. She turned on her large screen TV even though it was still too early for the news reports she was awaiting. She adjusted the set to CNN to have a front row seat when things start to happen and settled into her large comfortable chair that her staff disrespectfully referred to as her 'throne'. She then unlocked a side drawer in her desk and took out a folder which contained only one sheet of paper, her acceptance speech for when she was sworn in as President of the United States later in the day. The short speech had been re-written several times so that it would be received as exhibiting shocked surprise, sincere regrets, but at the same time, an air of confidence. The final draft of the speech had been hand written, scribbled actually, on plain lined paper to appear like a spontaneously and hastily prepared manuscript.

It was about 3:45 PM when CNN's regularly schedule broadcast was interrupted for a special announcement. The broadcaster's voice went up an octave as he announced, "We have just informed that there has been a bomb explosion of huge proportions in down town Belfast and a gruesome public electrocution in a hotel in Jerusalem. We will bring you further details as they come into our studio."

A thin smile formed at the corners of her lips as she thought to herself, "It's started, so far so good." She then sat back in her chair, crossed her hands on her chest, laid her head against the soft headrest and closed her eyes. There was a look of serene contentment on her face as she savored the thought of being addressed as, "Madame President".

The lack of specific details concerning the events did not surprise Mrs. Kavanaugh. She knew that reports of physical harm to the Vice-President and the Speaker of the House had to be thoroughly screened by the Secret Service before the lurid details of the deaths of the two politicians would be allowed to fill every TV screen in the world. There was still nothing regarding the President Pro-Tem of the Senate, but that did not bother her, because she really did not expect that his death would be discovered until someone from the Justice Department would try to contact him for his swearing in ceremony.

Mid afternoon turned into evening as she eagerly anticipated the bad news from the Pacific. Low rumblings of discontent ran through the large office outside her 'Den', as her staff chafed at being held after normal dismissal hours. Her pleasant reverie was suddenly shattered by a loud and persistent banging on the door to her office, followed by the unbidden entrance of a staffer, out of breath, excitedly waving a message form in the air. In a high pitched voice, she shrieked, "This just came in from our ambassador in Tokyo, we thought that you would want to see it as soon as possible. <u>The Premier of North Korea is dead!</u>"

Madame Secretary jumped from her chair and steadied herself with open palms flat on her desk. "<u>What</u>, that can't be, there must be some mistake," she shouted as a sudden look of shock and disbelief swept across her face. "When, where, how," she continued in a tone of voice that screamed of incredulity.

With less volume in her voice, the young lady who had burst into the office started to answer Madame Secretary's questions, "He died in the arrival lounge at Yokota Air Base on his way the greet President Alexander."

An expression of disbelief and deep consternation flashed across the Secretary's face. She rushed from behind her desk, shouting, "Something must be wrong, give me that," as she roughly grabbed the message form from the distraught girl. She read the message three times. With each reading, she paled a little bit more. The message read, "As he was going to greet President Alexander at Yokota Air Force Base, the North Korean Premier collapsed and died. More details to follow as they are received."

Her face was now purple with rage as she screamed at the girl, "You, get out of here." The puzzled and frightened girl started to cry at the vicious rebuke that had been leveled at her and turned on her heel and fled from the office. Madame Secretary's gait was now unsteady as she stumbled back to her chair, throwing the crumpled message into her waste bin.

Just as she was about to sit down, the CNN broadcaster, using a solemn voice tone announced, "We interrupt our usual program for a special bulletin just in from our afffiliates in Japan. Earlier this morning, Far East time, the Premier of North Korea suddenly collapsed as he was about to greet President Alexander on his arrival at Yokota Air Force Base near Tokyo. Immediate attempts at cardio-pulmonary resuscitation were unsuccessful and he was pronounced dead at the scene. The cause of death is presumed to be either a massive heart attack or stroke. Stay tuned to this station for further bulletins."

Madame Secretary sat down bolt upright on the edge of her chair, folded her hands on the desk top and stared unseeingly straight ahead into space. The color had completely drained from her face, her eyes had glazed over, her lips were partly open, and her rate of breathing had slowed considerably. She gave every appearance of being in a deep hypnotic trance.

After about ten minutes, as she was slowing becoming aware of her surroundings, the CNN newscaster was reporting, "We have an up-date on the bombing in Belfast and the electrocution in Jerusalem. While the Vice-President and the Speaker of the House of Representatives were in the vicinities of these unfortunate occurrences, neither man was injured and both are safely on their way back to the Capital."

Madame Secretary slowly stood up and fed her now useless acceptance speech into the paper shredder. As she shuffled towards her office door, a giant tidal wave of self pity engulfed her as she was thinking, "Why me? why me? What had gone so terribly wrong? All the planning, all the attention to minutia, all that money, and for what, nothing, absolutely nothing! The way things have gone, I wouldn't be at all surprised if the President Pro-Tem of the Senate were still alive."

Before she put her trembling hand on the door knob, she took a long sad look around office that she treasured so dearly, for deep in her broken heart was the stark realization that it wouldn't be hers much longer.

As she left her office, the same staff members, who had noted her sunny and confident expression on entering the building, were now struck with wonderment as she now had the appearance of a much older woman, who looked like she had been a victim of one of her own vicious tirades and tongue lashings. The Dragon Lady had lost her fire breathing capability and was now just another crushed and broken bureaucrat.

CHAPTER 31

WASHINGTON
November 19-20

On the weekend subsequent to the day that could have been another 'Date that will live in Infamy', the letdown after a prolonged period of maximum effort and angst set in. Admiral Billig slept all the way on the long flight from Guam to Hawaii. Fully refreshed and unstressed, he hit the beach at Waikiki and finally got to enjoy a meal with ComSubPac at John Domini's. By Sunday evening he was back in Washington and on Monday morning he was back in his office, where he hung out the 'Do Not Disturb' sign.

Kevin was welcomed back into his family and all the Jablonski's had a quiet reunion, thankful to have the head of the household back to his usual jovial self.

I cleaned and oiled my gun and put it back into its hiding place. Once the flush of combat had passed, Cindy Lou and I spent the quietest weekend I had enjoyed in years doing nothing but relaxing, watching 'oldies but goodies' on the VCR, sucking up a variety of beers and wines, and savoring good home cooked (hers) meals.

The President celebrated the removal of the monkey from his back and the success of the Trade Conference with jovial and spirited repartee with his companions in Air Force One on the long, but pleasant, return flight to Washington.

CHAPTER 32

THE WHITE HOUSE
November 21

It was 9:00 PM when President Alexander, fully recovered from his Far East trip, leapt from the high backed leather chair behind his desk in the Oval office as Admiral Billig came through the door. His greeting was effusive and he shook the Admiral's hand so vigorously that the Admiral thought, "It's a good thing I'm not an oil well, I'd have crude oil gushing from my ears."

Eventually the two old friends settled into the same sofa where they had discussed and planned the events that had recently taken place. As befitted the occasion, the low table in front of the sofa held an ice bucket with a bottle of chilled Dom Perignon and iced champagne glasses. Before getting down to business, they drank a toast to the United States of America.

The President could hardly contain his exuberance as he related what had happened since their last meeting. "I think the summit went well. It was subdued by the death of the North Korean Premier and his absence took the wind out of the sails of the North Korean delegation. There were almost no objections to my proposals. By the way, I'm sending Bill Clinton to represent us at the state funeral. He always likes to travel in an official status. Vice-President Carlton and Speaker Sidney returned home without any idea of how close they came to meeting their maker. Senator Willis is having second thoughts about becoming the Secretary of State. He is still recovering over how quickly and quietly, the threat to his life was handled, but he'll get over it."

"Now, to the one million dollar question,– What should I do about Maureen Kavanaugh? She's finished as Secretary of State, I will be accepting her resignation tomorrow, but where do we go from there?." The admiral was quick to pick up on the switch from "I" to "We," but discretion is always the better part of valor, so he let it pass.

The Admiral cautiously suggested, "She could be allowed to quietly fold her tent and melt into obscurity, thereby keeping the whole mess well buried."

The President shook his head, "I can think of several reasons why that solution won't work. First, I don't think she'd stay quiet forever and I wouldn't put it past her to try blackmail me for her silence. Second, the anxiety of wondering what she's brewing up would never give me any peace and third, I really do want this entire sequence of events kept out of the public eye and the history books. But, I sure as hell do not want her to walk away from this scott free, considering the seriousness of her crimes."

"OK, Mr. President," the Admiral offered less cautiously, "We have enough evidence to indict her and her father as the major co-conspirators. The same evidence will also implicate her son and daughter for their part in carrying the money to Europe for their grandfather, even though they were unknowingly involved. Once the entire scenario is laid out, I have no doubt that the trial would be short and sweet, with Maureen and Jack being convicted and going to prison."

"True, true Vincent," the President agreed, "but we would paint a very negative picture of the U.S. if we wash our dirty laundry openly in the courts, on the front pages of every newspaper, and on the wide screens of every TV network in the world. Every attorney in the ACLU would fight for the chance to represent her and get mega-tons of free publicity. The trial would be worse than the O.J. Simpson debacle. I think our friends would agree with us and not interfere, but our enemies would have a field day. They'd try their best to portray Maureen as a patriot, who was only trying, in the only way open to her, to place the country in the position of being the 'great peace maker' at any cost, just as Neville Chamberlain tried to do for England. Sure, we'd win the legal battle, but I'm not so sure about the political one."

The Admiral could not fault the President's analysis of the possible world wide reactions to a lengthy and messy legal battle. The liberal media would have a field day. The two men spent several minutes in silent reflection.

Finally, the Admiral emitted a sigh and in a somewhat reluctant tone of voice suggested, "Well, we could always try the Rommel solution."

"What are you talking about?," the President asked.

"Mr. President," Admiral Billig continued, "if you remember, towards the end of WWII, after the unsuccessful attempt on Hitler's life, he became convinced that his favorite Field Marshall, Erwin Rommel, was one of the conspirators. He was determined to punish Rommel but he didn't want to make a martyr of him. The solution was to offer Rommel the choice of committing suicide and to be buried with full military honors, or be court-martialed and branded publicly as a traitor and summarily executed. Because Rommel was so popular with the German populace, Hitler feared that the backlash would be devastating. It could even wipe out everything that Goebels was doing to maintain an optimistic front, in spite of the reality of the German military collapse. Rommel also feared that his wife and son would be tarred and feathered with the stigma of being the family of a traitor. As history recounts, he took poison. We could offer Maureen Kavanaugh the same choice."

The President looked at Admiral Billig with an expression of utter disbelief, and was aghast that his friend had even considered such a solution to the problem. The somber expression on the Admiral's face left no doubt that he was very serious. Without speaking, President Alexander rose and paced back and forth, for several minutes, in complete silence, his face betraying the agony he was experiencing. He was being asked to make an executive decision, one that if it backfired would bring his administration down in shambles and permanently disfigure the country's image in the eyes of the rest of the world.

Finally, he rejoined his friend on the sofa and spoke in the most solemn tone of voice the Admiral had ever heard stated, "What you have suggested is very repugnant to me but, in all practicality, is probably the best way to proceed. God forgive me for what I just said. But, before I sign her death warrant, do you have a way to do it tactfully, and with discretion?"

Without hesitation, the Admiral said firmly, "It can be done. You don't want to know the details."

The President again stood up and resumed his contemplative pacing. Then he stopped directly in front of the Admiral and looking down at him spoke his mind, "Vincent, you "Vincent, you are a devil. You know that, don't you. You had this all worked out before you came through the door didn't you?"

The Admiral only nodded.

The President sat down heavily, his face had lost its color and his voice was barely a whisper, "Do it, but do it quickly, and for all that is holy, don't screw it up."

The Admiral rose and said only, "It will be done," and turned to take his leave. As he closed the Oval office door, the President uttered a quiet prayer, "God forgive us."

November 22

At precisely 9:30AM the Secretary of State was admitted into the Oval Office. With a forced smile on her face, Mrs. Kavanaugh greeted President Alexander, "Good morning, Mr. President. Welcome back to–"

The President had not risen to greet her and the scowl on his face made her stop in mid sentence. On President Alexander's desk was her undated, but signed, letter of resignation. It was the form letter that Cabinet appointees give to the President. President Alexander picked up his pen, dated the letter, added the words "Accepted this date," and signed it.

"Maureen, I just accepted your resignation," was his blunt greeting to his visitor. Under Secretary of State Miles Roche will be here in ten minutes and I will inform him that he will be the Acting Secretary of State until the Senate confirms your successor. My Press Secretary has called a special news conference for 10:00 o'clock, at which I will make the official announcement. You have until 5:00 o'clock to clean out your desk. Dismissed!"

The color left Mrs. Kavanaugh's face and her expression betrayed shock and disbelief. She sputtered, "How can you do this to me? I demand an explanation!"

The President growled, "You know damn well why this is happening. End of discussion. <u>Dismissed!</u>"

Mrs. Kavanaugh spun on her heel and stormed out of the Oval Office and the White House, leaving raised eyebrows on all the Presidential staffers whom she flew past.

ASHBURN
November 22

I was enjoying reading the Admiral's after action report of the events that had played out in the Pacific when my office phone rang. It was the Admiral, "Glenn, the President has just announced on TV that he fired the Secretary of State. Do it!"

I walked down the hall to Kevin's office, stuck my head in the door and asked, "Kevin old buddy, what's the latest on Jack McCarthy?"

"Just a second," Kevin replied as he typed the inquiry into

his computer. "Other than going to church on Sunday, to pray for forgiveness I'll bet, he hasn't left Maureen's place. The only phone call he made was to book a flight from Reagan National to Boston on Friday morning the 24th."

"Thanks, Kevin," I answered. The nature of my upcoming meeting with the former Secretary of State required strict privacy and an uninterrupted confrontation. I would have to wait until Jack was gone before I would be able to carry out my orders.

I then returned to my own office and spent the rest of the day putting all the evidence against the former Secretary of State in a folder that I would confront her with. Included in the folder were:

- Timed and dated photos of her making her phone calls from the Ritz-Carlton to the Chairman of the North Korean Trade Commission, along with copies of her finger prints lifted from several places on and around the phone
- A copy of the details of her last conversation with the head of the Commission
- Pictures of her father meeting with the Gilhooley brothers in Paddy's grill
- Photos of her son and daughter transferring the funds they had carried to Paris to their grandfather's brief case
- Photos of her father passing wads of thousand dollar bills to Mutt and Jeff
- Photos of the dead bodies of Mutt and Jeff
- Copies of the State Department Visitors Log listing visits to and from the Chairman of the North Korean Trade Commission, the Chancellor of the Syrian Embassy, and a representative of the Palestine Liberation Organization
- Transcripts of conversations between the involved parties
- Photo copies of decoded incriminating messages
- Copies of all her self-incriminating utterances

revealing the depth of the obsession driving her to covet the Presidency
- Signed confessions from Paddy O'Rourke and Liam Gilhooley, spelling out in detail their part in the attempted assassination of the Vice-President, including implicating Jack McCarthy, and finally
- A copy of a plea bargain, executed by the Chairman of the North Korean Trade Commission, admitting his involvement with the then Secretary of State in the plot to shoot down Air Force One, in return for political asylum and entrance into the witness protection program.

CHAPTER 33

VARIOUS LOCATIONS
November 23

Thanksgiving Day was unusually balmy in New York City. The annual Macy's parade enjoyed brilliant sun and only soft breezes that barely affected the huge balloons. Coats and sweaters had been removed and the throng of viewers were sporting T-shirts, and even a few shorts. Santa Claus, in his tradition red suit and white fur collar, suffered in the heat, silently praying that he wouldn't faint from heat exhaustion.

At the opposite reaches of the country, Hawaii was experiencing its usual hot and sunny day. In the 50th state, Santa Claus arrived on a surf board, wearing gaily colored swim trunks and a gaudy Aloha shirt. Kalakaua Avenue, in the heart of Waikiki beach, was lined with tourists, enthusiastically applauding the hula dancers and equestrians who performed in the parade.

At the White House, President Alexander was hosting a special Thanksgiving feast for himself, his First Lady, the Vice-President and his lady, Speaker Rosen and his wife, and Senator Willis and his eldest daughter. As the President intoned the grace before meals, he waxed eloquently about the dedication and loyalty of all the civilian and military personnel, whose duty it was to protect the nation's leaders. The ladies bowed their heads respectfully, the Vice-President and the Speaker of the House looked at each other with expressions of puzzlement on their face, while Senator Willis nodded and smiled.

Somewhere, in the vast depths of the Pacific Ocean, Captain Savage had joined his crew for their traditional turkey dinner with all the trimmings. After saying the grace, he led his crew in the Navy hymn, "Eternal Father, strong to save."

In nearby Virginia, Admiral Billig, Miss Eagleton, Cindy Lou and I were guests at the home of Kevin Jablonski and his family. Prior to sitting down to the gourmet feast, the Admiral recited a prayer of serious thanks for the success of the recent events, and proposed a toast to the United States.

Across the metropolitan Washington area, Salvation Army leaders were giving heartfelt thanks for the generosity of the anonymous donors who had filled their red Christmas buckets with thousand dollar bills. It was going to be a good holiday season for the under privileged of the nation's capital.

While no other nation celebrates Thanksgiving like the Americans, Sir Malcolm in London and SgtMajor McGregor in Belfast offered prayers of thanks for being able to avert the catastrophic event that could have taken place. In Jerusalem, Brigadier Templem and invited Becky Zelman to join him at a Thanksgiving meal reminiscent of those his family had celebrated in Philadelphia.

The former Secretary of State and her father dined on an unappetizing Chinese take-in meal. There was no feasting, no joy, and nothing for which to be thankful.

CHAPTER 34

WASHINGTON
November 24

The nation's capital was experiencing a balmy late November evening. A light breeze rustled the remaining leaves on the almost barren trees and a low cover of fleecy clouds provided the shadows that hid me from sight. Across the street from where I was stood, the windows of Maureen Kavanaugh's large colonial house blazed with brilliant white light. Eventually, the lights in the house went out, one by one, and all the windows were black. It was now the wee hours of the 25th. I waited another half hour to be sure that Maureen had not changed her mind about retiring for the night.

I ran a quick check on the street and listened carefully for the sound of an approaching vehicle or a late night dog walker. Silence reigned. When I was positive that I could move without being seen, I sprinted across the street, my rubber-soled running shoes muffling my footsteps. When I was cloaked in darkness on the porch of her house, I paused to see if anyone had seen or heard me and put on my latex-free gloves. No lights came on in the neighboring homes and no dogs started to bark. I was ready to enter the enemy's camp.

Kevin had used his spare time while babysitting Senator Willis to learn all about the circuitry in his security system, the same system that the former Secretary of State had installed in her home. Using his wizardry, Kevin had constructed an electronic bypass devise that would allow me to open the front door without setting off the burglar alarm. When it was firmly attached to the dead bolt housing and securely grounded, the security company's display would show no irregularity. Kevin had also managed to provide me with a key to the dead bolt. He never would tell me how he had accomplished that feat. He had also discovered the codes that controlled all the functions incorporated into her system.

I thought to myself, "Show time." Prior to inserting the key, I coated the door hinges with WD-40 to prevent squeaks and positioned Kevin's by-pass device. The key worked smoothly and the door opened silently. No alarm went off and the only sound I heard was industrial strength snoring wafting down the stairwell. The security pad display read, "Armed-Stay". I could move about freely and go to work.

I tiptoed into her study, softly closed the door and turned on the desk lamp. All was exactly as it had been on my earlier clandestine recon mission to familiarize myself with the setting. I pulled her phone, fax machine and computer connections from their wall phone jacks and stuffed the three cords into the large pockets of my fatigues. I chuckled to myself when I deactivated the hidden camera and microphones that she had used to make recordings of what went on in her sanctum. I got on my hands and knees to deactivate a kneecap panic button on the underside of her desk. I knew that if it were pushed, the closest Metropolitan police station and/or Secret Service headquarters would respond instantly. The only window in the room had been bricked over, leaving the single door as the only access to the study. I was surprised at the degree of paranoia that had inspired all these extra security measures.

I turned my attention to her desk and removed a small .32

caliber pistol and a box of cartridges from the top drawer. I emptied the cylinder of all but one bullet and put the gun and the rest of the bullets into another of my large pockets. I also pocketed an Olympus camera and a Minolta hand held voice recorder. Into a small fabric sack went a box of matches, scissors, letter openers, and every other heavy and/or sharp instrument that could be used as a weapon against me. Next addressed was her wall safe, the last word in sophistication. It had a five number combination that Kevin had provided and a secret sensor, that unless deactivated within twenty seconds of opening the safe, would send an electronic signal to the same place as the knee activated device. I needed only a few minutes to change the combination, shut the door and spin the dial. When the room was prepared to my satisfaction, I laid the folder I had brought with me on her desk, opened the door wide, knocked over a small table in the hallway and stationed myself behind the doorway inside the study.

The sound evoked the desired response. I heard footsteps over my head, the stairwell lights came on and Mrs. Kavanaugh bounded down the steps, zipping up her robe as she descended. On reaching the foot of the steps, she removed a baseball bat from the hall closet, raised it to the attack position and charged into the room. She did not see me until I slammed the door shut. When she spun around, the first thing she saw was the business end of my nine millimeter pistol pointed straight at her chest and she froze.

"Stand still," I ordered, "And drop the bat!" When she hesitated, I raised my gun level with her eyes and added, "NOW!" The bat clattered to the floor. Without taking my eyes off her, I motioned her to sit at her desk. When she moved behind her desk, I kicked the bat towards the door.

For a brief moment, a gamut of emotions played across her face– shock, surprise, indignation, rage and finally hate. As she slowly settled into to her desk chair, the torrent of questions started,– "Who the hell are you? Where did you come from? Who sent you? How did you get in here? Why didn't the alarm go off? What do you want? Do you know who I am? Do you think that you can get away with whatever you're here for? What in hell is going on here?" Then the accusations and threats began, "You better get out of here before the police arrive. I'll see you in hell before I knuckle under to you. There is no way you can get away with this."

I listened to her tirade quietly, without once shifting my gaze from her eyes and keeping my gun pointed at her head. The ultimate emotions of terror and fear now crossed her face, as she finally realized the seriousness of the situation and fell silent. In measured tones, I answered some of her questions. Most of them I ignored.

"It doesn't make any difference who I am or who sent me. Yes, I do know who you are and yes, I am going to get away with this. How I got in here is irrelevant and you'll find out soon enough why I'm here."

Her mind started to work as she suddenly tried to push the panic button with her knee. When it was obvious that nothing was going to happen, she started to look around for some sort of weapon. A look of utter resignation crossed her face when she found none. She then played what she thought was her trump card saying, 'It'll only be a few minutes before someone important calls me. When I don't answer, he or she will become suspicious and notify the police."

I just shook my head, "Lady, you're a has-been now. No VIPs are going to be calling you anymore, especially at this hour."

When Mrs. Kavanaugh, at last, accepted the fact that she was cut off from the outside world and completely at my mercy, all semblance of bravado deserted her. She slumped back into her chair and stared at me with an expressionless gaze. It was time to get down to business, "Mrs. Kavanaugh, we have definite proof that you and your father engineered a plot for you to become President of the United States by the cold-blooded assassinations of President Alexander, Vice-President Flaherty, Speaker Rosen, and Senator Willis."

The torrent of denials, protestations and questions started again, "What, are you crazy? You're out of your mind. Your accusations are preposterous. I could never be guilty of such a heinous crime. What kind of proof do you have that you think will substantiate these outrageous accusations?"

I answered this last outburst by telling her to read the contents of the folder I had laid on the desk, documenting her involvement in the affair. When she finished reading the documents, there was no more fight left in her and her limp body said that she had resigned herself to being caught red-handed. Tears started to well up in her eyes.

Her voice returned, but it was barely above a whisper, "If you are so sure of your facts and proofs, why am I not in handcuffs or jail right now? I could have been arrested at any time."

"The President would like to avoid a long and messy trial," was my brief answer.

A smirk curled her lips, "If the President wants to avoid a trial, then nothing will happen to me or members of my family. All your alleged facts and proofs aren't worth the paper they're printed on without public disclosure. You are one big bluff. Maybe I'll write my memoirs and become more famous and richer."

"No, ma'am, no way are you going to walk away from this scott free. You have only two options– a trial, or the easiest way out for all concerned." I punctuated my last words by taking her pistol out of my pocket and aiming it at my head. A look of puzzlement crossed her face until she realized what I meant.

The smirk returned as she sneered, "And what if I don't take the easy way out, what happens then, Mr. Know-It-All?"

"The President will direct the Attorney-General to issue a warrant for your arrest, and to prosecute you on the following charges: conspiracy to commit multiple murders, treason/conspiracy to overthrow the duly elected government of the United States by violent acts, collaborating with foreign governments to commit treason, malfeasance in office, dereliction of duty, conduct unbecoming a Cabinet member, violation of the public trust, and whatever else the Attorney-General can come up with. Your father will be indicted as your co-conspirator on many of the same charges, and your children will also be indicted as accessories."

"You and your father will undoubtedly be convicted and sentenced to long prison terms. You would be a very old woman by the time you were eligible for parole, but your father, at his age, would end his life behind bars. Your children might escape jail, but their careers would be ruined and they would carry to their graves the stigma of a mother guilty of treason. The media would be in a frenzy to interview your estranged husband and every investigative reporter would have a field day digging up the juicy details of your tempestuous marriage. Mr. Kavanaugh is rich enough to retire and leave the country until everything blows over, but his legal career would be irreparable damaged."

"Think very carefully, lady. Do you really want to do that to your family. I'll give you three minutes to make a decision!"

Her reply was to spit out, "You son of a bitch, you dirty son of bitch!" At the end of the three minutes, she finally realized that she really didn't have any choice and nodded her consent to the easy way out.

I put the folder inside my shirt and took the one bullet out of her gun, laid it on her desk and told her not to move until I was out of the room. I laid the bullet on the carpet just inside the door, picked up the bat, and told her she had two minutes to write a short note, and to do *it*. Just before I opened the study door, I saw her gaze shift towards the wall safe. "Forget it," I said, "I changed the combination."

I stepped into the hall, locked the door, picked up the table I had overturned, put the bat back in the hall closet, and waited. A string of curses told me that she was unable to open her safe. Just before the end of the two minutes, I heard the muffled sound of a shot. I waited another thirty seconds before cautiously re-entering the study. Mrs. Kavanaugh was slumped over her desk, blood oozing from a round hole in her right temple. Her gun had fallen to the floor. I quickly crossed the room to her side and found no pulse.

The next thing I did was to reload her gun, leaving the spent casing in the chamber and repositioned it where it had fallen. I then reconnected every piece of gear that I had disconnected and returned everything I had put in my pockets to where I found them. My last step was to reset the combination of the wall safe.

I did a final visual check to insure that the room was exactly as it was when I had entered it. It was, except for the late Mrs. Kavanaugh and a short note, really scribbled this time, "To my family, I'm sorry."

She would be discovered by her cleaning lady later in the morning.

I returned the study key to its proper place on the inside of the door, left the house and retrieved Kevin's by-pass device. As I melted into the shadows and left the scene, my thoughts were, "The game is finally over!"

CHAPTER 35

November 26

This morning's **WASHINGTON POST'S** banner headline screamed:

EX-SECRETARY OF STATE SUICIDE VICTIM
Despondent Over Removal From Office

In several houses of worship in the Capital area, volumes of prayers were raised to the heavens in petition for the happy repose of her soul. Others, definitely not enamored with the lady, offered silent prayers in thanksgiving for the country being rid of her.

In Pyongyang, the Communist controlled newspaper printed a wreath surrounded double headline in red ink:

HERO OF THE PEOPLE
BURIED WITH HONORS

November 27

On the lower half of its front page, the **Boston Globe** reported:

Jack McCarthy Suffers Major Stroke
Partially Paralyzed, Unable To speak

In Guam, aboard the submarine tender, the *USS SCRANTON* and her captain and crew were awarded the **Meritorious Unit Commendation** by CNFM.

Pier side, at the Yokosuka Naval Base, the *USS SAN FRANCISCO* and her captain and crew were awarded the **Navy Unit Commendation** by ComSubRon 7.

Aboard the *USS Ronald Reagan,* in Fremantle harbor, the task force commander awarded the *USS SEA LION*, her captain and crew the **Presidential Unit Citation.** At a subsequent ceremony, at SubPac headquarters at Pearl Harbor, Captain Savage was presented with the **Defense Meritorious Service Medal** by ComSubPac.

In the office of the CNO in the Pentagon, Admiral Vincent T. Billig was awarded the **Distinguished Service Medal** by CNO himself. Later in the morning, Admiral Billig presented the **Medal of Freedom** to Glenn Stark, and Kevin Jablonski.

November 28

In a rare moment of magnanimous generosity, the Admiral granted himself, Kevin and me with 10 days of 'basket leave' (time off not charged to our normal vacation time) as a reward for 'services rendered'.

Cindy Lou and I basked in the not often available totally free time to just goof off for a few days and then we took Amtrak's Acela streamliner to New York for a holiday vacation for three days to enjoy the comforts of a safe and sane life style. The Admiral had even approved my request to leave my cell phone/pager in its charger in my kitchen. We played tourist to the nth degree—ice skating at Rockefeller Center, hearing the St. Petersburg Symphony play an all Tchaikovsky concert and on the next night watching the latest rendition of Riverdance at Lincoln Center, shopping on Fifth Avenue, enjoying the Christmas show of the Rockettes at Radio City Music Hall, and savoring sumptuous meals at five star restaurants. I had found the cloud with the silver lining.

Kevin took his family to Disney World and, on a side trip to Cape Canaveral, they were treated to the first launching of the new space shuttle **Excaliber.** His children were so enthralled that they talked about their vacation to their playmates well into the new year. Even the Admiral took a 'busman's holiday' on a Caribbean cruise. It was reported that he spent much time on the bridge, catching up on all the latest gimmicks and gadgets that have given a new definition to the sailor's old saying, 'steamin' an' dreamin'. He wisely declined the offer of the ship's captain for him to try driving the ship. The rest of his time at sea was spent taking part in the other creature comforts that the magnificent liner afforded her passengers. He was even seen to smile several times.

The result was exactly what the Admiral had planned, we all returned home well rested, with our attitudes adjusted, and ready to take on the next crisis.

EPILOGUE

President Alexander completed his second term in office without further major incidents and went on to become a respected elder statesman, earning the title of "Der Alte" of the United States.

Vice-President Flaherty succeeded President Alexander in the Presidency.

House Speaker Sidney Rosen stayed in the House of Representatives, where he served five more terms as Speaker.

President Pro-tem of the Senate, Senator Bryan Willis, had had enough of politics and graciously declined appointment as Secretary of State. He retired to Oahu, becoming a well recognized figure and scratch golfer at the Waialae golf course.

Sir Malcom Oliver Middleton retired early in 2007 and quickly faded into history..

SgtMajor Ian MacGregor was later awarded the Victoria Cross for gallantry during a fire fight against a band of terrorists in the Middle East.

Brigadier Jacob Templeman went on to become Prime Minister of Israel.

Agent Rebecca Zelman was promoted to Deputy-Director of Mossad.

Captain Bart Savage continued his successful naval career, culminating as Commander, Submarine Force Atlantic Fleet, retiring with the rank of Vice Admiral.

Jack McCarthy ended his days as a broken man in a total care facility.

Kevin Jablonski eventually left the Institute and founded his own computer empire that was as successful and well known as that of Bill Gates. He maintained his association with the Institute as a Senior Consultant.

Patrick 'Paddy' O'Rourke and Liam Gilhooley are serving life sentences for their roles in the plot to assassinate the Vice-President.

Admiral Vincent T. Billig finally retired (for the second time) but never strayed too far from Washington, where he was frequently consulted on matters of national security. He also got his fourth permanent star when a grateful President Alexander prevailed on the next U.S. Navy's flag promotion board to promote him to full Admiral for services rendered while he was on recall duty. In order to stay within the budget, the promotion did not include a raise in his retired pay, but it was the rank that mattered. Because the promotion had no effect on the Navy's active duty flag community or its budget, his promotion was not widely publicized. Those few curious reporters, who read the entire promotion list, labeled it, "A premature tomb stone promotion". They couldn't have been more wrong.

After Admiral Billig retired, his second-in-command moved into his office as the new Director, and Glenn Stark [me] was promoted to the Vice-Director's billet, complete with my own private secretary and parking place in the VIP garage. Cindy Lou was now my wife.

Miss Eagleton also retired shortly after the Admiral and became his social companion at the many receptions, etc. to which the Admiral was always being invited.

The North Korean news media never reported the loss of *Red Vengeance*. There was no investigation into the circumstances of her loss. The next of kin of her officers and crew were told only that, "She was lost at sea, cause unknown." A few very highly placed officials in the North Korean Navy Department suspected the true cause of her loss, but most others laid the blame on an accident related to an unsuccessful attempt to launch a missile from too great a depth.

GLOSSARY

ACLU	American Civil Liberties Union
AFB	Air Force Base
BOOMER	Ballistic Missile Submarine
CAG	Commander, Air Group
CIA	Central Intelligence Agency
CIC/CINC	Commander-in-Chief (the President)
CMC	Commandant, Marine Corps
CNFJ	Commander, Naval Forces, Japan
CNFM	Commander, Naval Forces, Marianas
CO/C.O.	Commanding Officer
CNO	Chief of Naval Operations
COB	Chief of the Boat
COD	Carrier On Board Delivery
COMPAC	Commander, U.S. Forces Pacific
COMPACFLT	Commander, U.S. Pacific Fleet
COMSEVEN	Commander, 7th Fleet
COMSUBPAC	Commander, Submarines, Pacific
COMSUBRON 7	Commander, Submarine Squadron 7
EOD	Explosives Ordinance Division
FITREP	Fitness Report
FMF	Fleet Marine Force
GQ	General Quarters
HRH	His Royal Highness/Her Royal Highness
HUMINT	Human Intelligence
IRA	Irish Republican Army
KGB	Russian Secret Service
MI6	British Foreign Intelligence Service
MOSSAD	Israeli Secret Service
OAS	Organization of American States
PLO	Palestine Liberation Organization
POW	Prisoner of War
SAM	Surface-to-Air Missile
VEEP/VP	Vice-President
VIP	Very Important Person
XO/X.O.	Executive Officer

ABOUT THE AUTHOR

Ed Novak, Jr. is a native of Scranton, Pa. He earned Bachelor of Science and Doctor of Medicine degrees from Georgetown University. He was in private practice as a Board Certified Ophthalmologist until his retirement in 1996. During a 35 year Naval Reserve career, he had eight years active duty, serving on board destroyers, diesel submarines and submarine tenders, and Qualified as a Submarine and Diving Medical Officer. He retired with the rank of Captain in 1991. He lives with his wife in Potomac Falls, Va., where this book was written. He is an active member of the Kiwanis Club of Arlington and enjoys world travel as his main hobby.

ISBN 142510970-5